T0147134

Books by Heather Grothaus

THE WARRIOR
THE CHAMPION
THE HIGHLANDER
TAMING THE BEAST
NEVER KISS A STRANGER
NEVER SEDUCE A SCOUNDREL
NEVER LOVE A LORD
VALENTINE
ADRIAN
ROMAN
CONSTANTINE
THE LAIRD'S VOW
THE HIGHLANDER'S PROMISE
THE SCOT'S OATH
HIGHLAND BEAST
(with Hannah Howell and Victoria Dahl)

Published by Kensington Publishing Corp.

The Scot's Oath

Heather Grothaus

LYRICAL PRESS
Kensington Publishing Corp.
www.kensingtonbooks.com

LYRICAL PRESS BOOKS are published by

Kensington Publishing Corp.
119 West 40th Street
New York, NY 10018

All Kensington titles, imprints, and distributed lines are available at special quantity discounts for bulk purchases for sales promotion, premiums, fund-raising, educational, or institutional use.

Special book excerpts or customized printings can also be created to fit specific needs. For details, write or phone the office of the Kensington Sales Manager: Kensington Publishing Corp., 119 West 40th Street, New York, NY 10018. Attn. Sales Department. Phone: 1-800-221-2647.

Lyrical Press and Lyrical Press logo Reg. U.S. Pat. & TM Off.

First Electronic Edition: February 2021
ISBN-13: 978-1-5161- 0709-4 (ebook)
ISBN-10: 1-5161-0709-8 (ebook)

First Print Edition: February 2021
ISBN-13: 978-1-5161-0713-1
ISBN-10: 1-5161-0713-6

Printed in the United States of America

For Sir Cheerio

Prologue

September 1428
Caedmaray, Western Isles
Scotland

The island looked like the loneliest place Thomas had ever seen—perhaps it was even the end of the earth.

The ever-present shrieks of the seabirds that had followed the supply boat from Thurso swelled as the living banner of white darts swooped beyond the bow to dive through the sea spray and fog surrounding the rolling green land mass. Caedmaray was small—like a crumpled hat floating upon the water—and seemed to grow no larger as they drew near. No structures penetrated the ceiling of mist, and, indeed, even the rounded crest of the isle's pinnacle seemed too meek or tired to attempt challenging the dense cloud surrounding it like a cloche.

The burly captain appeared at Thomas's side then, seizing the rail near the bow as the supply boat bucked and leaped over angry swells. "Caedmaray," he confirmed in a shout over the roar of the waves and wind. The stocky cog ship that bore them had departed from Thurso just that morning on indigo water sheeted with white-gray waves. And even though the wind was at their back, hurtling them over the rutted and bucking sea, the journey had taken hours.

"Nae beach to land upon," the captain continued. "We'll move the cargo ashore, gain our trade, and be gone. Storm rolling in, English. If we arenae gone within the hour, 'tis dead we'll all be, to a man. So move yer arse, ken?"

Thomas nodded. "Aye, Captain."

Apparently satisfied with Thomas's curt answer, the captain turned and stomped away as easily as if he were traversing the stone floor of a chapel while only comfortably drunk, but the wild dip of the clouds beyond the rail caused Thomas's stomach to spasm, even after these many months.

Eight months since he'd fled the woods beyond Loch Acras. The same length of time as would pass before the supplies ship made the dangerous and lengthy journey to Caedmaray once more.

Eight months since he'd bashed in the skull of the dead Carson on the hillside, hoping against hope that Vaughn Hargrave would think it was Thomas Annesley lying dead and would cease his scourging of the Highlands for him. Cease his determination to see destroyed anyone connected with Thomas.

Seven months since he'd crept into Thurso and gained the basest work as an anonymous ship hand on a trading vessel, earning just enough through the balmy summer to buy food to eat in a darkened doorway or filthy alley after the town had gone to sleep. His hands had bled for weeks at first, the sea water and rough work sucking the moisture from his skin and ripping thin, deep wounds into the folds of his fingers more deftly than any blade.

Thomas's hands no longer bled, the skin now tough and stiff and slicked like matted wool. Never of ample flesh to begin with, he was whip-thin now, his muscles like cording beneath his tanned skin, his hair long and curling and caught up with a leather strap most days. He looked like any of the other unfortunate young men hired on the trading ships now, and save for his crisp English accent, no one would ever guess that this young, starving worker—little more than a slave—was at one time Baron Annesley, Lord of Darlyrede. It was only when he spoke that the trouble was likely to ensue, and Thomas had spent many days recovering behind an inn from beatings doled out by drunken Scots.

Thomas watched Caedmaray slowly approach over the rutted, striped waves. The seas were rougher here than Thomas had ever known any sea could be, and it was nearly another hour before the ship dropped anchor some distance from the rocky shore. Then the ship hands slipped out like a strand of pearls, connected to one another by a rope lashed to a boulder on the island, chest deep in the icy, shoving water, passing heavy barrel and bundle and crate over head in vain attempts to keep the cargo dry as it ferried ashore. The sea burned in Thomas's eyes and nose, in his lungs and stomach, as he gasped to stay upright on the slick, submerged crags beneath his boots—any cargo lost would come out of his meager pay, and Thomas suspected that he already made half that of the other hands, thanks to his blasted English accent.

The final heavy bundle was passed overhead, and then his mates began slogging past him, pulling themselves hand over hand along the rope toward the ship.

"Low man untethers," one sailor growled at him as he passed, as if Thomas had somehow forgotten his lowly station. "That be you, English. Mind the slack."

Thomas turned his head to cast a grim look toward the termination of the rope on the rocky shore, which seemed leagues away as the waves buffeted him. The sky was growing darker, as if it was made of slate, and the angry waves reached up to wet it black. He struggled out of the loop but kept both hands firmly on the rough woven line as he labored up onto the sliding shore to where the rope was tethered. It grew taut, then limp, with no discernable pattern, sending dull twangs into Thomas's ears. On the next instance of slack, he tossed the loop from the gray stone and followed it back down into the waves as it jerked in his hand, wrenching his shoulder.

Slack. Jerk. Slack.

A wave hit him full force in the face, filling his head with seawater. He choked and sputtered, pulling himself onward, his boots leaving the rocky shelf beneath the waves with each swell.

And then the rope was suddenly gone from his hands with a zing of heat.

Thomas thrashed out into the water as the prow of the ship, still too far away, rose sharply into the air and he was thrown back toward the shore.

Thomas saw the line of men on board frantically pulling and gathering the tether rope. They hurled it over the side once more in Thomas's direction as he bobbed wildly in the undulating wilderness, but it landed out of his reach and vanished beneath the murk. And the ship was turning now. Turning to portside, wallowing a breathless moment. Thomas saw the burly captain clinging to the rail, peering through the spray as if searching for him. His mouth moved soundlessly, the roar of the wind stealing his words. The captain raised an arm.

"No!" Thomas shouted. He sputtered as water filled his mouth again, treading furiously to stay afloat. "No! Come back!" Another wave crashed over him, plunging him down onto a rock shelf. Thomas kicked up toward the surface again with every bit of strength remaining in his weakened legs, and when he at last gasped the misty air, the stern of the cargo ship was only just visible in the foggy gloom.

He turned and lashed out for the steep, rocky shore, his feet spinning madly at the firmness beneath them, scrambling up the treacherous surface before the next breaker could rush ashore and claim him. He crawled the last bit, dragging himself above the tidemark, falling onto his hip and then turning to his back on his elbows, his gaze searching the now-empty waves while the seabirds circled and screamed above his head. The icy wind cut his sodden clothes and exposed skin like a thousand knives.

They had left him. Left him on godforsaken Caedmaray.

The end of the earth.

He began to shake; from the cold, the wet, the shock—he didn't know. His limbs felt as if they were made from stone as he struggled to his feet. He turned and saw nothing beyond the beach but painful green—no trees, no brambles. Only long grass, cleaved by a narrow, wet path to the foggy crest of the hill where it met the thick, darkening sky. He started up.

He was afraid, in a nonsensical way, that he would gain the top of the rise only to discover naught but more green on the other side. A lonely island of empty nothing. He knew that was impossible—he'd seen the line of villagers carrying the cargo over the hill himself while he'd been tethered in the violent bay. And yet the loud silence of the wind and sea, the triune landscape of grass and water and sky, gave the impression that he was the only man left alive here at the edge of the world.

But no, just down the hill, there it was—the little cluster of village, figures transporting the cargo along its narrow alleys. Small stone houses sunken into the earth more than halfway up their walls, all parallel with the length of the island. Raised hillocks in the lee of the land—crop beds, perhaps? The little piles of white, striking against the green: sheep. Short, cylindrical stone towers, whose purpose Thomas didn't recognize, dotted the undulating green beyond the settlement.

The wind gusted, buffeting him on the hilltop path, turning his sodden clothes to ice. One of the villagers raised his head toward the hill, and then his arm to point at Thomas. The others paused in their work, turned, and stood, staring. Thomas couldn't see their faces from so far away, but he was well familiar with their postures.

Foreigner.

Intruder.

English.

His only choices were to return to the sea and throw himself in or venture into what was perhaps a hostile settlement. The sky grew thicker, then; lower, like layers of icy batting being rolled out and pushed down over Thomas's head—so low that he fancied he could feel them brushing the top, aching and wet from the cold.

He shivered his way down the steep, narrow path toward the figures who stared openly at him. The first few stinging drops of rain cut through his slicked-back hair to his scalp, stung his face. The wind burned his sea-seared lungs; his empty stomach squirmed against his backbone. Each jarring footstep brought him closer and closer to the people who watched him, slack-faced, as if they'd never seen another man before, and Thomas grew even more uneasy.

Would the people of Caedmaray give him shelter and sustenance through the long winter to come, until the supply boat returned from Thurso? Would he be safe on Caedmaray?

Was he safe anywhere?

He came to a halt at the corner of the nearest buried house, and still the villagers stared at him as if he were a strange, dangerous creature. Thomas thought of all the times he had been initially welcomed at a table or hearth only to have the kindling kindness dashed by the accent that rolled from his tongue, and he hesitated to speak. But no one hailed him, no one questioned him. They only stared.

"I'm from the ship," he muttered quickly, his teeth clacking together. No one blinked, and so he gestured with an arm back the way he had come, flicked his head inanely, as if the people of the island had so soon forgotten the vessel that had brought the cargo some still held in their arms; as if they didn't know the way to their own rocky bay. "I lost the tether line."

"Dè a tha thu ag iarraidh bhuainn?" an old, bonneted man barked.

Thomas blinked at the foreign words, swallowed down the razors in his throat. "I'm from the ship—"

"He heard ye," a woman's voice called out, and then a figure emerged from a hidden doorway behind the man. Her skirts were long and gray, almost identical in shade to the leaden clouds above the island. The long rope of hair that emerged over her shoulder from the faded kerchief wrapped across her forehead was the color of dark honey. She was young, but she did not smile at him. "My father has only the old tongue."

She touched the man's shoulder. *"Chaill e am bàta, athair."* What she said Thomas could only guess, for the man's stern countenance didn't change. Then she looked to Thomas. "Have they left ye?"

"Aye."

She looked him up and down. "Yer English."

Thomas nodded curtly. "Aye."

"He canna stay here," a sneering voice cut through the tense silence, the drizzle around them suddenly sounding like the crackle of flames. A boulder of a man rolled through the villagers to stand next to the young woman. "He's an outsider."

"Where else is he to go, Dragan?"

"They likely left him a-purpose. Likely for a thief," Dragan argued, staring with unabashed hatred at Thomas. They looked at one another uneasily; obviously there were others in the village who spoke English.

"I'm no thief," Thomas spoke up. His shivering had increased, although now his skin felt fevered, as if he had been standing near a roaring fire. "I only lost the tether line."

"They didnae think ye worth turnin' back for, now did they?" Dragan jeered and took a step forward. "Likely happy to be rid of ye. Thief, I say." He had a hungry look in his eyes then, like a starved wolf who can't believe his luck at a lamb wandering into his territory.

The woman stepped in front of Dragan. "Ye know the ship would have been dashed to pieces in the swell had it turned back. I saw him workin' the line, just the same as ye."

The old man suddenly barked another stream of unintelligible words, causing Dragan's scowl to deepen.

She looked to Thomas once more and gestured toward the doorway from which she'd emerged. "My father bids ye welcome. Ye will stay with us, in his house."

Thomas could barely force his throat to swallow as he at once reached down to the pouch that was still tied tightly around his middle, beneath his soaked vest. In it was all the coin he had managed to save from his meager earnings working the ship. He had hoped to use it one day to make his way back south and, somehow, some way, redeem himself. But if he was to survive the long winter on this remote island with already one enemy made, perhaps it would be better used to repay the old man's generosity.

He undid the ties carefully, feeling the eyes of all those strangers gathered on the path on him, watching his every movement. The leather pouch felt heavier in his shaking hands then, heavy with seawater and wet coin and fear.

"I know my presence will be an added burden to your village," he said quietly and paused, glancing up at the woman, and then looking to her father pointedly.

She translated his words into the guttural Gaelic.

He withdrew a handful of the coins, looked at them in his palm, and then looked at the woman's father, presumably the patriarch of the tiny community. "Perhaps this will help offset the cost of my lodgings." Thomas held out the silver to the old man. "I will, of course, share in the work."

The woman's quiet translation was snatched away by the wind as the old man took the coins with an expression of grim confusion. Whispers broke out between the villagers.

Suddenly, Dragan roared and stepped forward, slapping the coins from the old man's hand and ranting in Gaelic. The villagers turned horrified faces to Thomas.

"Chan eil! Chan eil!" the woman protested, and looked around them frantically. Her unintelligible words continued, and then she looked at Thomas. "He said you want to buy me from my father. To take me as your wife."

The old man looked suspiciously at Thomas.

"No." Thomas held out his hand to the old man. "I didn't—" He looked to Dragan. "That's not what I said. You understand English—you know."

"I heard what ye said, but I see more clearly what ye mean," Dragan growled. "I'm nae stupid Englishman can be lied to, and I'll nae have ye lyin' to the folk."

"Yer the one what's lyin'," the woman shouted. She broke out in another stream of Gaelic, ending with a pleading look to her father.

The old man turned to Dragan with a low query.

Dragan's expression darkened further, and his fists clenched. "Christian or nae, I'll nae have it," he growled. And then he spun on Thomas. "I'll nae have it, I say."

He lunged for Thomas and seized him by his wet hair. Thomas ducked, but it was of no use—the man's reach and hands were mythological in proportion and there was no escape. Thomas struggled, but the cold and the wet, the shock of being abandoned on the tiny Scots isle had sapped his strength, and each blow he landed on the gargantuan man seemed to have as much effect as a child's as Dragan dragged him further into the village. A sharp blow to the side of Thomas's head caused colors to explode behind his eyes and his right ear to ring like the giant bells of a cathedral. He went momentarily limp as they passed the last of the houses on the opposite end of the settlement, headed toward a long point of land strewn with boulders that appeared to have been tossed about like toys.

The sea crashed onto the shore with ferocious intensity, as if the water had declared war on Caedmaray, and the beach was the point of engagement.

"I'll send ye back meself," Dragan said, shaking Thomas by his head, stomping through the muck so that great showers of mud splashed from his boots. "The devil take ye!" He plunged into the surf, dragging Thomas with him into a wall of water, and Thomas was thrust beneath a wave, the hand on the back of his neck holding him down as surely as any broken-off granite from a cliff slide.

He struggled against Dragan's grip, squirmed and writhed and managed to get his face above water between waves to gasp a breath.

"She's mine!" the Scot screamed into his face before he again plunged Thomas beneath the salty, icy water.

She's dead. As the water pushed inside his skull, Thomas saw Vaughn Hargrave's face on that dreadful night. The night Cordelia lay in the dungeon, her perfect, white skin slashed open. The night before they would have wed. The night all the secrets—all the shocking confidences of everyone at Darlyrede House—had been discovered.

He had not been strong enough to save Cordelia. He had possessed neither the courage nor the physical prowess to overpower such evil—evil he hadn't known until that night could even exist.

He had run away and left her at Darlyrede.

He had run away and left Harriet behind.

He had run from his mother's clan.

And now he would meet his end on Caedmaray, at the hands of yet another evil man. Dragan wanted the honey-haired woman, and perhaps one day this would be her same fate—Thomas could foresee it now, as the cold waves stole the present from him, showing him with startling clarity the future and the past at once.

There would be no retribution. There would be no truth. Not for Thomas. Not for the woman or the villagers of Caedmaray. He had failed everyone who had ever dared be kind to him, and now there was no one and nothing left. He grew limp.

Hargrave would win, and not ever know his accomplice.

Fight, you coward, a quiet, fierce voice whispered inside his frozen brain. *For once in your life, fight.*

Thomas fought the powerful surge of water and the lack of air to raise his right hand and clutch a handful of Dragan's inner thigh through the man's thick woolen trews—the hand that had pulled miles and miles of wet, heavy rope over the summer. He curled his fingertips into a claw and squeezed with all the strength left in his body, imagining that he gripped Vaughn Hargrave's throat, and he felt the ends of his fingers plunging into warmth.

And then he was free. Miraculously free, there at the end of the earth, and full of a deafening, red rage the likes of which young Thomas Annesley had never before felt.

He erupted from the crashing surf with a gasp, and then a great scream of fury, as he lunged at the goliath Dragan in the same moment the surprised and furious Scot came at him again. But this time Thomas did not try to duck and evade. He met the man's blows to his head as if he had lost the capacity for feeling, and perhaps he had. For his blows gave no heed to the ones that landed on his own body. Thomas's inexperienced fists flew faster and faster, striking Dragan's face, his throat, the tender place behind the man's ear. He climbed the dangerous weapon that was the islander, every protuberance on his body acting like a lance as he channeled his fury.

Dragan's blows began to slow. And then a massive wave overcame them both and twirled them together in the storm surge, whipping the heavier man to the rocky bottom, shoving the entwined pair higher up on the shore.

Thomas wrapped his hands around Dragan's throat, holding him beneath the foamy, detritus-strewn shallows while the man squirmed and kicked beneath him. Thomas squeezed his bloodied fingers, pressed with all his might, in his mind waiting for the bones of Dragan's neck to finally give, give, *give* under the pressure.

He would stop running now. He would stop running, and stop being afraid.

"Stop! Stop!" The woman's arms were around his neck, pulling vainly at Thomas. He was like an iron band, bent over Dragan—he could not be moved. He would not be moved.

"Please," her voice shuddered in his ear. "Nae matter his cruelty, he's one of them, and they'll never let ye live if ye kill him! *Stop!*"

It was another wave that did her work for her, separating Thomas's death grip on the man and sending him tumbling onto the shore. He was shaking once more, but no longer with cold. No longer with fear. He swiped the seawater from his eyes as he saw the handful of village men dragging Dragan's limp bulk out of the foam. They awkwardly maneuvered him onto the path and away toward the village, leaving Thomas alone in the rain with the woman and, standing some distance away, her father.

She stared at him, her eyes red, her chest heaving through her soaked gown.

"Who are you?" she asked incredulously, her voice breaking.

Thomas returned her confused gaze for a long moment. Who was he? He couldn't be Thomas Annesley—that man was dead, killed at Darlyrede along with Cordelia; killed by betrayal on the bridge to Carson Town; killed on the wooded slope of Town Blair, just beyond Starving Lake by the stone in his own hand. Thomas Annesley was dead and buried so many times over, he could never be resurrected again.

And that was perhaps the way it must be if he was to survive, here at the end of the earth.

"Tommy," he croaked at last. "I'm Tommy."

"All right," the woman whispered. "All right, Tommy. I'm Jessie Boyd. Come on now, back to the house. There's a storm blowin' in."

Chapter 1

October 1458
Darlyrede House
Northumberland, England

"Is it done?"

The rasping whisper and skeletal fingertips digging through the sleeve of her gown caused the maid to gasp and freeze in her movements—she hadn't known the lady was awake, she'd been so still, her eyelids drooping so low.

"Yes, milady. All is ready."

"Then I am also ready," Caris Hargrave said. She opened her hand and turned it palm up toward the maid, who took it in a firm but gentle grip and then seized the woman's forearm, pulling her into a sitting position on the thick mattress, forested by towering piles of cushions and throws. The noblewoman dragged her thin legs from beneath the coverlet and, at first glimpse of the woman's bare feet, the maid dropped to her knees to fit the fine, tall, calfskin slippers over the pale, blue-veined skin.

"Cordelia? No, of course that's not right." Lady Hargrave sighed crossly. "Forgive me; I...I haven't been sleeping, and—"

"Think nothing of it," the maid said, pulling the ties of the slippers tight—but not too tight—against the fragile bones of the lady's foot. It was like fitting a songbird with armored boots. "I am called Beryl, milady. Remember?"

And that was true. The first rule was to tell the truth as much as possible.

"Beryl, of course. How could I..." Her words trailed away.

Beryl helped Lady Hargrave to stand, then held the thick robe while the woman slid her arms inside. She braced her with an arm around her waist and then, together, they turned toward the door and began a slow advance.

The maid reached out an arm to open the ornately carved door leading to the adjoining chamber.

"I remember now," Caris Hargrave said as they entered the glowing chamber, lit by exactly fifteen candles. "The abbey."

"That's right, milady," Beryl murmured, leading the woman through to the long, lead-paned window. "I will try to remind you."

"No, no," Caris said dismissively as she lowered herself gingerly onto the window seat. "It is only a remnant of my nightmares, Beryl."

As soon as Lady Hargrave was settled, Beryl took a step backward and folded her hands at her waist, prepared to wait silently. She would be standing here for at least an hour, and while there would be little conversation, it was an opportunity to further observe, and Beryl would take full advantage of it.

Lady Caris Hargrave. Aged three score, if reports were averaged. Her dark brown hair contained not even one strand of silver, her face pale and lovely still, even if the skin was thin and draped over the fine bones of her face like fragile pastry over a tart. Her eyes were the same dark shade as her hair, her brows wispy and arched.

Beryl thought that this woman could have passed for her own mother, and it made her heart ache quietly in her chest.

Lady Hargrave wore no veil in such private attire as her sleeping gown and robe; none of the heavy jewels Beryl had occasionally glimpsed. But, then again, she never wore them at night when she took up the vigil in the hauntingly still apartment of rooms that was Beryl's primary domain. The entirety of her duties at Darlyrede House took place here, and they must be done with absolute precision.

Fresh linens. A pitcher of cold milk and a plate of cheese and crisp bread. Fifteen new candles lit and kept burning as night crept across the moors toward Darlyrede House. Every night. And for the first hour of the vigil, Caris Hargrave would keep watch at the window, waiting for the return of her missing niece. Fifteen candles to mark the age Euphemia Hargrave had been when she had disappeared.

"He hasn't touched you, has he?"

The question—both the noise of and the subject matter—startled Beryl. "Milady?"

"My husband. Lord Hargrave," Lady Caris clarified in her soft, vulnerable tone. "Has he touched you in any way?"

Beryl stared at the woman, her heart pounding, her mouth dumb.

Lady Hargrave tucked her chin, and her deep brown gaze bore into Beryl's. "Be not afraid to tell me, child. You would not be punished."

"Nay, milady," Beryl answered, dismayed at her raspy whisper. "He has not. I swear it."

And that too was, thankfully, true.

Caris held her gaze an instant longer before turning back to the black window that showed only the woman's specterly reflection. "Good," she said. "Sometimes he…takes liberties beyond what he is entitled to. I don't like it when he touches my girls. I wonder sometimes…"

Beryl forced herself to swallow past her constricted throat.

"You will tell me, won't you?" Lady Hargrave said abruptly, her gaze still fixed upon the nothing through the window. "If he is…untoward?"

"Of course, milady," Beryl said. "If you wish it."

"I do wish it," Caris Hargrave murmured to her reflection. "I wish it very much."

The woman was quiet for a long time, and so Beryl thought that her mistress had reverted to the silence that had marked these nightly rituals for the six months of Beryl's employment at Darlyrede House. Six months of watching, waiting; of rebuffing the offers of friendship from the other maids, rejecting the advances of the male servants of the estate. She was known as the cold French girl now. Airs, they said.

Perhaps that was also true.

But then Caris Hargrave whispered again, and this time Beryl did actually jump.

"She's dead, isn't she? Fifteen years with no word, no sign. She must be dead. Out there, somewhere."

Beryl swallowed forcibly. "We must have faith, milady."

"'Faith'?" The noblewoman repeated the word as if it was a foreign term she couldn't comprehend. "When I think of where she could have gone, who she could have encountered…" She paused, and Beryl could see the shining, silver trails of the tears on Lady Hargrave's face reflected in the window glass.

"It haunts me. Every moment of every day. Even into my dreams. I pray that she is dead. That she stumbled into a ravine and broke her neck at once. The alternative is unthinkable."

"Your devotion is admirable," Beryl dared offer, her heart pounding. It was a risky game she played, but the lady had never spoken so freely.

"She was mine," Caris murmured. "After Cordelia…it was another chance, I suppose. To protect her properly."

"I will continue to pray for you, milady," Beryl murmured. "And for the soul of Lady Cordelia and Lady Euphemia's safe return."

"You are a blessing from God, Beryl," Caris Hargrave spoke to her reflection. "Such kindness you've shown me." She stilled, and her head turned so that Beryl could see her profile, but the woman kept her gaze cast toward the floor. "Would you...might I impose a favor on you? It's foolish and improper of me to ask. I know I am often confused, but I'll not punish you if you refuse me."

"Anything, milady," Beryl replied.

Lady Hargrave turned her face more fully to Beryl. "Would you lie with me upon her bed for a while? Keep me company? Euphemia and I would oft share stories before retiring and..." The woman's thin shoulders jerked. "It is fifteen years. Tonight."

Beryl felt her own eyes ache with unshed tears. "Of course, milady. Here, come." She helped Caris Hargrave from the window seat, and the woman seemed to lean all her slight weight upon Beryl's arm as they reached the side of the bed. Caris climbed upon the pristine, white surface of the fresh coverlet, rested her fragile-looking skull upon her open palm while Beryl rushed to the other side and gained the mattress, facing Lady Hargrave.

She wore an exhausted, saintlike smile as she reached out a skeletal but somehow graceful hand to tuck a strand of Beryl's hair behind her ear.

"When Lady Paget told me of your...uncomfortable circumstance that forced you to the abbey, I wondered: Did you have no parents to return to, my dear?"

Beryl shook her head, mesmerized by the sight of the woman's face before her, the heartbreak so clear as to be exquisitely outlined on her face.

"They are dead, milady." True.

"No family at all?"

"A brother," she admitted.

"And where is he?"

"I don't know." Also true. "He could be anywhere."

"He does not care for you?"

"He is ambitious, milady."

Caris's eyes narrowed and her mouth turned up in a hammock of folds. "That is the way with men, is it not?" She reached out again and stroked Beryl's cheek with a forefinger. "They leave us to our own devices. Only returning when they have made a great mess of something and require our assistance."

Beryl felt her own mouth curve. "They underestimate us when it suits them."

Lady Hargrave's smile widened with pleased surprise. "Just so. And you are a bit older now, to know so much better after your ordeal." Her hand fell away to tuck itself between her waist and the plush bedclothes, embracing her own thin form. "I shall sleep here tonight, Beryl. I think it fitting. Will you stay with me? Please say you will. It is an unfair request after all you have done, but…"

"Of course," Beryl interrupted, and moved closer to the woman, as if she were a magnet and Beryl composed of ore. "Of course I will, milady. I would not leave you so alone on a night such as this." She reached over and drew the coverlet up from behind Lady Hargrave and tucked it around her. "Rest easy," Beryl insisted. "I will be right here."

The lady gave a series of dainty although forceful sneezes as Beryl withdrew.

"Oh dear," she said with a sniff. "Have you by chance been in the unfortunate company of a *cat*, Beryl?"

Beryl hesitated only the briefest moment, her heart pounding. "Nay, milady, I—" She swallowed the lie. "Oh, yes! Yes, I have. When I was in the kitchen preparing the tray. Looking for an easy supper, I suppose. I removed it forthwith." True.

The lady wore an expression of relief. "The next time you see it, do have it killed. Dreadful creatures. I cannot abide them. The asthma, it is brought on by the horrid things. I nearly died once. You've probably heard."

"I have, milady." Unfortunately, true.

Lady Hargrave's solemn countenance was luminous in the candlelight, her pupils enlarged so that all the iris appeared black. "I want to tell you a secret—"

The hinges of the door squealed as it opened with a whoosh of air, causing the fifteen candle flames to duck and then dance in indignation. Nothing so loud, so sudden, ever went on inside this sacred chamber, with its thick draperies and carpets.

Beryl's eyes went wide, and she looked over her shoulder to see Darlyrede's steward step into the chamber, his hand still on the door latch.

"How dare you," Lady Hargrave whispered, pushing her slight form up onto one hip, the coverlet Beryl had so carefully tucked sliding away.

"Forgive me the intrusion, Lady Hargrave," Rolf rushed, one palm held toward her beseechingly. "Forgive me. We have a visitor."

"A visitor?" the lady hissed. "*A visitor*? Why would I ca—"

"A man claiming right to Darlyrede House, my lady," Rolf interrupted, and it was only then that Beryl could make out the sheen of sweat glistening on the usually collected servant's forehead. "He is demanding entrance."

"Well, turn him away and be done with it," Caris sputtered. "I have had enough of these tales of errant heirs. Is Lord Hargrave not in attendance?"

"He is, my lady."

"Well?"

Rolf's face was expressionless, but Beryl could see the distress just under the man's pale skin. "The watchman has spotted an army riding behind him, my lady. His lordship has suggested that perhaps you would prefer to remain within the safety of your own chamber. With the bolts thrown."

Beryl couldn't help her gasp. "An army riding on Darlyrede?" She turned her gaze to the lady once more.

But rather than showing frightened dismay, Caris Hargrave's chest heaved—the high neck of her dressing gown gaping around her spindly throat, emphasizing the anatomy of her windpipe and tendons. "I would not prefer," she said through her clenched teeth. "Beryl, go below in my stead. Find out who this person is, and if we are truly to be laid siege to."

"Of course, my lady," Beryl said, scrambling from the bed.

"And take him with you," Caris added bitterly. "It is well known that there are to be no men in Lady Euphemia's chamber. Rolf?"

"Milady?"

"Should your boots ever again cross the threshold of this chamber, you will be set from this house, and I care not what Lord Hargrave should say. Do you understand?"

Rolf bowed awkwardly as he backed through the doorway. "Aye, milady. Forgive me, milady."

"Come on," Beryl muttered as she swept past the nonplussed steward and into the corridor.

She struggled to keep pace with the long-legged man as they fairly flew down the polished stone staircase. They were yet two floors above the entry of Darlyrede House, and already Beryl could hear the echoes of angry shouts, words without form; blustering accusations and loud reports of footfalls from below.

Beryl's heart pounded as she rounded the balustrade on the second floor, but it was not from exertion or fear; she was angry.

I want to tell you a secret...

What had Lady Hargrave wanted to tell her? Was it something more about Euphemia's disappearance? Perhaps she was poised to incriminate her husband. So many whispers of Vaughn Hargrave, so many peculiarities about the man. The way he sometimes looked at Beryl made her skin crawl.

Has he touched you? I don't like it when he touches my girls...

The missing servants, the missing villagers. They couldn't be blamed on Thomas Annesley, gone from Darlyrede House for more than thirty years. He was supposed to have been located early that year, executed in London. But he had vanished again.

Like Euphemia Hargrave.

Like the villagers.

Like the purses of the wealthy nobles who dared travel unguarded over the road of the moor.

Perhaps it could all be blamed on the band of criminals inhabiting the wood beyond Darlyrede. Caris Hargrave was likely justified in her heartbreaking hope that her niece had met a quick and accidental end. If young Euphemia—a physically frail, sheltered noblewoman barely out of childhood—had had the misfortune of encountering those base thieves, her fate would likely have been quite gruesome indeed. Beryl had stood for what probably amounted to days now, staring at the portraits of Euphemia Hargrave that welcomed visitors in the entry hall of Darlyrede House. Euphemia at seven, with her wolfhound; Euphemia at ten and two, in close profile; Euphemia at fifteen, one pale hand resting on the back of a chair, a single white lily in the other.

Her hair had been the color of winter sunshine, her blue eyes too big for her dainty, heart-shaped face, and always she wore an expression that hinted she was watching something frightening unfold just beyond the gilt frame.

I want to tell you a secret...

Damn it all! Whoever this person was who had destroyed the moment of victory Beryl had been working toward so diligently, so carefully, for six months, had better brought a large army with him, for if Vaughn Hargrave didn't see the interloper dead, Beryl felt she might just be so inclined.

She hastily crossed herself for the sinful thought out of habit.

Beryl and Rolf gained the main floor in nearly the same instant, and both slowed their running to brisk strides as they came upon the rear of the motley group gathered on the marble paving before the large main door. A collection of servants and men-at-arms formed a barrier behind the tall, gray-haired figure in the center.

Lord Vaughn Hargrave.

Rolf penetrated the line easily, slipping between the house servants and disappearing, while Beryl was left to struggle against the flank of the older head maid.

"Let me through," she said, seeking to wedge her body into the crowd.

The woman buffeted her back with such force that Beryl staggered on her feet. She felt her eyebrows lower and then she charged forward again, pulling at the woman's gown.

"*I said, let me through*—Lady Hargrave sent me."

The woman jerked the folds of her gown from Beryl's hand with an ugly frown and then sent her through to the center of the group with a shove.

The sheer number of people pressed together should have prevented her fall, but as Beryl tried to regain her balance, the servants moved away from her as if on cue, and she went down on the marble with a frightened shriek, her palms slapping the cold stone, her nose only a hair's breadth from smashing against the floor as she slid to a stop nearly at the toes of Lord Hargrave's costly boots.

And another set of footwear—this one dark and dull and old; gouged and stained and mended. If this was the visitor, he was not worldly.

"What in the devil's name is this about?" Vaughn Hargrave demanded in a series of barks.

Beryl got her knees under her and then felt a hand grasp the crook of her elbow firmly, helping her to stand. "Forgive me, my lord."

She raised her face at last and saw that it was not the barrel-chested, malevolent lord of Darlyrede who had assisted her, but the owner of the old boots. She looked into his face and her heart fluttered a half beat, throwing off the rhythm of her anger, her humiliation.

His hair was the color of polished oak, curling in a lock over his forehead, his eyes blue like the sky in their depth and clarity; his features seemed to be set with precision within the frame of his face, his skin bronzed and supple-looking beneath the stubbled beard of a traveler even in this late time of the year, when all other Englishmen were already pale and wan. Her pulse beat in her elbow beneath her skin, and Beryl realized the stranger still gripped her.

"Are ye all right, lass?" he inquired in a low voice, his brow creased, the rich, rolling timbre of his voice causing her heart to stutter once more.

This was no Englishman.

"Lay no hand on a servant in my house," Hargrave growled, and then he jerked her away from the stranger. "Beryl?" Lord Hargrave blurted in annoyed surprise. "What are you doing here? I have already sent word to my lady."

Beryl dared a final glance at the Scotsman before turning her reluctant gaze up to Vaughn Hargrave. "She has requested my report, my lord."

"There shall be naught to report," Vaughn Hargrave said, and as he once more looked to the stranger, Beryl did the same. "Yet another imposter intent on affixing himself to Darlyrede's teat for a rich drink."

Beryl felt her face heat and wanted to cringe at the nobleman's crudeness, even before a man who by all appearances was no more than a striking beggar.

"I'm nae imposter," the man retorted, and his voice held not the slightest trace of doubt or concern as he stood in the midst of the clearly hostile group in his tattered clothing. In fact he raised it, as if intent that everyone should hear him clearly. "I'm the one you've been waiting for: Padraig Boyd, the only legitimate heir of the man known in this land as Thomas Annesley." He turned to look directly at Beryl now, and a shiver raced up her back at the intensity of his gaze.

"Darlyrede belongs to *me*."

Chapter 2

Throughout the rough and treacherous sea journey from Caedmaray to the mainland—selling his boat down the coast when the late autumn seas became too rough to navigate even the bays; through more than a fortnight of cold, wet foot travel along foreign roads, Padraig had held in his mind an image of Darlyrede House. A stone keep—he'd already been told that. He'd supposed it owned a good-size village. Rich grazing land, likely, just beyond the Scots border; most certainly a fair river or loch.

Padraig had fantasized how he would take it all back from the thieving bastard, Hargrave. He would clear Tommy Boyd's name, and he just hoped someone tried to stop him.

But when he had seen the shape of the place on the rise beyond the wood edging the moor, the light-colored stone reflecting the hazy glow from the sun setting behind him, he had caught his breath, hanging in the chill of the evening like the smoke from a warming fire he so longed for. Surely this fortress—this palace—could not be Darlyrede House, his father's childhood home.

There was a curtain wall extending to either side of the tall main building, which could not be described as merely a keep. The fortifications snaked over the shoulders of the rise, meeting at the rear crest above the river and sitting on the hill as a crown rests upon the head of a king. It could—and likely did—house hundreds of people.

Padraig had stood alone on that far hill for a long while in the cold, considering the now apparent folly of what he had come to do. He'd brought no companion. He wore the only set of clothes he owned—rough island garb, the woolen shirt and breeches woven by his own mother in the year before she'd died. The shawl wound about his head and shoulders was his father's, old and faded, and of a Highland design Padraig didn't know, but it was still thick and warm. His boots had seen many years and veritable lochs of seawater and dung. The seams were more like netting now, the soles thin enough to cause him to curse the sharper stones hidden beneath the yellowed grass.

He carried only a blade, and his knapsack, which was largely empty save for a deflated skin pouch, an already worn parchment, and an intricately carved piece of tapered wood that was also Tommy Boyd's. Padraig didn't know what its original purpose had been, but once, when he'd been yet a boy, his father had said that the little decorative spear had saved his life.

Padraig had carried the carved wooden piece as a sort of talisman on his journey to claim Darlyrede House, but looking upon the truth of that immense, formidable stronghold, he had felt foolish and unsure. He had no defense, no proof of his claim besides the brief writing scrawled over the parchment in his sack.

But he had come to do this thing for his father, and he would not fail.

Now, eye to eye with Vaughn Hargrave, the elaborate entry to Darlyrede House was so silent that Padraig fancied everyone gathered there staring at him could hear the pounding of his own heart beneath his worn shirt and shawl. The beautiful servant girl's eyes widened at his proclamation and her lips parted as though she were about to scold him.

Or warn him, more likely.

And so Padraig lifted his chin higher in this grand entry, meeting Vaughn Hargrave's incredulous and scornful gaze.

A chuckle suddenly bubbled from the lips of the Englishman, and the corners of his eyes crinkled. "Your house, is it now, lad? Ho-ho!" Then he did give a true laugh. "I do have the feeling the king might have something to advise about that, but I'll not have it said that the lord of Darlyrede ever turned away a man in want of a rest and a warm meal." He glanced down toward Padraig's feet. "Perhaps a new set of boots as well, to serve you on your return journey."

Padraig's pride took the blow, although his mind left the bait lay.

"I've a message in my bag," he began.

"Yes, yes—I'm sure you do," Hargrave cut him off in a condescending tone. "Why don't you come through to the kitchens and fortify yourself with some sustenance, and then perhaps I will read your message to you and explain to you what it means."

"I can read just fine," Padraig shot back. "I ken who ye are, *Hargrave*. You stole my father's life. I've come to retrieve it."

The rumbling sound of many hooves began to push itself into the crowded entry, and although Padraig had no desire to turn his back on Vaughn Hargrave, the man's frown of displeasure caused Padraig to hope for a miracle as he dared a glance over his shoulder.

Shadows separated themselves from the gloom of night across the bridge spanning the deep, protective ditch. Tall shadows, bouncing and rolling forward, peak upon peak. Riders, Padraig realized. The horses arrived with thunder upon the bridge, and a lone rider pulled ahead, his sharp features becoming clear in the torchlight to either side of Darlyrede's entrance.

A miracle, aye.

"I told you to wait for me," Lucan Montague chastised as he neared.

"An' I told *you* I wouldna," Padraig replied.

The knight swung from the magnificent black Agrios before it came to a complete halt and flung the reins across the saddle, his irritation clear. He strode forward, removing his black gauntlets with sharp efficiency, tucking them into his belt and then reaching into his quilted doublet in a series of seamless motions. His face was hard, and Padraig knew the man was used to those around him following his commands.

"Montague?" Hargrave said as Padraig turned back to the entry. The pretty maid was suddenly nowhere to be seen. "I thought I'd given you all that you required when last you tried my hospitality with your cryptic messages. Did you send this…this *beggar* to my door as some sort of grotesque joke? If I didn't know better, I should take these soldiers as a sign of aggression."

Lucan came to a stop just forward of Padraig. "Lord Hargrave. You received the message from London, I presume?"

"I did," Hargrave blustered. "But it made no allusion to this chaos. The king's men, I say?! I don't see—"

Lucan Montague held forth one of two folded and sealed squares of parchment toward the lord. "From Henry himself." After Hargrave had taken the packet with a frown, the knight held forth the remaining message toward Padraig. "Your own copy," he said, meeting Padraig's gaze. He lowered his voice. "Did you think to take on the whole of Darlyrede's men-at-arms on your own?"

"If I'd had to, aye," Padraig answered in an equally soft voice as he used his knife to break the wax seal of the parchment. He was carefully unfolding the missive when Hargrave's outburst caused the servants in the entry to jump en masse.

"This is outrageous!" he shouted. "Is this your doing, Lucan?"

"Forgive me, my lord, but this is not the first instance of forewarning. You know I am only the king's messenger," Lucan Montague replied.

Hargrave sneered. "And enforcer, apparently."

Padraig held the paper toward the nearest torch and scanned the words scrawled there. The bottom seemed to fall out of Padraig's stomach, and it took all his pride to keep him from staggering on his feet.

A miracle indeed.

He looked up and found Lucan Montague watching him intently. "I told you to wait."

Hargrave's furious shouts filled the entry again. "Surely Henry cannot expect I would house a veritable stranger while he thinks of a way to scheme from me all I have rightfully earned. Why, this man looks like any vagrant found on the streets of any burg. He is no one!"

"I am Thomas Annesley's son," Padraig offered calmly, drawing the nobleman's glare. "When Darlyrede's ownership is in question the only heir of the man born to it must be considered. The king agrees."

Hargrave turned his attention from Padraig without comment. "I thought you were employed by the Crown, Lucan? I may still call you Lucan now, mayn't I? Or is such a knight too lofty to address in a personal manner?"

"I have been charged with investigating the truth of Darlyrede's rightful claimant," Montague replied evenly. "While I am in the king's employ, it would be best that our relationship remain formal, Lord Hargrave."

Padraig found himself looking between the two men, the older of whom made no further pretense of looking benevolently upon the dark-haired knight. Lucan Montague himself remained unmoved by any passion.

There was history here. History that Padraig could not fathom.

"The king is coming?" Padraig shook the message in the space between them for emphasis. "And I ken that I am to be given residence at Darlyrede House until he arrives?"

"There will be a hearing," Lucan conceded with a nod. "But whether here or London, I do not yet know."

"I'll not give this...this pretender so much as a stall in the stable," Hargrave declared.

"Very well," Montague responded. "If you do not agree to the king's terms, you immediately forfeit right of a hearing. It says so just here—" He leaned over Hargrave's copy of the message, his finger trailing over the page. "Very clea—"

Hargrave jerked the parchment from Montague's touch. "I can read, *Lucan.*"

Padraig knew a moment of satisfaction at the man's phrasing, spoken by Padraig himself only moments before.

"Both claimants must occupy Darlyrede House until Henry's determination, and be wholly present at the trial—in both body and mind. Any deviation from the terms shall result in a forfeit." Montague looked directly at Vaughn Hargrave. "I do doubt that the king would consider a stall in the stables adequate."

"He has no right," Hargrave said through clenched teeth.

"I've more right than you," Padraig spoke up, meeting the man's gaze. "My claim is by blood—yours is by treachery."

Hargrave leaned forward, as if to make a move toward Padraig; Padraig answered the motion.

Montague stepped between them. "Until the king's decision, Darlyrede belongs to neither of you," he interjected. "Lord Hargrave shall continue to see to the business interests of the hold, in light of his experience and station."

"False station," Padraig muttered.

"The hold will be divided between your households to prevent unnecessary conflict," Lucan continued pointedly.

Hargrave interrupted. "But he has no household."

"*However*, the resources shall be shared proportionately." He looked to Hargrave. "I have been given leave to assign servants and *appropriate* quarters to Master Boyd fairly, and to thereafter divide the hold as I see fit."

"Ah, administrator now," Hargrave challenged. "You wear many caps, Lucan."

"I've only come for the truth, Lord Hargrave."

The way the knight said the words tickled at Padraig's curiosity, but now was not the time to indulge in imaginative theories.

"He should stay in the village," Hargrave insisted. "He is a stranger to this house, and possibly a danger to those in my care."

"I claim full responsibility to the Crown for his actions," Lucan answered back at once. "And, yes, I—and the troops that accompany me—shall enforce the terms. Fully," he emphasized.

Hargrave held Padraig's gaze for what seemed an eternity—his perfectly coiffed hair seeming to make Padraig's scalp itch, his immaculate costume causing Padraig's own rough garb to chafe and emit the odor of so many days' travel. But Padraig never let his chin drop, never let his glance stray in any sign of submission.

"I see that I have little choice but to defend that which is rightfully mine against foreign usurpers. Again," Hargrave insisted bitterly. His tone had modulated, the high color in his cheeks fading, but the man's eyes had narrowed the tiniest bit, as if desperate to view a thing that was just out of focus. "But as I am confident that the king will not only reward me finally with what I deserve but redress others accordingly, I will, of course, cooperate." He broke gaze with Padraig to flick a nasty and meaningful glance at Montague. "The redress will be far-reaching, I do hope."

"I have no fear of the truth," Lucan said calmly, and there was so much meaning behind the simple declaration, before he added the deferential "my lord," almost as an afterthought.

Hargrave's noble countenance turned stony, but he did not bother to look at Montague again. Instead, he barked, "Beryl!" The hall was silent. "Beryl, where are you, girl?" He looked over his shoulder with an irritated jerk.

"I am here, my lord," a lilting voice answered reluctantly.

"Well, come *here*," Hargrave insisted, his words so obviously strained that the command was gritty and forced.

The crowd parted, and the beautiful servant girl who had fallen at his feet moved near Hargrave's side, her pretty face downcast, seeming to try to keep herself turned away from Padraig so that he could barely see her porcelain skin beyond the edge of her veil.

Already his enemy, was she?

"My lord?" she queried softly, and Padraig could hear the accented lilt behind her words. Perhaps she wasn't native to Darlyrede House either.

"Make your report to Lady Hargrave as she requested," Hargrave ordered. "And then advise her that I would seek her council before she retires for the evening."

Beryl fidgeted. "But, my lord, she is already—"

"Go," Hargrave insisted.

The maid curtsied stiffly and began to slip into the crowd, but then Montague's arm shot out, grabbing her arm and jerking her back around to face him. Padraig thought there was fear in her gray eyes as she stared up at the knight.

"What the devil, Montague?" Hargrave demanded.

Lucan Montague's glare seemed to slowly sink beneath his high cheekbones and he abruptly released her with a shallow bow. "Forgive me. I only wished to have the girl convey my regards to Lady Hargrave."

"Very well." Hargrave sighed and waved his hand. "See that you do so, Beryl."

Beryl disappeared into the crowd so quickly that Padraig could not tell the direction of her flight. She seemed to simply vanish before his eyes.

"The hour is late," Lucan announced, and although his words were once more crisp and matter-of-fact, Padraig could sense a note of disquiet beneath the cool façade. "The king's men have ridden far, and I would not detain you further from your evening, my lord. Tomorrow is soon enough for us to lay out the details of the thing."

"Upon that point, I find I do agree with you," Hargrave said. "I assume you will take up your usual quarters?"

"The barracks will be adequate, my lord," Montague responded.

The older man looked upon Padraig as if he were a bit of dung dragged onto the marble floor of the grand entry. "My steward shall show you to a chamber—Boyd, is it?"

Padraig answered with a curt nod as a dark-haired man with a neatly trimmed, pointed beard stepped forward.

"In that case," Hargrave looked between Montague and Padraig, "you are all dismissed." He turned on his heel and strode toward a staircase springing from the marble paving in the left rear corner of the soaring entry, and the servants scattered like beetles before a torch at night. In a moment the entry was empty save for Padraig, Lucan, and the steward.

"Rolf," the knight said. "Please forgive the inconvenience this might cause you in your duties."

"Have no care for it, Sir Lucan," the man said. His face was fish-belly pale within the tight frame of his rich, dark red hair, his eyes like glistening jet. "I am at your service, always." The man then turned to Padraig. "If you will follow me, lord."

Lord.

Padraig looked to Lucan, suddenly unsure but loath to show it. The great house was cathedral-silent now—the scores of servants vanished and leaving an echoing stillness that somehow seemed ominous to Padraig as he noticed the portraits soaring up a wood-paneled wall, their subjects staring at him accusingly, judging him.

Montague seemed to read Padraig's thoughts. "It is well," he advised quietly. "I would not let you go alone otherwise. However, I would advise that you not take it upon yourself to go exploring in the night."

"I shall provide Master Boyd with anything he requires before I retire," Rolf volunteered.

"Very good." Lucan looked back to Padraig. "Keep the bolt thrown until morning."

Padraig gave him a nod, but then held up his open hand before Lucan's doublet to stop him when he would have gone. "The maid you spoke to. Beryl."

"What of her?"

"Do you know her?"

"She was certainly not employed by the Lady Hargrave when last I visited," he replied.

Rolf cleared his throat quietly, drawing Padraig's attention. "If I may; Beryl has only been at Darlyrede for the half year. She is under special duties to the lady." The man looked back to Lucan. "I don't believe we've had the pleasure of Sir Lucan's calling since the turn of the year; is that not so, sir?"

"Indeed. January, if I recall, Rolf," Lucan confirmed. "Until the morn, then." He gave a shallow bow in Padraig's direction and then strode quickly toward the rear of the entry, disappearing into a darkened archway.

Lucan Montague knew Darlyrede House well, obviously—its servants, its corridors.

"This way, lord," Rolf repeated, his words barely louder than a whisper, and yet they seemed to carry in a spiral to the very height of the tall ceiling, where they evaporated into heavy, pressing silence brought on by the glares of the portraits.

Padraig followed the steward from the entry, unable to help the feeling that the quiet of Darlyrede House was nothing more than the insulating thickness of decades of secrets.

And it caused him to wonder where the pretty Beryl had gone, and why she had seemed so afraid.

Chapter 3

Euphemia Hargrave's chamber was empty upon Beryl's return. The fifteen candles burned low, the tray untouched as usual. The connecting door was shut tight, but, pressed by Lord Hargrave's directive, Beryl crossed the floor to rap upon it lightly. She would have done so even had Lord Hargrave not bidden her.

"My lady?" she called. "It is Beryl."

There was no answer, and so Beryl pressed the latch, but the door had been bolted on the other side. The woman was so frail, so fragile, Beryl imagined a hundred tragic scenarios that could have befallen the lady in her absence.

She rapped again, slightly louder. "Lady Hargrave, please, are you well?"

"Beryl?" The call was faint beyond the stout door. "Are you alone?"

"Yes, milady." She swallowed her relief and tried to steady her voice. "I've come to tell you of the happenings."

There was a scraping of metal on wood, and then the door opened a crack, revealing a pale slice of the noblewoman's face.

"I dared journey on my own to the top of the stair," Caris whispered, and Beryl could see even in the shadow of the portal the woman's dry, trembling lips.

Beryl gasped. "Alone? My lady, forgive me, but what if you had stumbled?"

"How could I not see for myself, though? Such chaos. I heard everything."

"Shall I stay with you?" Beryl wanted her—needed her—to open the door. Perhaps there were a few moments to spare before the terrible lord made his appearance. Moments in which Beryl might reclaim the confidence of the woman, might somehow encourage her to tell that which she had been on the verge of. And if she was present in the chamber, perhaps she might glean details of the evil man's plans for Darlyrede's bold claimant.

Darlyrede belongs to me, he'd said.

Beryl shook the image from her mind. "I might be of some comfort."

"It is unnecessary," Caris said. "I will be with my lord husband."

"I know," Beryl blurted out, and then felt her cheeks heat. She hadn't meant to be so bold. "Forgive me, my lady. But...if I may speak plainly, I worry—"

"Nay. Hush. You may not speak plainly," Caris snapped. But then her hand—pale and cool and dry—shot out from the darkness and clutched at Beryl's wrist. Beryl turned it to wrap her fingers around the lady's own—it was like gripping the tiny bones of a bird encased in the thinnest, softest leather.

"He would never harm me," Caris whispered. Her fingers tightened, like thin, strong twine. "Never."

"If anything were to happen to you, milady, I could not forgive myself."

True.

A ghostly sigh came from the darkened chamber. "Ah, my girl. Seek your bed, and let no dire worries trouble your young dreams. All is well. Think upon it no more."

Beryl hesitated, noting the woman had not relinquished her grip. Was she only putting on a brave front?

"Shall I return later? To see if there is anything you desire?"

Lady Hargrave gave a rare, low chuckle, and Beryl could imagine the soft lines near her eyes and mouth pressing into her sad, gentle smile. And then she did slip her hand from Beryl's.

"Good night, Beryl." She closed the door soundlessly.

"Good night, milady," Beryl whispered, hot, stinging tears coming unbidden to her eyes. She leaned her forehead against the wood and pressed against the door with both splayed hands, wishing in that moment that she could vanish the barrier, or turn it transparent at least.

But she had been given her instructions, and she would carry them out faithfully.

Beryl pushed herself away from the door and moved efficiently about the chamber, pulling the heavy drapes closed, straightening the bedclothes. She removed the piece of cheese from the platter and rolled it into a corner of her apron, which she tucked into her waist, and then carried the tray to the corridor, where she placed it on the floor to the side of the doorway. She returned to the chamber to blow out the candles, one by one, save the last, which she pulled from the holder and carried with her to the door.

She paused in the doorway, the single flame barely pressing back the darkness that wept from the corners, from the seams of floor and ceiling and walls. The chamber seemed pregnant with secrets, and perhaps Beryl had come close to witnessing the bearing of them tonight.

Fifteen years of darkness. Of mourning and misery and quiet, tragic ritual. Her breath caught in her throat at her sigh. She closed the door with a silent prayer for the noblewoman waiting alone, just out of her reach.

But as soon as the latch clicked sure, fear for her own safety occupied her thoughts. It was a test of will for Beryl to walk calmly during the long trek to her own chamber from Lady Caris's wing of Darlyrede House. Her heart pounded in her chest so that her blood crackled against her ears. Every whisper of her own slippers against corridor floor or stair she imagined was a footstep behind her; every creak of rafter or window caressed by the wind outside was a door easing open in the darkness. She met not another visible soul on her downward journey, then into the dark corridor inside the curtain wall, and yet she thought she could feel evil eyes watching her just beyond the meager circle of light provided by the diminishing flame of the candle she carried. The hot wax ran in a sudden, burning rivulet over her knuckles and she gasped, instinctively dropping the tiny stub, and the corridor was at once cloaked in total darkness.

Beryl gave up all pretense of bravery now, picking up her skirts in her left hand and running down the passage, her right hand skimming the stones for bearing. The archway to the courtyard near the stables was open, and even though it was fully night, there was enough ambient light from the torches around the barracks for Beryl to reorient herself. She heard the laughter and conversation of the soldiers outside, but she didn't pause to look through the doorway—in fact she ran faster past the opening, praying that she wouldn't be seen.

Stone; wood. Stone; wood. Her fingertips read the corridor like a map. Here, the wall curved into emptiness to the right; to the left was her own passage. Stone, going on forever it seemed, and then, finally, wood again. Beryl threw herself against the door, fumbling with the latch until her trembling fingers could make it work, and then she was at last inside, gasping, her back against the door. She grasped blindly with her left hand, sliding the bolt into place.

The chamber was black, cold, silent. No one had come to lay her fire, as usual. And still she stood there for another pair of moments, giving her heart time to slow, listening to the darkness. She blew out a long, relieved breath, in control of herself once more, and then pushed herself away from the door, shaking off the weak feeling in her limbs.

It took her several moments to build a fire in the tiny alcove. It wouldn't give off very much heat, but the chamber was small enough that it was sufficient. She lit a pair of candles and set one on the little wooden table near her shallow cot and the other in the long, narrow stone inset of what could laughably be referred to as a window. It had at one time been an arrow slit in the exterior side of Darlyrede House's original curtain wall, whose wide, inner corridor had been made over into a wing of tiny servant cells many years ago. The opening was now covered over with a sheet of horn scraped thin and set in a wooden frame, and although it admitted little light, Beryl appreciated being able to open the small portal on nice days to let some of the chill out. It was far too small to ever admit a person. But...

The familiar, scalp-tingling scrape of claw on the bone glazing sounded in the next moment, and Beryl returned to the window, removing the candle and holding it aloft while turning the crude closure and swinging the frame inward. A slithering white stream poured itself through the opening and leaped gracefully to the floor.

"You nearly had me in the muck today." Beryl quickly closed the window and replaced the candle. "How many times must I tell you to keep out of the kitchens?"

"Meow." He was sitting on the edge of the bed now, looking regal, as always.

She crossed the floor and bent to frame his face in her hands, stroking his cheeks with her thumbs. "It's not as if I don't feed you like a prince, Satin."

He pulled out of her hands and stretched out his neck to sniff at the waist of her apron.

"Not even a proper hello. Oh, all right." She took up the candle from her small table and moved to the foot of her bed, squatting to pry at the wooden panel that made up her wall. It came loose easily now, after so many times being removed. She slid it aside and reached into the blackness, finding at once the small, dinged metal dish she kept hidden.

Beryl placed the container on the stingy rug covering the stones and then rose up to fetch the pitcher of water on the table, pouring a little into the flat bowl. She unwrapped the stolen piece of cheese laid in pointless anticipation of a vanished girl's repast and then squatted once more to the floor, placing the cheese near the bowl. The cat plopped to the floor gracefully and reseated himself, nibbling at once on the pale cheese.

Beryl left him to his meal while she replaced the pitcher and then returned to the secret compartment behind the paneling, reaching inside to retrieve the thick, square leather packet and then the smaller linen sack. She placed her belongings on the mattress and then returned the candle to the table before feeding the fire that was now crackling comfortingly. At last she was crawling upon the cot to rest her back against the wall.

She sighed, her hands in her lap for a moment, her gaze turned up to the low ceiling. Satin's lapping at the water out of sight on the floor soothed her. The night had been a complete disaster, but at least here, she could be herself.

She pulled the heavy leather packet onto her lap and unwound the leather thong holding it closed. Once open, the day's events began to recede into a more orderly fashion, the emotion of it falling away as she sifted through the pages gathered together inside the portfolio. Handwritten journals, calendars, sketches of chambers and wings of Darlyrede and other holds in the area of Northumberland, and even beyond.

She came to the most recent entry of her notes and then reached for the linen bag, removing her small pot of ink and pen. She sharpened the tip and opened the pot, pausing a moment to collect her thoughts before dipping the quill and setting it to the paper in the flickering candlelight.

1 October, 1458. C. H. seemed more distraught than usual. Fifteen years since E. H.'s disappearance. Darlyrede was visited by a man claiming to be a legitimate heir to T. A. He is almost certainly Scottish. Quite destitute. Bold. L. M. arrived nearly atop him and appears to be staying, in anticipation of the king. What time is left for the investigation is unknown. C. H. is to meet with V. H. alone this evening. I fear for her health.

Beryl set the page aside to dry while riffling through the stack until she located the drawing she sought. She dipped her quill and dabbed it well on the neck of the pot before turning the tip to its finest edge and leaning her face close to the page. She drew a short line emanating from within a thin rectangle, indicating the doorway between Lady Hargrave's chamber and the one previously belonging to Euphemia Hargrave.

Bolted, C. H. side.

Beryl raised up and looked at the overall sketch, her eyes going at once to a similar rectangle that marked the exit of the chamber into the corridor, and the note she'd made weeks ago.

Bolted, inside. Keyed at corridor.

Her lips pressed together. Euphemia Hargrave's chamber was capable of being secured from the inside against anyone attempting to enter it from the corridor, but it was also outfitted with an intricate mechanism requiring a metal key from the outside, which, to Beryl's mind, would only be required if one wished to keep whoever was in the chamber from leaving. The inner door between the chambers was only able to be secured from Lady Caris's chamber. There was no nurse's quarters attached to the chamber, and as far as Beryl knew, there had never been a nurse assigned to sleep in the chamber with the girl—Lady Caris had been the sole carer. Perhaps the locks were measures that remained from when Euphemia was a young child, and no one had ever seen reason to change it.

Or perhaps the lady had been trying to protect her niece from someone.

The small addition to the map took only a moment to dry, and then Beryl shuffled all the pages together again and secured them within the leather portfolio. Satin chose that moment to leap onto the cot, picking his way daintily around the obstacles until he reached her lap. He circled and then laid himself in the valley of her thighs, his eyes squinting drowsily as he began to purr.

Now Beryl's mind was free to dwell on Padraig Boyd.

He didn't appear to be a man descended from nobility and entitled to a grand manor such as Darlyrede House. As much as she hated to agree with the detestable Lord Hargrave—save for the Scotsman's proud face and his well-muscled frame—Padraig Boyd would be nearly indiscernible from any beggar on a city street. Beryl had certainly seen her share of the destitute masses in Chartres. Rough men and women with no home, no money, no family, begging for the church's charity. But if Padraig Boyd's claims were true, he did have family—Thomas Annesley.

Which turned her reluctant thoughts at last to Lucan. It was all his doing, Beryl was certain. She dreaded the moment when she would have to face him again—now that he had seen her, she knew there was little hope of avoiding him.

There came a light rapping on her door, and Beryl froze, daring not even to breathe. No one came to her chamber in the night—not since she'd first arrived at Darlyrede and a handful of the men employed at the hold had thought to woo her in their rough, clumsy manner. Her wide eyes fixed on the wooden barrier, the candlelight rippling gently over it.

Had her thoughts of Lucan summoned him? Perchance it was the stranger, Padraig Boyd, who pursued her. He had been kind to her in the entry, yes, and there had been something else in his eyes when he'd looked at her—almost as if he was truly speaking to her as a person and not a servant. But despite his handsome looks, his situation was desperate, and Beryl knew from experience that one could never predict the actions of a desperate person.

The door latch rattled insistently once, twice.

Perhaps it was Vaughn Hargrave who sought her at last, ready to bring to life all the dreadful imaginings of her nightmares. Beryl covered her mouth with her hands to stifle any anxious cry, and her gaze flicked nervously to the thick, leather portfolio. In her mind's eye, she saw the wood splintering as the bolt gave way, the dark, hulking figure striding into her chamber, discovering her and her secrets. It seemed that the very roots of her hair ached with the strain.

But the bolt held firm, and no further attempt was made.

Beryl let out her breath slowly through her nose. Her hands drifted down as if sinking through deep water to hover over the mound of warm, white fur. Satin slept on, still curled in her lap, oblivious to the potential danger that lurked in the black corridor beyond the chamber door. He gave a pitiful mew of objection when she gently scooped him up and set him on the rough woven coverlet.

Moving gingerly lest her cot make the faintest betraying creak, Beryl gained her feet and took up the portfolio. She rolled her steps, heel to toe, soundlessly to the black hole in the wall where she deposited the packet without so much as a whisper of leather against stone. She replaced the panel with painstaking slowness, not bothering to go back for the linen sack containing her writing utensils; pen and ink could be replaced.

The pages were exceptional, and a potential death sentence if discovered.

She rose and turned noiselessly, facing the door. With the same careful gait, she crossed the floor and stood nearly touching the wood. Beryl turned her face aside and leaned her ear near the seam of door and wall, holding her breath once more, listening, listening…

A pair of light, percussive taps sounded at her cheekbone, the sudden reverberations against her skin so startling that Beryl gasped aloud and stumbled away from the door, her heart threatening to explode in her chest.

Then footsteps, carelessly loud, receded into the silence of the night.

It was a very long time before she slept.

Chapter 4

Padraig's chamber was invaded just after dawn, Lucan Montague preceding Rolf and a pair of maids carrying trays of food and the items required for a thorough toilette. Padraig washed while Montague ate, his pride unwilling to allow him to sit at the small table in his current state. Even in his plain garb, Lucan Montague seemed a wild gentleman, a snowy linen cloth tossed over his left shoulder, his manner relaxed and yet elegant as he partook heartily of the fragrant nourishment provided. The eating knife seemed a fine instrument in the man's hand, choosing this and that in turn, never hesitating, even as his attention was fixed on Padraig while he gave his initial advice for the morning's affair.

But being clean of body did little to bolster Padraig's confidence when he had no choice but to redon his worn clothes, and it seemed that they had grown more threadbare and filthy since his arrival. He sat down at the table stiffly as Lucan continued.

"He'll not be pleased," Lucan said, pausing to chew and then turn his head slightly to wipe his mouth with the cloth over his shoulder. "But there is little protest he can put forth, lest he wishes to incur the king's displeasure."

Padraig picked up the heavy chalice of watered wine—at least he knew how to drink. "He'll only choose those loyal to him. Nae sane man would lend his enemy his best weapon." He brought the cup to his mouth.

"It's not only up to him." Lucan seemed to pause pointedly while Padraig drained the chalice. Padraig set down the metal cup with a solid thunk and then released a belch before he thought better of it. The knight stared at him.

"What?" Padraig demanded, but his ears burned.

"Nothing. Any matter, I have leave to choose the majority of your camp from Darlyrede's staff. I believe there are few here with any real love for

Hargrave, but most hold such fear of him that there are equally few who will be willing to lend you their support at once." Lucan reached out to flick the tip of his knife over his trencher; it came away with a hunk of tender-looking meat that he promptly plucked from the blade and then placed in his mouth.

"Do I have nae say?" Padraig asked, eyeing the halved roasted birds lying on the platter alongside a pile of dried figs and a round of bread. He was hungry. He picked up the knife alongside his trencher.

"If you like," Lucan said with a touch of surprise, and Padraig could feel the man's eyes on him as he speared the half carcass with his blade.

Padraig caught the other side of the bird with his left hand. It smelled delicious. He would do his best not to embarrass himself, but it was only Montague, after all. "Rolf." He held the fowl suspended between his hand and knife and brought it to his mouth, ripping off a large bite.

Lucan blinked. "Not possible. The steward must remain neutral. Master Boyd, is your blade not sharp?"

Padraig spoke around his food. "I reckon it is. Why?"

"Perhaps you might *use* it. Rolf is in service to Darlyrede House. His sole responsibility is keeping the hold in order."

"He'll have a faggin' hard time o' that, is my wager." Padraig wiped his mouth with his sleeve reflexively, regretting it almost before the wool touched his face.

Lucan reached across the table and lifted a square of cloth—another snowy piece of linen—and handed it to Padraig. "Indeed. Any matter." He dabbed at his mouth with his own napkin again, as if as an example, and then whipped it from his shoulder as he stood. "Forgive me for cutting short your…meal, but they will be gathering in the hall. It's best we arrive before Hargrave has a chance to turn too many ears to his cause through trickery or outright lies."

Padraig nodded and stood, still chewing. His napkin fell to the floor. He peered into the pitcher, but it was already empty. He gestured to Lucan's cup. "You through?"

"What?" the knight asked, and then his eyes went to the chalice Padraig had indicated. "Oh. Yes, I've fini—"

But Padraig had already lifted the cup to his mouth, draining the contents. He sighed in satisfaction, although it would have been more heartening had the wine not been watered.

"I'm ready," Padraig said. Lucan was looking at him queerly again, and so Padraig held up his palms. "Well? Are we to get on or nae?"

Padraig followed Lucan Montague from the chamber and through the maze of corridors, running his hands through his still-damp hair as the knight walked confidently before him. He felt as though the stone passageways were closing in around him, narrowing the farther he walked, until he fancied he could feel them brushing against his shoulders like specters.

His home on Caedmaray was not much wider in breadth than the corridor, true, but with only a trio of steps he could be out the door, under the endless dome of the sky, perched on the top of a world made entirely of the wide sea, the wind tearing through his hair, filling his senses. Padraig felt already as though he hadn't seen the sky in days. His chest tightened, his breathing grew ragged, and he thought he might now understand the panic and distress of the young rams when they needed to be confined.

But at last the corridor opened up into a high-ceilinged chamber—the largest Padraig had ever seen. The great hall, then. Its timbered lofts seemed impossibly tall, its hearth wide enough to shelter a fishing skiff. The stone floor was covered over with rows of trestle tables, and seated on the benches were scattered what had to be two score people. Padraig's eyes scanned the somber faces for the dark-haired maid from last night…

"Ah, you at last grace us with your presence, Lucan," a voice called out in a mocking tone, drawing Padraig's attention to a table on a raised dais near the hearth. At his side was seated a ghost of a woman, paler than snow, her dark hair swooping away from either side of her face like the heavy-looking draperies at the long, narrow windows. Her eyes were hollow, dark, haunted. The Lady Hargrave, she must be. And at *her* side was the only other person in the chamber save Hargrave whom Padraig recognized.

She would not look at him.

Lucan Montague gave a shallow bow. "Lord Hargrave."

The older man's steely gaze swung to Padraig, and his face was expectant.

"I'll nae bow to you, if that's what you're waiting for. You're nae lord o' mine."

Hargrave's brow rose. "My, my. Defensive at the start, are we not, Master Boyd? It's only common courtesy to pay respect to one's host when one is a guest. Especially when they are your better. But I suppose I shouldn't be overly expectant of a show of manners from one seemingly raised in the wild."

Padraig's pride burned at being so blatantly insulted before the beautiful woman who as yet refused to acknowledge his presence. "I'm nae your guest, Hargrave. Darlyrede belongs to my father."

"Back to that, are we? Well, I confess I'm not really surprised. The jingle of a purse tends to bring out all manner of beggars from the cracks."

"You—" Padraig began, but Montague turned quickly and stepped between Padraig and the hall, effectively blocking his view.

"Stop," he commanded in a low voice. "He's baiting you before everyone gathered and you're playing right into his hands. *Stop,* before he turns you into a fool. I assure you, he will." Lucan turned. "Gentlemen, may I remind you that there will be a time and a place to present your cases before the king? We have gathered this morning to do no more than determine the division of the hold."

"*Gentlemen*—ha! Ah, well—the voice of reason, as always, Lucan," Hargrave condescended, but Padraig could tell by the man's smug expression that he felt he had already scored a point. "You will be happy to know that while we were waiting interminably for your arrival, I chose a suitable staff for your ambitious indigent." He waved a hand toward a nearby table, and a trio of brawny and scowling men stood from the benches.

"You should be quite pleased." Hargrave smirked. "They are most suitable to your…specific needs."

"Thank you, Lord Hargrave," Lucan said. "We shall certainly begin with these three."

"Oh, they're all I can spare, I'm afraid."

"Master Boyd shall require personal attendants for his chambers. I do doubt any of these lads has experience as a chambermaid."

"I can throw out me own piss," Padraig muttered.

"Very well," Hargrave agreed quickly. Too quickly, in Padraig's mind. "Searrach?"

A raven-haired woman seated at a table near the first six men rose. She was shapely of body, but her features were sharp. "Aye, milord."

"Are you amenable to serving our guest for the remainder of his—very brief, I'm certain—stay?"

"As you wish, Lord Hargrave."

Padraig felt his eyebrows raise. The woman was a Scot.

Hargrave looked back to Lucan, a thin smile on his face. "There you are. Happy now?"

Padraig suspected he was the only person in the chamber to hear Montague's curt sigh before he strode through the hall, weaving between the tables and benches. He stopped in the center of the gathering, turning in a slow circle.

"You," he said, pointing to a large, somber-looking young man. "And you, there. Yes. You, mistress—is that your daughter with you? Very good; the pair of you, if you please. You, and…also you."

Now Lucan looked back to Hargrave. "That should be a sufficient number for now. I reserve the right to reevaluate in the coming days once Master Boyd becomes settled."

"You reserve the—?" Hargrave grasped both arms of his chair and leaned forward with an incredulous expression. And then he laughed.

"Wait," Padraig interjected, crossing the floor to where Lucan stood and drawing the attention of all in the hall. He cleared his throat. "I'd have my say."

Lucan Montague fixed Padraig with a glare full of daggers.

Padraig ignored him, turning toward the dais fully and pointing toward the woman sitting rigid as a post next to Lady Hargrave. Her gaze seemed fixed on some point away from where Padraig stood at Montague's side.

In the daylight of the hall, Padraig knew she was the most beautiful woman he'd had ever seen. Quite possibly the most beautiful woman in all the world.

She would give him her attention now.

"Her," he said clearly. "Beryl, you called her. I want her."

* * * *

Beryl raised her head so quickly the bones in her neck crackled. She knew her eyes were too wide, her expression full of shocked abhorrence.

"What?" she blurted out and then looked quickly to Caris Hargrave. "My lady," she pleaded quietly.

But Lady Hargrave was already smiling serenely and laid a cool, comforting hand on her arm, even as she spoke toward the hall in her soothing, melodic voice.

"I'm afraid that's not possible, my dear Lucan. Beryl is wholly a lady's maid, and her duties are such that I simply cannot do without her. I'm sure you understand."

Beryl silently let out the breath she'd been holding.

Lucan nodded deferentially. "Of course, my lady. Perhaps someone else, Master Boyd," he suggested.

But the Scotsman was already shaking his head. He crossed his arms over his wide chest, and Beryl noticed then that his hair was curling over his shoulders, his eyes sparkling as they continued to look upon her boldly. He'd had a bath at least, if not a change of clothes. The way he pinned her with his gaze was offensive—that could be the only reason her heart was beating wildly in her chest. Of course she was insulted.

Did he know nothing of how to behave?

"Nae," he said. "She'll do."

Lucan closed the spare distance separating him from Padraig Boyd, and Beryl watched them closely, although she could not hear the terse tones exchanged between the two. After a moment Lucan turned once more toward the dais, and the rigid expression on his handsome features was one she well recognized.

"Master Boyd insists, my lady," he said through obviously clenched teeth. "He has need of a woman servant."

"I have little care for his insistence," Caris said wonderingly. "And my lord husband has already given him a wench from his own…tribe. Regardless of Master Boyd's alleged claim to this hold, Beryl is mine. And I shall not turn her over to…to such a base stranger to be abused."

Warm affection for the woman bloomed anew in Beryl's chest and her eyes prickled with grateful tears.

"Montague, you are upsetting my wife," Lord Hargrave warned.

"That is not at all my intention, my lord," Lucan replied, and Beryl could sense the strained patience in his tone. "If I may speak with candor, I have advised Master Boyd that he may be better served by individuals who perhaps"—here Lucan looked directly at Beryl, and his accusation was loud, even if Beryl was the only one who could hear it—"do not hold such loyalty to your family."

Beryl looked at the nobleman from the corner of her eye and saw his brow raise. "Indeed."

"The answer is no," Caris Hargrave interjected.

It seemed as though everyone's gaze now turned to the Scotsman standing like an oak in the center of the hall. Patient. Immovable. He shook his head again.

"'Tis her I'll be having," he said. "Else I'll take my grievance and proof of my claim to the king's court myself."

Hargrave laughed. "You can't do that, you buffoon. He'll have you thrown in jail."

"Let's just see if he doos, then," Padraig Boyd answered curiously and then turned on his heel and strode toward the doorway of the hall. The echoes of his footfalls dying away were the only sounds in the cavernous space for a pair of moments.

"What proof does this fool think he has against me, Montague?" Lord Hargrave demanded suddenly.

Lucan's face was stony, and he didn't so much as twitch to go after the vanished Scotsman. "I don't know, my lord. Regardless, Henry will be much displeased with us all at having his very clear commands disobeyed when he has already set aside his schedule for the business of Darlyrede House."

"*Fool*," Hargrave muttered again. He rubbed his lips in an agitated fashion with his fingertips and glanced at his wife, who appeared to Beryl to be not at all concerned with this turn of events.

Then the old nobleman let out a string of whispered curses. "Very well," he said smoothly at last, obviously recovered of his composure. "Go fetch your beggar pet. If I can spare the king any upset, we shall all endure for his sake."

"My lord," Caris whispered, "I will not allow it."

"Only for a short time, my dear," Lord Hargrave soothed. His gaze flicked to Lucan. "Go on, before he escapes us."

The hair on Beryl's neck rose at the phrase.

Lady Hargrave's chair legs screeched against the wood as she gained her feet, her pale, frail fingertips on the tabletop holding her steady.

"No!" she shouted. "No, I say! I need her—she shall not be some...some pawn," Caris gasped, and Beryl could see the woman's veins standing out on her fragile neck, could see the trembling of her whole person.

"My lady." Beryl rose and pinched a fold of the woman's fine sleeve. "Please, be not distressed on my account."

The woman flung off her touch with a wild motion that caused her to sway. "You will not go against my wishes!" Her voice was thin, raspy in her passion. "*Lord Hargrave!* I shall die!" The woman's knees buckled, and Beryl caught her mistress in her arms, lowering her back into the chair.

"My lady, I beg of you," Beryl whispered, patting the woman's arm, her hair, fanning her with her hand. "Calm yourself. I can perform both duties, I swear it. I'll not leave you. I shall be at your chamber every night, as always. Everything shall be as it is now. I swear it. Please." Beryl's voice broke on her plea. If the woman worked herself in to apoplexy, died on Beryl's behalf after all that she had already endured, Beryl would never forgive herself.

She would never forgive Lucan, or Padraig Boyd, whoever he revealed himself to be.

"We have little choice, my dear," Vaughn Hargrave said in a sinister voice. "We must bear it until we can be rid of him. I would not ask it of you if it weren't necessary."

"You ask me nothing," Caris rasped. "You do things without my knowledge. I know it." Her breathy words trembled and broke.

Beryl's eyes widened, but she dared not lift her gaze to look upon Lord Hargrave. She had never heard his wife speak in such a way to him directly, and the undercurrent of her statement was deep and dark and swift.

"You mustn't think such things of me, my dear," Lord Hargrave warned quietly.

Beryl's heart pounded as she dared intervene. "Everything shall be as it has always been," she repeated. "Please, my lady. I will take care of you."

Commotion in the hall signaled that Lucan had successfully located his prey, but Beryl did not give them the consideration of her attention, for Caris Hargrave at last turned her face toward Beryl, the motion so slow that it seemed as though it must have taken every drop of strength left in the frail woman's body. Painful uncertainty filled her eyes. And fear. She was afraid.

"He'll take you from me, too," she breathed, her head on Beryl's shoulder, her mouth by her ear.

Beryl's heart pounded as she shook her head. "Never," she whispered down. The hand on her arm tightened.

Lord Hargrave's hateful voice called out, "Now that you have sent my wife into distress and caused discord between us, are we in agreement, Boyd?"

"Aye," the Scotsman allowed. "For now."

Beryl did look up then, in shock at the man's seemingly reckless nerve, as Hargrave banged his fist on the table.

"*Get out of my hall*," he demanded through clenched teeth.

Padraig Boyd stood in the midst of the tables and gawking residents, but rather than appear intimidated or shamed, he wore a slight smile across the wide planes of his face.

His bright gaze found Beryl's, and he winked at her.

Then he turned and preceded Lucan into the corridor from which they'd emerged.

Chapter 5

Padraig knew he had won that first battle, but his triumphant exit was ruined shortly after gaining the corridor by Lucan Montague's swift yank on his arm.

"This way," the knight ordered crisply, walking at once in the opposite direction into a dark tributary of the main passage.

Padraig quashed his newly birthed pride and followed. "Where are we going?"

"The barracks."

"What for?"

"To meet with your servants."

"Why?"

"So they might be educated on their expected duties."

"They doona already ken what they're about?"

Lucan's only answer was a curt sigh.

Padraig obviously didn't understand something that was perhaps very basic, and it was clear that the Englishman was already running out of patience with him this first full day at Darlyrede. Padraig wasn't used to and didn't like feeling unsure, ignorant, vulnerable. And so he asked no more questions while he followed Lucan out of the keep proper and into Darlyrede's wide, busy inner courtyard.

No sooner had the pair of men entered into the low-ceilinged common room attached to the stables than the appointed staff from the hall began to file in, singly and in pairs. Scottish Searrach came alone, and her gaze immediately sought Padraig's. She looked him over boldly.

She was striking, and Padraig's interest was stirred. What was she, a Scottish lass with the wild look of the Highlands in her hollowed cheeks, doing here at English Darlyrede?

Lucan drew Padraig's attention from the woman when he pulled out a rough stool from the end of the common table and gestured to Padraig before sitting in the seat to the right. Padraig eased himself down, feeling all the eyes in the chamber on him now as the servants lined the walls. The burly men appointed by Hargrave were the last to arrive.

Beryl had yet to appear.

Lucan cleared his throat. "In the time until the king's decision, you have been appointed to serve Master Boyd. I expect that you all will fulfill your roles properly. Your loyalty, until you are informed otherwise, is to him."

One of the burliest men chuckled. He was ugly and bald and greasy. "My loyalty is to him that pays my wage. And that be Lord Hargrave."

Lucan paused and pinned the man with a cool stare. "Your loyalty shall be to Master Boyd. And if I receive word otherwise, you will be dismissed from Darlyrede altogether."

The ugly man's condescending smile never left his face. "I'd like to see you try, me fair lad."

The entire chamber seemed to be holding its breath, waiting for Lucan's response.

Padraig felt like a child, seated at table and yet forced to remain silent while the adults conversed. The more the image turned in his mind, the angrier and more resentful he became. This was not Lucan Montague's battle.

"I am here on the direct command of the king," Lucan began in a stern voice.

Padraig gained his feet, but no one paid him any heed as they were too enraptured with the exchange between the rough servant and the fine knight. It was only until Padraig put himself directly in front of the contentious man that the servant took notice of him in an annoyed fashion.

Padraig realized the man wasn't actually very tall.

"What's your name?" Padraig asked in a low, curious tone.

The man huffed a laugh and glanced to either side of him at his mates before lifting his chin in an arrogant fashion, so as to look Padraig in the eye.

The man spat a mouthful of warm saliva at Padraig. It struck his throat and slid down thickly.

"That's my name to you." His grin was challenging, mocking. "I can say it again, if you wish. *Master Boyd.*"

The chamber was tomb silent.

Padraig's mind swirled with indecision. He knew this would be a crucial moment in his future—how the people in the chamber would forever remember his first actions at Darlyrede House, his first actions as the lord of the hold. Although his instinct wanted him to send his forehead into the man's wide nose, Padraig did not want loyalty through fear of punishment.

But he could not be seen a coward by the rest of the servants, and certainly not by the man's cronies.

What had his da always said? "Padraig, it is verra fine to have a friend at your side. But it is greater to keep those who are nae your friend in your sight at all times."

This man was clearly not invested in Padraig's success.

"Nae need for that," Padraig said easily. He took out a kerchief from his belt and swiped at his neck. "Let it be noted that I've found my chambermaid, Sir Lucan."

The crowd gathered in the chamber gasped.

"Aye, this man here shall be my own attendant."

The servant's eyes widened for a moment, and then his heavy brows dropped. "Not a chance."

"Verra well," Padraig acquiesced. "If the job doesnae suit, you can, the lot of you, take yourselves back to Hargrave and tell him you've been dismissed." Padraig's gaze did not waver.

It was clear that the man was now backed into a corner, and it confirmed Padraig's suspicions: Vaughn Hargrave had chosen the band of rough, brawny servants to spy on Padraig and cause trouble—perhaps worse. If one of them was refused and they were all sent away, it would diminish the evil man's assets, and Padraig thought the punishment doled out by Hargrave would likely be worse than any retaliation Padraig could think of in the moment for the man's insult.

"Your choice," Padraig urged. "Stay or leave. If you're to stay, 'tis a chambermaid you'll be."

The man's jowls quivered, his nostrils flared.

"What say you"—Lucan called out from behind Padraig—"Booger, is it?"

"It's Cletus," he said at last, through clenched teeth. His chin lifted again. "Chamberlain is the more proper title."

"Cletus," Lucan said airily, and Padraig could hear the scratching of Montague's quill as he muttered, *Chambermaid to Master Boyd.* He paused. "There. I am sorry, but Master Boyd doesn't know better at this point, and so chambermaid it is. It has a certain quality to it, though, I must say."

The man's face was nearly violet now.

"You're dismissed," Padraig said quietly.

Cletus's chest heaved for a moment, but then he jerked his shoulders to the left, ducking through the doorway and from the chamber.

Padraig turned in a slow circle, meeting everyone's gaze who stared openly at him. "Anyone else care to air a grievance? I will hear you." He had turned almost full circle when Searrach caught his eye. He stopped.

Her lips parted and her tongue sneaked out to dampen them, her dark eyes sultry. "I'd hoped to be chosen as the lord's maid," she protested quietly and took Padraig's measure down to his boots.

He cleared his throat. "I'm certain his...knightship will find you a fitting place."

Her lips curved in a smile.

Padraig turned his back to the woman and made his way to his seat once more while his ears burned. He ignored Lucan's squinting, quizzical glance as he sat down.

Knightship?

"Very well," Lucan said at last, rescuing Padraig with a return to his gruff, businesslike tone. "One at a time; state your name and your regular duty in the hold."

* * * *

It was over in less than an hour, and the common room of the soldiers was emptied save for Padraig and Lucan. Padraig leaned his elbows on the table as if he'd spent all day fighting the waves of the North Sea to the mainland. He was already exhausted.

But, at his side, Lucan rose briskly, his demeanor that of one who had just awoken from a refreshing nap. "I've some business to take care of for the next hour. How might you occupy yourself until then?"

"I'm nae child, Lucan."

"From your earlier behavior in the hall, I remain unconvinced."

Padraig's brows lowered. "Hargrave needed to understand that he canna coo me. It was one wee request—I left the rest of it to the pair of you."

Lucan sighed. "Aye, Padraig, it was but one request. But it was the maid of Lady Hargrave. Do you not think that was perhaps pressing it a bit much?"

Padraig shrugged, not wanting to admit to the man that he had done little but think of the woman's lovely face since she'd been thrown at his feet upon his arrival.

"She didna come, any matter, did she?" he said, trying to squeeze the petulance from his tone.

"She did not," Lucan agreed curtly. "And although it might sting your pride, it is perhaps fortuitous that she has been this once disobedient."

"Surely she doesna appease the woman's every whim."

"That very thing describes the whole of her duty," Lucan said, and he sounded none the happier for it.

Padraig sniffed. "Thinks herself too good for the likes of me."

Lucan paused for a moment, then looked at Padraig squarely. "At this point, and you must believe me, she is most certainly too good for you."

"I thought you were for me?"

"I am," Lucan insisted dryly. Then a sound from the doorway drew his attention. "Ah, Rolf," he said as the steward entered. "Excellent timing, as usual. Would you be free to show Master Boyd about the grounds?"

"Certainly, Sir Lucan. In fact I had intended to suggest Master Boyd might appreciate a tour of the various industries Darlyrede employs within her walls."

"Och, I've a keeper?" Padraig lamented. "Jesus, Lucan, what's an hour? The ignorant Scot shallna drown himself in a privy."

Lucan cocked his head. "Padraig. You are a stranger here, in more ways than one, surrounded by very dangerous enemies. I'm trying to keep you alive until you have learned to recognize the hazards—and allies—for yourself. They are where and whom you might least suspect."

Padraig paused for a moment, weighing his response. Who else in the world could he trust? At last he stood from the stool and nodded.

"Verra well." He looked to Rolf expectantly.

Rolf cocked his head. "This way, Master Boyd."

* * * *

Beryl paced her small chamber floor, wringing her hands. Her pages were still scattered on her narrow cot, the ink still drying, but she found she could not sit still with her thoughts.

He'll take you from me, too.

What had Lady Hargrave meant? The other servants rumored to have gone missing from the household over the years?

Or Cordelia? Euphemia?

You do things without my knowledge. I know it.

Beryl shuddered at the thinly veiled implications the lady had dared in the hall. There had been no one else close enough to hear the accusations save herself, and for that very reason, Beryl knew the stakes had only gone up for her. Hargrave would surely put her under closer watch now. It was unlikely she could glean any useful information about his movements without placing herself directly within his dangerous reach, and then it might be impossible to extract herself. She was already risking so much...

A pair of raps fell upon her door, causing her breath to freeze in her chest. Everyone in the hall had likely thought her to have followed the other servants chosen for the Scots' camp when she left, and so whoever knocked could only be one who knew she had not been present at the muster.

As if in answer, another quick pair of raps fell, followed by a single knock. Two, two, one. The old signal from the abbey. She could put him off no longer, for either of their sakes.

She walked to the door and placed her mouth near the seam of wall. "Who is it?" she called quietly.

"You bloody well know who it is, *Beryl*."

She slid the bolt and opened the door, allowing Lucan Montague to slip inside. She secured the door once more and turned to face him. His face was stony—she had no idea in which direction he would go.

But then he held out his arms. "I am so very glad to see you."

Beryl flew into them with a cry of relief and pressed her face into his chest.

"I may take a strap to you later," he amended, "but I am truly glad."

"Oh, Lucan, I had no idea you would be here so soon." She pulled away. "Why *are* you here, and with that Scottish man?"

"Why am *I* here?" he queried with a stern look. "Iris Montague, you know bloody well why I'm here. Why are *you* bloody here? And as Lady Hargrave's bloody maid, no less! Are you mad? Why are you called Beryl? When did you arrive? Rolf implied—"

Iris held up a palm. "Come, sit down," she said. "I don't have long, but I can tell you the very first of it. Or show you, rather." She gathered the pages and her leather portfolio together and held them out to him.

He took them. "What is all this?"

"What I'm bloody doing at Darlyrede House, dear brother."

Lucan sifted through the pages as she spoke, quickly at first, and then his movements slowed, his eyes widening.

"After you last visited, we had a girl come to the abbey; a lady's maid from an English household traveling in France had gotten herself with child and been left behind to bear the baby. Her name was Beryl and she was under my care."

Lucan tore his eyes away from the pages to look at her. "That doesn't explain how *you* came to be *here*."

"The lady Beryl served sent messages occasionally, to ask after her welfare. She was quite awful from the sounds of them, and I knew that her home in England was not far from Darlyrede. I read them all, and replied for Beryl. But then Beryl died in childbirth," Iris explained. "As did her baby. And that very day another message came from Beryl's lady. So I again responded, telling Lady Paget that the child had died, and that I—as Beryl—was too heartbroken and ashamed to return to her employ. I begged her mercy to recommend me to another house."

Lucan's expression seemed to freeze. She had managed to surprise her stiff-lipped brother. "*Lady Paget* got you the position here?"

Iris's eyes widened and she clasped her hands together at her chest. "Yes," she hissed. "Caris Hargrave sent funds and an escort for my travel. Isn't it amazing?"

"No, it's not amazing," Lucan insisted. "It's mad! The maid came from *the Pagets*? And the Hargraves didn't recognize you?"

"Of course not; the last time they saw me, I was a child, Lucan. It was clearly God's will."

"Speaking of God, how did you escape the abbey? Surely when the escort arrived for Beryl, the abbess told him she was dead."

"He didn't come as far as the abbess," Iris said with a grin. "When I heard he'd come I packed all Beryl's things, which I had hidden after her death, into the market basket, and left the abbey as usual for the village. Once at the willow grove near the river, I changed into Beryl's clothes and met my escort at the inn."

Lucan appeared stunned into speechlessness. "But...but I've received no word from the abbess that you were missing."

She smiled sweetly. "I flung my habit into the river. They likely think I drowned but still wish for my stipend to continue. Since you never sent any letters inquiring as to my welfare," she pointed out.

"Sly," her brother mused. Then his face dropped back to the sheaves of papers scattered over his lap. "Iris, this is..."

"Helpful? Remarkable? Vital to our investigation?"

"*My* investigation," Lucan corrected distractedly and then looked up to meet her eyes again. "But, yes, all of that. It's also incredibly dangerous."

"I know," she agreed. She grew solemn and then turned to sit on the cot next to her brother. "But I couldn't just stay there in France, waiting for you. You *never* wrote. I never knew where you were, if you were safe, if you had learned anything new. I was desperate."

"I couldn't send the kind of information you wanted," he protested. "It would have been too hazardous if it fell into the wrong hands."

"I understood—I understand," she rushed to assure him. "But they were my parents; Castle Dare my home too. I may not remember them as you do, but I remember how I felt after they died. I remember the fire, the smell of the smoke, the blackened walls of our home. I remember the ship, and arriving at the abbey. I remember those years we were scared and alone in a foreign land." Her brows drew down. "And I remember when the rumors reached all the way to France. I couldn't stay there any longer. Lucan, I wanted to come *home*."

Lucan looked at the pages for a moment longer, nodding his head distractedly, and then sighed. "I cannot say you've not done well. But now that I've arrived at Darlyrede, there is absolutely no need for you to stay on. I have the papers."

Iris's eyes widened. "I'm not leaving," she insisted. "Not now. I can't. I promised Lady Hargrave I'd—"

"Iris, listen to yourself; you just cited a vow to a Hargrave as the reason you cannot leave a highly perilous situation. If Vaughn Hargrave finds out you've been spying on the household, making these notes—*maps*, for God's sake!" He gestured toward her with the pages.

"That's another thing," Iris said quickly. "Lucan, there's no cellar in all of Darlyrede. The house is ancient, and yet—"

"Yes, it's ancient," her brother interjected. "And so, like many others, the cellar likely collapsed or was so unstable that it was filled as new additions to the hold were made. It won't matter if Lord Hargrave—"

"He won't find the pages."

"Well, he won't now," Lucan allowed, "for I'll have them."

"Oh, no," Iris warned, and then pulled at the stack. Only half of them came away before Lucan tightened his grip on them and the portfolio. Without fully realizing it, Iris resorted to the French they both had spoken for so many years. "I've risked my neck to accumulate this information—I'll not have you taking all the credit. Give me the rest."

"I'll not," Lucan answered her in French without hesitation, twisting the pages out of her reach. "You shall leave at once. As soon as I can make arrangements."

"No, I shan't. I've nowhere to go, any matter," Iris argued. "Lucan, I know you think this is the best way to keep me safe, but it's not. If I leave suddenly, it will be suspect."

"It won't be suspect," Lucan argued. "You made it very clear in the hall that you did not wish to serve Master Boyd. Servants run away."

"It's not that," Iris continued. "Lady Hargrave is in very real danger from that monster who is her husband. She confides in no one else save me." She pleaded with him with her eyes. "I'm all she has. If I leave her, Lady Hargrave will die—either at the hands of Vaughn Hargrave or from a broken heart."

"Iris—"

"Just listen to me, please," she pressed. "I have insight here that you do not. I am trusted. Isn't that worth something?"

Lucan looked at her for a long time without saying anything, and Iris knew her reasoning was working. Lucan was rarely swayed from his decisions, but she could hear the creaking of his resolve.

"Why didn't you come to the barracks?"

"I needed to make my notes while they were still fresh in my mind," she said. "I'll not play chambermaid to that stubborn Scots lout, any matter."

"No, you shan't," Lucan agreed. "Cletus has been assigned his chambermaid."

Iris snorted reflexively and brought a hand to her mouth. "Cletus? Hargrave's minion? Perhaps I should have attended, if only for the entertainment."

"Yes, you should have," Lucan continued. "Especially because you seem determined to stay on at Darlyrede. You must take up a position in his camp, now that it's been allowed."

"In both camps," Iris lamented. "In what possible capacity could a lady's maid benefit a rough Scotsman intent on defeating a member of the English nobility?"

Lucan stared at her for a long moment, as if she'd said something extremely stupid—or brilliant.

"*Exactly.*" He'd had the same look about him on the day when he was ten and six and he'd told her he'd decided to become employed by the king of England. "You shall be Master Boyd's tutor."

Iris frowned. "His...tutor?"

"Yes," Lucan mused, putting the portfolio and pages aside on the cot and, rising, working out his plan to himself as he paced the small chamber, while Iris scrambled to gather all her work together once more. "That could encompass any number of things. We might also say you are teaching him to read—that will amuse Lord Hargrave."

"I don't understand," Iris said, glancing over her shoulder before shoving the portfolio beneath the coverlet. She straightened and turned to face her brother. "What do you *actually* want me to do with the man, Lucan?"

"Padraig Boyd is...ah," Lucan paused, squinted a bit. "Rough."

Iris called to mind at once an image of the large Scotsman standing in his rugged clothes, his muscles straining at the cloth, his square jaw that only—

She cleared her throat as her cheeks began to tingle. "Yes, I've noticed."

Lucan nodded. "So you can imagine the difficulties he will encounter once Hargrave calls his cronies to descend upon Darlyrede, as he surely will. And should the king arrive...well."

Iris pulled a face as she imagined the Scot dropped into the center of the crowd of nobility that Hargrave considered his circle. "He isn't quite eloquent."

"Believe me, his table manners are worse than his speech."

"He'll be completely humiliated. The king will laugh at the idea of giving a man like that Darlyrede and its title."

"Which is why it shall be *your* job to educate him on the ways of the nobility. By the time Padraig Boyd encounters Henry, he needs to be a perfect gentleman."

Iris paused. "How can you be sure this is the right thing to do? Aren't we placing ourselves—you, especially, with your position in the Order—at risk of losing everything if the king sides with Hargrave? If we let it play out without interfering—"

"It's the right thing to do," Lucan interrupted, "because Padraig Boyd is Thomas Annesley's only legitimate heir. He is our only chance of toppling Hargrave from this lofty perch he seems to have grown so comfortable upon. If I cannot prove who had a hand in the fire that killed our parents and forfeited their lands to the Baron Annesley, I can at least do my best to see that Vaughn Hargrave loses everything he has to a man who deserves it, by rights."

Iris stared at her brother. She could see the ardor in his eyes beneath his perpetually composed exterior. He was ready and willing to risk it all for this rough Scotsman. But would the reward be worth it?

"Will we regain our lands? If Padraig Boyd succeeds?"

Lucan gave the slightest shrug. "I don't know. Sheep and cattle graze about the ruin. Have you been?"

A scratching sounded upon the window, prompting Iris to huff in annoyance when in reality she was glad for the interruption that prevented her from answering her brother's question. "He must have heard you."

"Who?" Lucan asked, and then almost immediately, "Surely not—"

Iris opened the window and the white, slithering fog that was Satin slid through the opening and bounded to the floor, trotting at once to Lucan to wind about his ankles.

"*Bon jour, mon petit ami*," Lucan said, a smile in his voice as he bent and scooped up the cat. "My God, I thought I'd never see this scoundrel again. I can't believe you brought him."

"I couldn't leave him," Iris lamented as she stepped forward to scratch Satin's forehead. "Unfortunately, cats bring out hectics and choking asthma in Lady Hargrave. It's been all I can do to keep him hidden, and keep Cook from taking a cleaver to him every time her ladyship sneezes."

Lucan chuckled. "Well, I say a bit of a tickle is a small price to pay for a maid as devoted as you."

"It's more serious an aversion than just a tickle, Lucan. It could truly kill her. I must be very careful. And now I'll need to change my gown before I visit her tonight. Even one hair…"

Lucan sobered and looked down into Iris's face. "It's obvious that you have become attached to her, Iris. But you must remember, regardless of the danger that Lady Hargrave might be in, *your* safety is paramount. Tread carefully. Caris Hargrave was friends with our mother, remember."

"Maybe that's why I feel so protective of her," Iris mused. "She is the closest thing I have to a parent. Will you tell Padraig Boyd I am your sister?"

Lucan shook his head. "It's too soon. Everything here is too foreign, and he is yet too impulsive. We cannot trust that he would understand our motivations, nor that he might not slip at the wrong moment or with the wrong person. I don't think he realizes just how deadly a place Darlyrede House is. But he will."

Iris nodded and sighed, dropping her hand. "When shall I begin?"

"Today," Lucan insisted. "Now that we have decided our path, we can waste not another moment. Upon my honor, we shall need each one." Lucan took Satin to the window and prodded him out.

"I trust that I'll not be receiving any more surprise visits from you in my chamber," Iris said as she followed her brother to the door. She stepped around him to place her hand on the latch.

"We shall see enough of each other in Master Boyd's presence, I think." He leaned in to press a kiss to her temple. "I'm glad you are here, Iris."

She smiled up at him. "As am I." Iris opened the door and peered both ways down the dark corridor before stepping aside and letting him pass.

"Wait," Lucan whispered, trying to turn back into the chamber. "The portfolio…"

Iris shoved the door closed and bolted it, resting her back against it with a grin.

Chapter 6

By the time Padraig was led back to his chamber by Lucan Montague, his head was spinning, and not only from being overwhelmed at Darlyrede's prosperity—the place was indeed a veritable empire. The steward had walked him about the grounds within the tall stone walls, passing innumerable industries of the hold, and all the servants employed there were busy at their tasks, unsmiling, unfriendly. The majority of them wouldn't raise their eyes to meet Padraig's gaze, and those who did regarded him with outright suspicion.

It was a rich man's home, that was certain. Padraig guessed the whole of the habitable part of the island of Caedmaray could be set down neatly within the walls, with no risk of rubbing up against the stone. Padraig had asked stupidly where the grazing animals were, and Rolf's confused expression before he composed himself to answer that they were with the shepherds in the fields had prompted him to keep any further rash inquiries to himself for the time being. But as they strolled briskly between cottages and stalls and canopies housing the trades of Darlyrede, Padraig's worry increased.

This had been his father's home. All this wealth had belonged to Thomas Annesley, third Baron Annesley. How could that be reconciled with Tommy Boyd—the gruff, strong, quiet man Padraig knew simply as Da. Darlyrede still belonged to him. Or belonged perhaps to Padraig now.

What was he to do with it all? Padraig knew only sheep, and fishing, and the weather, and the sea.

They were walking back along the wall toward the keep when the projectile glanced off Padraig's skull from above. His vision flickered, he staggered, and Rolf grabbed his arm. The servants gathered nearby gasped in fright.

"Lord, are you all right?"

Padraig brought his hand away from his bloody scalp; he could feel the gash beneath his hair. He looked down at the burst wooden pail at his feet, its load of stones spilled in the dirt. He and Rolf looked to the top of the wall in the same moment, but there was nothing to be seen along the walk.

"Fell off the ledge, you think, Rolf?" Padraig muttered.

The steward didn't answer, although his expression was dark with anger. The knight didn't seem surprised. "And so it begins," Lucan mused grimly.

A thorny lump had grown in Padraig's stomach—along with the throbbing ache in his head—by the time Rolf made his excuses and left Padraig with the English knight once more.

They were not truly alone, though—the chamber held a handful of the servants Padraig had met earlier in the barracks and, after Padraig's head wound had been tended, they all seemed bent to some task; the chamber was a quiet hive of activity.

"We shall commence with your wardrobe," Montague announced in a businesslike tone, moving around the bed to set up his ever-present packet of ink and quill and parchment on the small table, as if Padraig hadn't just nearly been killed in the bailey.

The matronly woman Lucan had chosen in the hall, whom Padraig now knew was called Marta, approached him, a long ribbon stretched between her hands.

"If you'd be so kind as to hold out your arms, Master Boyd?" she queried. Upon Padraig's hesitation, she demonstrated, lifting her thick arms to her sides like a seabird coasting on a warm current of air.

Padraig cautiously raised his arms to shoulder height, and the *slip-slip* sound of the ribbon between Marta's fingers sliced the air like swallows over a field.

She called out a series of seemingly random numbers and then said to him, "Turn 'round, please." Another series of numbers. Padraig tried not to jump when her plump arms came about his waist from behind, then his hips. But he could not help flinching when her fingertips came between his thighs with a firm prod.

"Step apart, please." *Slip-slip.*

Marta called out more numbers, and then Padraig noticed her daughter at the bedside, a piece of chalk in her hand over a length of dark, rough fabric. Rynn finished her scribbling and then straightened, coming toward him with a square of the stiff fabric.

Rynn dropped to her knees before Padraig. "Your boots, please, Master Boyd."

Lucan looked around briefly from his papers. "Don't forget his head. I think he should perhaps be fitted for a helm."

Padraig's brow lowered into a momentary frown, but it only increased the pounding in his head.

Marta held up a finger with a nod. "Bless you, Sir Lucan." She came at him again while Padraig was still struggling out of his right boot.

Rynn pushed the fabric square toward his toes. "Step on, please."

As Padraig did, trying to ignore the rags that were the stockings on his feet—more hole than cloth—a screech on the wood floor directly behind him prompted him to turn his head.

"Master Boyd! Hold still, please," Rynn chastised from the floor.

Marta frowned into his face from her new vantage point of standing on a stool, then took hold of his skull with gentle fingers and swiveled his head forward once more. Padraig stood obediently as Rynn's chalk tickled along the edges of his feet onto the burlap. Marta's ribbon swooped about his forehead and tightened. He heard the chamber door open and close.

"Master Boyd wants a trim if he is to have any hope of fitting into a helm, and to avoid being referred to as 'mistress,'" Marta announced, before the ribbon whispered away from his head and she popped down off the stool.

Lucan nodded but didn't raise his head. "Very good. Right away."

"Step away, please." Rynn whisked the tracing from beneath his feet and rose.

The brisk drafts caused by the women's coming and going left Padraig standing on the floor in his pathetic stocking feet feeling very unsure. His arms were still slightly akimbo and he wasn't certain that he should move or not, lest he be politely chastised—or worse, tethered by his aching head—again. He turned slowly, testing his freedom.

She was standing not six paces from him, her arms laden with cloth draped over her elbow, a tray in her hands. Her rich, brown hair—like a paste of oil and costly spices—was glossy smooth over her ears, her light complexion composed as she regarded him.

Beryl. She'd come at last.

Should he bow? Clasp her hand? Before he could decide, his breath left him in a rush as he was pulled backward through the air and his teeth clacked together as his rear connected with a hard stool. An instant later, a cloth was whisked around his chest and tied tightly against his Adam's apple.

Beryl's pink lips crept up, but then she dropped her eyes and rolled her lips inward as she strode forward toward the bed.

Padraig was trying to force his lips to form *something*, but his voice seemed stuck in his throat just below the strangling cloth. His hair was yanked from behind with the sharp teeth of a comb, and then the crisp sounds of a chunk of hair being severed sizzled in his ear. Beryl set down the tray on his bed, ignoring him still.

"Where've you been?" he blurted out.

All sound and movement in the chamber seemed to still. From the corner of his eye, Padraig saw even Montague turn his head from his papers to regard him.

Fool!

Beryl straightened slowly and then turned to face him, her expression serene, her hands folded together before her.

"Good day, Beryl," she said pointedly, inclining her head just so.

Padraig glanced around the chamber, his breathing shallow. Marta yanked on a lock of his hair just then, causing him to yelp. He cleared his throat. "Good day, Beryl," he repeated at last.

"Good day, Master Boyd," she replied. "Forgive my tardiness. I had prior obligations to attend to before my facilities were secured to your service."

Padraig hesitated. "Nae harm," he ventured.

Her mouth quirked, her expression that of one who was not entirely satisfied but willing to accept his offering. The chamber fell back into its pattern of busyness at once, and Padraig released his breath.

"Good day, Marta, Rynn," she said to the maids, who seemed to be taking turns cutting at both the length of cloth Rynn had marked with chalk and Padraig's hair.

"Beryl."

"Mistress."

Beryl looked at Padraig pointedly, and he thought he understood—everything at Darlyrede revolved around one's station.

Beryl cleared her throat as she turned her gaze toward the seated knight.

Lucan turned around. "Ah, yes—forgive me. I see the lessons have started. Good day...Beryl, is it?"

"How kind of you to remember. A good day to you, Sir."

"Lessons?" Padraig repeated.

"Yes, lessons, Master Boyd," she answered briskly, and then her gray eyes grew round. "What on earth has happened to your head?"

"'Tis naught," Padraig scoffed, his ears heating.

Lucan muttered from the table without raising his head. "Someone dropped a bucket of stones on him. Don't worry, he's being fitted for a helm."

"I see." Beryl's expression was solemn as she held his gaze for a long moment. He saw her chest rise and fall in a sigh before she resumed her practical interrogation. "Marta, have you much longer at the master's hair?"

"Just finishing up now, mistress."

"Excellent." She strode across the table and spoke quietly to two young men stacking wood near the hearth. When she returned across the floor, the men followed her, bearing a small table and the other chair.

They positioned the furniture before Padraig just as Marta whisked the cloth from around his shoulders.

Beryl transferred the tray to the tabletop and then shook out a snowy linen. "I've brought your midday meal," she announced.

"Good." Padraig was starving. He reached for the domed cover.

"Ah," she said sharply, with a sideways look.

Padraig froze, his hand hovering over the filigreed handle. "Thank you?"

"*This*," she said, ignoring his thanks and draping the linen over her palm with the delicate, pinched fingers of her other hand, "is a *napkin*."

Padraig didn't wish to frown at the lass, but…"I ken what a napkin is."

She stepped around the table toward him, and in a moment Padraig was enveloped by her light, floral scent. "When you sit down to dine, you place it here"—she held it lightly against his shoulder, where Lucan had worn his that morning—"or here." Now she draped it over his left forearm. Padraig's skin broke out in gooseflesh, and he was glad of his sleeves, which hid her effect on him.

She straightened and looked at him expectantly.

Padraig reached out and took the napkin and attempted to jauntily toss it over his shoulder as he'd remembered the knight doing. The thing went flying behind him entirely and landed on the floor.

Beryl retrieved it and offered it to him once more, without a word or even a look of reproach.

Padraig kept firm hold of the corner this time, and although he didn't think the cloth was positioned so artfully, Beryl obviously approved for she moved closer to the table and picked up a brass bowl filled with what appeared to be water.

"Depending on the household at which you are dining, you may be considered equal in status to the host or beneath him."

Padraig felt a frown coming on, but he didn't argue with her, wishing to hear her continue to speak in her clipped, accented voice.

"If you are a guest of a greater lord, you will cleanse your hands upon entering the hall, before you are seated," she said. "However, in your own chamber, you are the master, and so a washing basin will be brought to you." She stepped fully to his side and offered the bowl.

Padraig reached out to take it.

Beryl pulled it away. "Ah. You dip your fingers into it." She held it forth once more.

Padraig wiggled his fingers in the water and then lifted them out.

"Now, dry them."

He moved to wipe his hands on his pants.

"With your *napkin*, Master Boyd."

Padraig complied, his lips set together firmly. *Idiot.*

"Very good." Beryl set the bowl aside and moved around the table to seat herself in the chair opposite Padraig. She placed a napkin over her arm and then lifted the dome of the tray.

There was a modest feast laid before him: a wide dish of pottage, a round of bread, a small bowl of dried apples and walnuts, and boiled eggs. It looked and smelled delicious.

But Padraig did not reach for anything, instead raising his gaze to Beryl, who watched him closely. A small smile played about her lips—she was pleased with his caution.

"Those seated shall rise as the host enters, and then again when the host or his chamberlain or priest say grace," Beryl said, and looked about the chamber, her lips parted as if to call for assistance.

"In this chamber," Padraig reminded her, "I am the master. And so should it nae be me what says the grace?"

Beryl looked unconvinced for only a moment; then she steeled her expression once more and rose from her seat.

Padraig stood and cleared his throat. "Thanks be to Thee, O Lord Jesus Christ, for all the blessings Thou hast given us; for all the sufferings and shame Thou didst endure for us. Have mercy upon us, O most merciful Redeemer, that we may know these Thy blessings and use them to Thine glory. For Thine own sake, amen."

"Amen," Beryl said, and her eyes held clear pleasure.

"I might nae be a fancy lord," Padraig advised her as he sat, "but I'm nae savage. Me da said the grace over every meal." He gave a proud nod.

Beryl seemed to float gracefully down to her seat while her lips curved. "A fine grace it was, Master Boyd. Perhaps you will yet surprise the both of us with things your father has taught you."

Padraig was so fascinated by her refined beauty that he spoke without thinking. "If it will make you smile, I'll resolve to surprise you each day."

Beryl blinked, and her expression softened for only a moment before she was back to business. "Let's not get ahead of ourselves. For now, we must study the use of the eating knife. Helm or nay, you will be expected to take meals in the great hall with the rest of the hold, starting tonight."

* * * *

Iris stood, along with the rest of the hold, as Lady Hargrave entered the hall on her husband's arm. She wondered briefly at the seat left empty to the right of the lord's before she sat and felt the fluttering brush of Caris's hand on her sleeve. She looked up.

"How do you fare, my dear?" the lady whispered discreetly. Her eyes were keen, full of compassion.

Iris smiled. "I am well, my lady."

"That savage has not overworked you, has he?" she pressed, although she had by all accounts turned her attention to arranging her napkin. "I shall put a halt to it at once, if so, and I care not for what he should tell the king. You look tired."

Iris took her cue from the woman, draping her own napkin over her arm. "Nothing so taxing beyond a lesson of manners, milady." She tried not to think about the way Padraig Boyd had seemed to watch her every move, much in the same way that Satin was keen on prey in the shadows. But the look in his eyes hadn't been malicious—only...fascinated, perhaps. It had made Iris feel self-conscious and more than a little flattered. "Although I'll admit, it has been a long day."

"Like teaching a hound to recite, I should imagine," Lady Caris breathed, her mouth barely moving as the seated crowd stirred. "We'll talk later."

Padraig Boyd stood framed in the corridor entrance, Lucan at his side. It seemed as though the motley company of servants grudgingly given into his service were gathered in the passage at his back. Lucan made a motion as if to step into the hall, but the slightest raising of Boyd's hand stopped him. Everyone waited.

Iris looked out of the corner of her eye at Hargrave, who seemed to be enjoying the palpable indecision of those seated between him and the Scot.

Should they rise as he entered? Padraig Boyd, remembering his earlier lesson with Iris, seemed to think so. Iris felt a rising tension in her middle at the challenge that was being played out.

"You're late," Hargrave called out flatly as the chaplain appeared near the lord's table. "The blessing of the food is about to be said."

Iris realized in that moment Padraig Boyd's strategy and bit the inside of her cheek in annoyance. He played a dangerous game, and Iris had unwittingly lent him the pawns.

"Then I'm nae 'tall late, am I?" Boyd challenged.

Father Kettering cleared his throat. "Let us pray."

Hargrave grudgingly gained his feet.

The hall followed suit.

Padraig Boyd, without even a hint of triumph on his face, gave a shallow bow toward Hargrave and then strode toward the open table placed conspicuously along the wall nearest the corridor and standing apart from the other trestles, with only two chairs to its side. His servants dispersed at once to the common tables in the center, leaving Lucan standing alone.

Iris glanced again at Hargrave and saw the red in his cheeks deepen, even as he motioned to the chaplain.

"Heavenly Father, we thank Thee that in Thy great mercy..."

A long moment later, it seemed, the shuffling of feet and stools grew loud as the people once more sat, and servers began circulating about the chamber with the platters. Lucan now made his way toward the lord's table and gave a bow.

"Good evening, Lord Hargrave. Where would you have me sit?"

"Ah, Sir Lucan," Hargrave said, picking up his chalice. He spoke in a voice too low for most of those seated at the common tables to hear, but Iris understood each clipped word. "Since it is yet unclear to me what you hope to gain through this little aided rebellion in my home, I thought perhaps the choice would be better left up to you." He motioned with the cup toward the empty chair at his side. "As always, there is a place for you at my table. Or"—here he paused pointedly—"there seems to be an excess of space available in the area reserved for our Scottish occupier. You may choose the location you think best serves you. Although, from all appearances, Master Boyd's side might be a dangerous location to one's person. Then again, perhaps he only stumbled and fell." He took a sip.

Iris daren't look up, but her heart pounded. Hargrave was calling on Lucan to declare a side, as if giving him one final opportunity to repent of what Hargrave must surely see as a betrayal. Should Lucan choose the seat at Hargrave's side, he would be indebted to the man; if he chose to sit at Padraig Boyd's table, it would be a clear signal that Lucan was determined to aid the Scotsman in his coup.

"My lord, you mistake my intent," Lucan protested. "I am here only as an envoy to the king. My sole purpose is to ensure that his commands are heeded."

Hargrave was silent for an awkward pair of moments while Lucan remained standing before him, pretending to decide over the dishes placed before him. "I mistake nothing, Lucan," he said distractedly. "As I see it, you can carry out the king's commands just as well from either table. It shouldn't be so troublesome a choice. Choose, and stop disrupting the meal."

Hargrave knew exactly what he was doing, Iris thought. She only hoped that Lucan did as well. She looked up at him through her lashes.

"Very well, my lord," he said calmly, his face as composed as ever. "I thank you for your courtesy." He gave a slight bow and then turned away from the table, and Iris could see all eyes in the hall watching him surreptitiously.

They had heard more than Iris had suspected.

Lucan walked to the nearest common table. "May I join you?" he asked the man seated next to the empty end of the bench.

The man's eyes widened and he said nothing, only stood from his bench while staring at the knight. The others seated at the table quickly gained their feet.

"My thanks," Lucan said, and sat as easily as if it were the high table in the king's house. He reached inside his gambeson and withdrew a black silken kerchief, tossing it over his shoulder before helping himself to the pitcher in the center of the table.

Iris let a shaky exhalation pass through her nose, then her gaze was drawn reflexively to where Padraig Boyd sat alone.

He was staring at her openly again, and she felt her attention caught by his eyes just as suddenly and firmly as a skirt hem on a thorn bush. He was still in the same clothes, yes, but with his hair freshly trimmed and the napkin on his shoulder, his unique, solitary presence behind the table didn't seem at all out of place. He seemed to belong there, with the stone wall behind him a perfect foil—a large man, a handsome man, a quiet man.

He frowned suddenly at her.

"Where's the finger bowl?" he demanded to the chamber at large.

Iris winced.

Perhaps not a quiet man, after all.

Chapter 7

Padraig was glad to be back in his chamber after the evening meal. The hour of sitting on display alone at his table while his head pounded and all eyes in the hall constantly flicked in his direction had worn on him. Well, all eyes save Beryl's. She looked as though she'd been carved from ivory, the way she sat so perfect and erect, her expression never deviating from its composed peace. Her hand lifted food to her mouth smoothly, rhythmically; Padraig fancied he could almost detect a pattern in her meal: food, food, food, napkin, cup.

Looking upon her was the only pleasure to be had at the long, awkward meal, even though the food had likely been quite good. He'd used all his concentration to hide his discomfort and strive to remember Beryl's many rules for eating, and now he felt as though he'd been wrung out like an old rag and draped over a stone to dry.

He pushed open his door. It was quiet inside, dark save for the cheery glow of the fire. It suited Padraig well—he longed for dark and quiet, like the inside of his cottage on Caedmaray—to soothe his skull. He closed the door behind him and slid the bolt, already loosening his shirt ties as he walked toward the bed.

The coverlet moved. Padraig froze.

"*Feasgar math*, Maighstir Boyd." Searrach's exotic features flickered in the firelight, the covers around her waist, naught but a thin, white, sleeveless underdress covering her upper body. Padraig could clearly see the outline of her breasts through the gauzy material. Her dark hair was down over her shoulders.

"What are you doing here?" Padraig blurted out.

Searrach smiled. "Your voice is a salve to my ears." She pushed down the covers and leaned forward to crawl toward the end of the bed, her heavy breasts swaying with her movements. "I'm sick of hearing these English, their stuffy ways, their foolish rules. You've the sound of the Highlands about you. Lord Hargrave has done me a favor."

Padraig backed up a step as she reached the edge of the mattress. "You must be a favorite of his, then."

Her smile flickered, but Padraig wondered if he'd only imagined it, for her expression immediately brightened once more. "He has given me my fondest wish." She drew her legs around from beneath her and slid from the bed.

Padraig took another step back. "Your fondest wish?"

"Next best thing," Searrach said, padding up to him on her bare feet and taking hold of his shirt ties. She looked up at him and then leaned forward until her breasts were pressed against him. "I want to go home. But…" She twirled the ties around her forefingers until the length of them was gripped in both her fists, and she drew Padraig's head toward her upturned face. "There's naught left for either of us in Scotland now, is there? We can be home for each other, for as long as you're here."

Padraig halted what had just a moment ago seemed his inevitable descent to her mouth. "I'm nae going anywhere, Searrach. Darlyrede belongs to my father, and soon it will belong to me."

The woman gave a careless shrug and then rose on her tiptoes to press her soft lips to the corner of his mouth. "You'll nae be able to prove that," she scoffed lightly.

"I can, and I will." Padraig was trying to remain focused, but Searrach's mouth was moving along his jaw, and now down to his neck. Some physical comfort would be welcome after such a trying day.

"How?" she murmured against his skin. Padraig opened his mouth but then closed it again, remembering almost too late Lucan's warning about enemies and allies.

"I will," he repeated.

But she didn't press him, only hummed against his skin while she pulled away the placket of his shirt and kissed his chest.

"We might enjoy each other's company either way then, aye? Let me tend your wounds in a more pleasant manner."

Padraig scraped together his meager reserves and took hold of the woman's shoulders, stepping from the reach of that seductive mouth.

"I doona think it's a good idea that we…have that sort of relationship."

"Sounds like aught that haughty Beryl would say. Were you hoping I was her?"

"What?" Padraig winced and pulled the ties of his shirt from her grip. "Nay." He moved to a chair to sit and take off his boots.

"Everyone's seen you watching her," Searrach continued, coming to sit in the other chair at the small table. She rested her chin on one fist and leaned toward him, her breasts propped on the tabletop and straining at the underdress. "Already, there's talk. Surely you expected it after you demanded her to your service. But you're a fool if you think she'll bed you."

Padraig paused in his actions and looked up at her sideways. "I'm nae trying to bed Beryl."

"Well, that's fine, then," Searrach soothed. "Since she's already spoken for."

Padraig kicked off his boots. "Nae my concern."

Spoken for by whom?

"It's nae surprising, really," Searrach continued. "Him thinking he's so high-and-mighty, and Beryl the same—Lady Hargrave's little French pet. The rumor is she got in trouble with a man in France and had to stay behind to bear the bastard. It wasna a full day after you'd come before she had lured his prissy self with that doona-touch-me manner of hers. Made for each other, they are."

Padraig sat back in his chair with a sigh, as if he was bored with the conversation.

"Sir Lucan, you mean."

"Aye, Sir Lucan. I heard them myself in her chamber while I was coming back from fetching bolts of cloth for that coo, Rynn."

"Is that so?" he asked in a bored tone.

"I couldna help it. I *had* to pass her chamber. I heard them speakin' that ugly language to each other."

Padraig swallowed. It had to have been when Lucan foisted Padraig off on Rolf. And not long after that, Beryl had deigned to finally appear. It had obviously been Lucan who had convinced her to come—Padraig supposed he should be grateful.

"What Sir Lucan chooses to do is nae concern o' mine. Beryl is only serving me as a maid."

"As am I," Searrach said with a mischievous grin. "But in a much more enjoyable...*position* is my hope."

Suddenly, the passion Padraig had had to fight for the Scotswoman across from him was no longer there. His head ached; he was tired, and a little angry with Lucan, although he was not ready to explore the reason why just yet.

"I'm going to bed, Searrach," he said, and then added, "alone, for tonight."

Her pout deepened, but only for a beat of time. "Verra well," she conceded. She got up in a fluid motion and seemed to pour herself across the space separating them to lean into Padraig. Her hand caressed the front of his trousers. "I'll be back on the morrow, *Master.*" Her hand cupped him firmly and then she pulled away, strolling to the door barefoot and without so much as a wrapper against the chill. In a moment she had unbolted the door and was gone.

Beryl and Lucan. Already.

Padraig recalled their meeting in the foyer, the way Lucan had reached out and grabbed Beryl's arm. And then, later, the way she'd spoken to him in this very chamber, demanding his attention; the casual way he'd regarded her. Casual because they were no longer strangers?

It was fine, he told himself. Fine.

He didn't know Beryl. She was a beautiful woman, that was all. A woman with manners of the sort that Padraig was not yet used to. A woman with manners of the sort that Lucan Montague appreciated. After his life on Caedmaray, Padraig was only taken with Beryl because she was a novelty. And because she was helping him.

It didn't matter that no other woman he'd seen before or since had caused such a visceral reaction within him.

It was *fine.* Good for Lucan, finding a woman with a bit of experience with whom to pass his evenings while held here at Darlyrede. Lucan obviously didn't think *too* much of her, for he'd forsaken the place at her table at dinner. In a few days, Padraig was certain, he himself wouldn't even be able to stand the sight of Beryl, with her lessons and her little sounds of disapproval. Her shiny hair and sweet smell and soft hands and—

Padraig's teeth ground together. Maybe Searrach was wrong.

Her chamber is just down the corridor...

He sat up in the chair once more and pulled his boots toward him but then paused, one boot dangling between his knees.

"Idiot," he muttered aloud.

He began to pull on his boot anyway; then kicked it off again, leaning his temple on his fist with a sigh. He looked down at the limp, thin leather of his shoe—evidence of his rough, meager livelihood. Nay, his subsistence on Caedmaray. The only home he'd ever known. Now he was sitting in a chamber as big as his island cottage, on a grand English estate, considering venturing out in the unfamiliar dark to spy on a maid.

Padraig got up, kicking at the boot for good measure. "I'm tired," he muttered at it accusingly as he crossed to the tall bed. He took off his pants and crawled beneath the cold coverlet and stared at the ceiling with his head pounding. Searrach could be lying. And he found he was curious as to why a lone Scottish lass should be at a place such as Darlyrede when she obviously longed for their shared Scottish homeland. What had she said?

I want to go home...

If Searrach wasn't lying about the knight and the maid, how had Lucan convinced Beryl to cooperate? Had he threatened her? Had he promised her something?

Had he slept with her?

Stop, he told himself. He closed his eyes.

Maybe they're together even now, while you're tucked abed like a wee laddie. All that shiny hair of hers falling down...

It was a long time before Padraig was able to sleep.

Chapter 8

Padraig had assured Lucan Montague that he could find his way to the barracks on his own the next morning, but now he was relatively certain he had just passed a particular tapestry for the third time.

He paused in the mouth of the corridor, looking in both directions again, trying to get his bearings. He scrubbed at his face with a growl of frustration. He could navigate the featureless sea between Caedmaray and Thurso in a gale, and yet he couldn't escape one bloody wing of Darlyrede. He turned around and headed in the direction in which he thought the entry hall lay, hoping to reset his internal map.

Servants crisscrossed the marble paving like ghosts, going about their errands and chores in solemn silence beneath the watchful eyes of the portraits. Padraig stopped in the center of the patterned floor and looked up, studying the figures and their features while the household staff flowed around him without acknowledgment.

Who were all these people? he wondered. There were several portraits of what appeared to be the same girl, as well as much older portraits of people wearing the dress of another age. None of them were Tommy Boyd, though, which was not surprising since the current occupiers of the home had accused Padraig's father of murder, among other heinous crimes. Padraig didn't really expect to see a portrait of his father hanging in a place of honor.

"Lost your way, have you?"

He was both relieved and dismayed to see Searrach. "Nae at all," Padraig lied, looking back up at the portraits. "Only wondering who all these people are. Do you know?"

The Scotswoman came to a stop at his side, mimicking his upward-looking posture, although unlike Padraig, her arms were burdened with evidence of employment—more of the dreaded bolts of cloth for Marta and Rynn.

"Nae bloody idea," she replied at once. "Nor do I care to." After a moment, she commanded, "Look at me." And when Padraig turned his gaze toward her, she seemed to examine his face.

"Huh," she huffed. "Must be the English of you."

"What?"

"Your eyes," Searrach said. "The color of them."

Padraig frowned. "What do you mean?"

"Good morning," another woman's voice called out, and Padraig didn't have to turn to know at once that it was Beryl.

Searrach tossed a bitter glare over her shoulder before giving Padraig a warm, slow smile. "Until tonight, Master Boyd," she said in a raised voice. "This time, wait for me to help you undress." And then she turned and left the entry as Beryl came to stand before Padraig.

His mouth went dry, so he cleared his throat before speaking solemnly. "Good morning, Beryl."

"Master Boyd," she replied. "Have you forgotten your lesson with Sir Lucan this morning?"

"I've nae," he said. "I was…ah…just asking Searrach about the people in the portraits. Do you know who they are? Besides the Hargraves, obviously."

"I'm sorry, I can only point out the portraits of Lady Euphemia," she said stiffly. "Lord and Lady Hargrave's niece. I never met her, though, of course."

"Lots of her," Padraig said, looking back up and mentally counting the portraits he recognized as the young woman.

"Yes, she was very much adored," Beryl said.

"Searrach said I have English eyes." Padraig didn't know what had prompted him to confess it, but now that he had, he turned his head to look at the beautiful maid, and to offer them up for her own inspection.

Beryl's porcelain features cocked thoughtfully, and Padraig thought he saw her own gray eyes widen the tiniest bit, perhaps in surprise.

"Perhaps," she admitted, but then her lovely pink lips pressed together like some of the grandmothers' he'd known on Caedmaray. "Although I don't know that I would place much value in Searrach's opinion. Shall we meet Sir Lucan?"

Was she jealous of Searrach? The very notion of it caused a warmth in his stomach, but he marked himself as nothing more than a hopeful fool—he'd no business speculating on his value to the enchanting woman when he couldn't even find his way to the bailey.

Then Padraig remembered a queer habit his da had always kept with Padraig's mother.

"O' course," he said, gesturing toward the open area of the entry with a palm. "After you."

Beryl's thin lips softened and she inclined her head. "Thank you, Master Boyd." She turned with a swirl of gray skirts.

Padraig blew out a silent breath of relief as he followed her from the chamber.

* * * *

Iris felt Padraig Boyd's gaze touching her the entire way through the corridor. He at last came to her side as they passed into the courtyard, but neither of them said anything and the silence was awkward.

Had Searrach spent the night with him? He'd only just arrived at Darlyrede.

He is a handsome man, she told herself reasonably. *And if he succeeds, he could be a powerful man.*

Regardless, whoever Padraig Boyd chose to spend his time with was absolutely none of her business.

Lucan was waiting for them, along with the captain of the guard, when they arrived outside the barracks, but rather than pause to talk, Lucan only motioned them to follow. The captain accompanied them with a sort of long quiver strapped to his back, and Iris thought she saw at least one sword hilt from beneath the soft flap of the bag.

Their small party departed through a postern gate in the wall, then trekked down the steep slope away from the hold, and the sun's bright rays warmed the air in a welcome change from the recent cold weather. Iris was wearing her sturdy servant's cape and was glad for its protection from the breeze, but Padraig Boyd seemed quite comfortable in nothing more than his—now clean—shirt and trousers, his old plaid across his chest.

"This will do," Lucan said abruptly, coming to a stop at the bottom of the hill, where a trickling brook coursed through the narrow valley toward the river on the north side of the grounds. The captain swung the bag from his back, laying it on the ground with a clatter, then kneeling at once and flipping open the flap.

"Master Boyd," Lucan continued, "this is the king's captain, Ulric."

The captain glanced up with a curt, "Lord."

"He shall give you your first combat lesson," Lucan continued.

"Combat lesson?" Padraig repeated, just catching the wooden sword Ulric tossed to him as he gained his feet, wielding a similar weapon.

"Yes," Lucan said. "A lord must be ready and able to defend himself and his hold. In any case, I don't think it would hurt to familiarize yourself with a weapon in case you are again attacked."

"With a wooden sword?" Padraig said, looking down at the thing with disdain.

"So I don't inadvertently injure you, lord," Ulric said apologetically, and then handed him a metal helm. "At Sir Lucan's insistence."

"Then he can wear it," Padraig muttered, and flung the helm to Lucan. The corners of his fine mouth pulled down, he spun the smooth, wooden handle in his palm and then raised his gaze to Ulric. "Come on."

The captain hesitated. "Prepare yourself, lord."

"I'm prepared."

Ulric looked to Lucan as if for help, but when Iris's brother only shrugged, Ulric turned his attention back to Padraig, his brows lowering.

He charged without a sound, and although Padraig tried to block the captain's blow, the man had not earned his rank through privilege. Iris gasped as the wooden sword went flying out of the Scotsman's hand with an "Oof" and then a muffled cry of surprise as Ulric kicked out Padraig's legs from beneath him. In a blink, the captain stood over Padraig's prone body, the wooden sword poised over his heart.

Iris cringed as she glanced at Lucan, but her brother seemed unbothered by the sight of the large Scotsman so quickly laid upon his back.

Ulric extended his hand and helped Padraig to his feet, even fetching his weapon and returning it to his hand once more. Then Ulric tucked his sword beneath his arm, taking hold of Padraig by his elbow and wrist.

"Like this." He swung down Padraig's hand sharply. "And get your weight behind it—elbow up. On your back foot, there—brace. Now an upward thrust. Look." The captain released him and brought down his sword slowly, allowing Padraig to repeat the motion on his own.

"Good, lord," Ulric said. "Now, step forward, hard; come around with it, full circle at my shoulder, here"—Ulric slapped his own arm—"or here, at the ribs." The pantomime played out. "Again."

The crack of the wooden swords rang in the air as the two men repeated the motion a score of times, Ulric adding in words of encouragement or correction. Each time Padraig defended and then counterattacked, his movements became faster, harder, and Iris noticed his feet moving more naturally beneath him.

Lucan, too, appeared to be watching closely.

"Your sword is an extension of your arm, lord," Ulric said. "A sharp extension. Do not leave yourself open to your enemy—here"—he reached out and thumped Padraig's chest and then his flank—"or here, yes? And keep your legs beneath your shoulders."

"Aye," Padraig said and then nodded, readying himself. "Again."

Ulric laughed, and even Iris could see the gleam in Padraig's eyes. The captain stilled, postured with his weapon, and then moved forward like a blur, swinging the wooden sword from a different angle. Iris winced, waiting for Padraig to lose his weapon once more, but to her surprise, the swords met with a crash, a slide; twin arcs raised in attack, parry. The sound of wood grating on wood filled the narrow valley as Padraig twisted and swung against Ulric's efforts, matching the captain's blows with such surprising, powerful grace that Iris was mesmerized.

They parted after several moments, both men breathing hard, and Ulric threw back his head and laughed.

"By God, me thinks we have a soldier in our midst, Sir Lucan."

Iris found her heart was beating very fast and she tried to calm herself with a long breath through her nose. But Padraig Boyd chose that moment to look over at her and his grin took her breath once more. She caught her lip between her teeth.

"Good," Lucan called out, breaking the spell, but Iris was infinitely glad. He walked toward the two men. "Very good, actually. You have a natural ability, Master Boyd."

"We're nae finished, are we?" he asked, surprised disappointment coloring his words.

Lucan chuckled as he plucked the wooden sword from Padraig's hand. "With these, we are." He handed it to Ulric, who at once returned them to the case and withdrew two metal weapons. "It will do you no favors to become too used to a weapon of such light weight. These are dulled but will still cause injury to the lazy."

Padraig took the sword in his hand, and Iris watched him heft it appreciatively, the muscles in his forearm flexing in the sunlight.

Iris's stomach fluttered.

Stop it, ninny, she scolded herself. *It's only a child's toy.*

But when the two men engaged once more, she could not help her gasps of surprise, her little sounds of dismay, as Padraig struggled to hold his own before the seasoned soldier. The sound of steel on steel rang clear in the air, and Iris was rapt by the Scotsman's efforts.

Ulric cried out and dropped his sword as Padraig's clipped his bare knuckles. But rather than a curse, a laugh was again on the captain's lips.

"I'll know to wear my gauntlets tomorrow, lord," he said in a voice full of admiration.

Lucan clapped Padraig's shoulder. "Well done. Next time we should have a boon to pay."

Padraig looked to her suddenly, his smile still broad and sparkling on his face. "From the lass, perhaps?"

Iris's breath caught in her chest, but she composed herself. "That is a highly inappropriate suggestion, Master Boyd. Now, if you boys are finished with your sport, Master Boyd must return to the hold for diction."

She turned away to begin the trek up the hill as the men groaned in sympathetic dismay, but Iris's cheeks were aflame and her lips were curved in a smile.

* * * *

A hunt has been scheduled. All the nobility within a day's ride of Darlyrede are being invited. It is a dangerous time when so many strangers are gathered as—

A solid but muffled thud coming from the corridor beyond the door caused Iris to lift the nib of her quill. She froze, listening to what sounded like garbled conversation. Another thud—a door, it must be—and then all was silent. She looked back to the page.

—as there have been several—

Another thud, this one closer. It was a door farther down the corridor, and if the echoing slam was any indication, doors were opening and closing all along her passage.

And drawing closer. A search? Had someone else gone missing?

Iris scrambled her pages together, sending up a little prayer that the ink wouldn't smear too badly as she shoved them into the portfolio. She scooted from the edge of the bed, causing Satin to blink and regard her disinterestedly for a moment before curling back into himself and closing his eyes. Iris placed the portfolio and bag into the hole in the panel and fastened it into place just as the knock sounded on her door.

She straightened and composed her expression as she rested her hand on the latch. "Who is it?"

"Beryl?"

"Master Boyd?" She slid back the bolt and opened the door a crack. His wide form blocked the corridor beyond him so that she had no idea if he was alone.

He stood there, his chiseled face in the shadows, staring at her, saying nothing for a long moment.

"Master Boyd?" she prompted.

"Is Sir Lucan with you?"

Iris knew her eyes widened. "Why would you ask that?"

"Och." He gave an awkward, hitching bow. "Good evening, Beryl," he said solemnly.

Her face softened. He'd thought she'd been questioning his manners.

"Good evening, Master Boyd. No, Sir Lucan is not here. What made you think he would be?"

"I…I doona know where his chamber lies. I assumed it was along this corridor…" He trailed off.

"I believe Sir Lucan is residing in the soldiers' quarters," she supplied. "In the bailey. Remember?"

"Oh, aye. That's right." He nodded, his handsome face a mask of seriousness. "He's nae here at all, then."

"No, he's not."

"You're certain?"

"He's in the bailey." She began to push the door closed. "Good night, Master Boyd."

"Wait," he said, grasping the edge of the door and moving forward. "Beryl."

Her heart skipped a beat. "Yes?"

"Could I…could I come in?"

Iris's eyes widened again. "Master Boyd, that is not at all proper for a gentleman to suggest to a lady."

"But you're nae lady," he rushed, and then at her indignant expression, he realized his faux pas. "What I mean is that I have some questions about—" He glanced down once and then backed up suddenly into the corridor. "What the hell's that?"

Satin slinked through the crack in the door and into the corridor toward Padraig, his tail stiff in the air, only the tip waving.

"Oh, God, get him," Iris whispered frantically as she came into the corridor.

Padraig was still backing up. "Get him?"

"Pick him up!" Iris hissed. "Please!"

Padraig stopped his retreat at once and then bent down obediently and reached his hands like two giant baskets held sideways.

Satin likewise ceased his advance and began to shrink back on his haunches, a low, ominous mew his only warning.

"Oh, no," Iris whispered as she quickened her footsteps. "No, no; Satin, don't—"

The moment Padraig's hands closed around Satin's middle, the cat turned into a screaming white dervish.

"Jesus Christ!" Padraig shouted, straightening and flinging up his arms, a living stole seemingly attached to his wrist. "Get it off!"

Satin was growling low in his throat, his front paws wrapped around Padraig's forearm, his mouth clamped down on the fleshy part of the man's palm below the thumb.

"Satin! Stop it this instant!" Iris hissed, reaching out to take hold of the cat by the scruff, but it was proving quite impossible with Padraig swinging his arm like a truncheon. "Master Boyd, hold still!"

She finally sank her fingers into Satin's thick fur, causing the cat to uncouple from his victim and whip his head toward Iris.

"*Don't you dare*," she warned him through her teeth as she peeled the cat from Padraig Boyd's person.

But he only yowled at her crossly for her effort, and Iris rolled him into a ball against her chest, still keeping firm hold on his scruff.

A door down the corridor opened. "What the bloody hell is goin' on down there?"

Iris reached out and grabbed Padraig's shirt and jerked him through the doorway and into her chamber, closing and bolting the door behind her.

She glared down at the cat, still restrained in the crook of her arm. "That was bad, Satin. Very bad."

"Good God, what sort of hell beast is that?" Padraig Boyd demanded as he stood with the backs of his legs touching her bed, his right hand gripping his left wrist where a small trickle of blood was finding its way up his forearm into his sleeve.

Iris walked to the chair and sat, drawing Satin beneath her neck in a snuggling embrace. "He's my cat, Satin." She kissed his naughty, furry head. "Mind his dish there behind you, if you please. The pitcher is empty and I've no desire to trek to the kitchens again."

Padraig snorted. "Fitting name, Satan."

Iris sighed. "It's Satin."

"'S'what I said."

"No, you said *Satan*," she mimicked. "Perhaps, as we've discussed in our diction lessons, if you attempted enunciating clearly the whole sounds of each word you mean to speak." They stared at each other for a long moment. "Satin," she repeated slowly, her patience strained by both his large, unnerving presence in her tiny chamber and the interruption to her work.

"Satan," Padraig repeated.

"He's not the devil," Iris said through clenched teeth.

Padraig drew back his head and looked away, muttering, "Me arm and me speech say different."

Iris sighed around a reluctant smile. "Satin was born in an abbey of nuns, and thus doesn't at all care for the company of men. But I couldn't allow him to escape into the hold."

True.

"He'd nae be hard to find—just follow the trail of blood. I prefer a dog, meself."

Iris bit her lip, but the corners of her mouth ached from the urge to draw upward. "I'm not actually supposed to have him." She winced toward his arm. "Is it very bad?"

He gave her an indifferent frown. "A scratch."

"I think he bit you," she ventured.

"I'm fine," Padraig insisted, clasping his hands behind his back. He suddenly seemed at a loss for what to do with himself inside the chamber. He was too large for the little cell and seemed to take up all the space between where Iris sat in the chair and where her bed pressed up against the wall.

Iris wondered how old he was. She shook herself.

"You wanted to ask me something?" she prompted.

He blinked at her. "Aye. Aye, I did," he rushed. "Ah…Searrach."

Iris tried to steel her expression against the distaste she felt. "What of her?"

"How long has she lived at Darlyrede?"

Iris frowned. "Perhaps two months. Why?"

"Do you know from where she hails?"

"Don't you?"

And then Padraig smiled too, and like all the other times he had forgotten himself, his face transformed, emphasizing the grand shape of his mouth, the merry tilt of his eyes. Iris didn't think she'd ever met a man so blatantly…sensual.

"Scotland, aye," he allowed. "But how did she come to be here? I assume she's nae family with her."

Iris shook her head. "She appeared on the bridge one day. Not unlike someone else recently. Only she claimed to have been attacked. She stayed on to work, once she had recovered from her injuries."

Padraig's face bore a keen expression. "Attacked?"

Iris's cheeks tingled. "I can only speak to what the woman said. The band of criminals terrorizing Darlyrede's wood and road are well known."

He nodded. "Nae family, then."

Iris shrugged. "I suppose not."

"Is she to be trusted?" he asked suddenly, as if unsure whether it was the right question but desperate to know the answer.

Iris paused, feeling that she was suddenly on unsteady ground. She could see the discomfort on his face. "Trusted to what?"

His ears went red. "Hargrave was eager enough to offer her up. Either she's worthless or he's sent her to spy on me."

Iris was impressed. For all Padraig Boyd's inexperience, he seemed to have taken quick measure of the Scottish woman whom most of the other servants regarded with extreme wariness.

"I'm sorry, Master Boyd," Iris said, letting Satin go when he slithered from beneath her hand and bounded to the floor. She stood. "You seem to have mistook my position at Darlyrede. I have been in the employ of Lady Hargrave, exclusively, until your arrival. Perhaps it would be better to pose your question to Sir Lucan, as you intended. I believe he is more familiar with such matters."

True.

Padraig's eyes narrowed the tiniest fraction. Perhaps someone else would have missed it, but Iris's brother had taught her well.

"Should I nae tell him about your hellcat when I see him?"

Iris couldn't help her smile. "They've already met. Our secret is safe with him."

"Ah, I see." Now Padraig's smile was enigmatic, and his eyes bored into hers and rattled her in a way Iris couldn't recall since his arrival at Darlyrede. "I reckon it is safe with me as well."

He had formed an opinion of her somehow. And perhaps it wasn't a good one.

She followed him to the door, where he paused, turning to face her. "Good night, Beryl. I'm looking forward to our lessons tomorrow."

Iris knew she should smile at him, ease his suspicions, whatever they were. But despite the fact that she seemed to have done nothing but smile since he'd come into her chamber, looking up into his face now, she could not. Something in his eyes made a sound in her head like the loud hush of wind over waves, surface peace hiding dangerous depths below. Not the danger of Vaughn Hargrave, where the end was painful and sudden, but a slow, sinking descent that meant holding your breath for years and years and years.

Did she see the danger Padraig Boyd faced reflected in his eyes, or was it the potential danger of the man himself?

"Good night, Master Boyd."

Satin swirled around her ankles after she had closed and bolted the door, meowing as if his best friend had just abandoned him.

"Your behavior tonight is why some people kick cats," she lectured.

Chapter 9

"Nae more!" Padraig moaned as he collapsed onto his back on his bed. "I canna do it again."

"Master Boyd, you're being dramatic," Beryl accused. "I'm doing most of the work. Surely it's not your legs that are tired."

"It's me brains," he complained staring at the gathered fabric over his bed. "If it's this, make a bow; but if this, just a nod. The lady goes first, except when you should. Doona touch her, but offer your arm. Never offer your hand, except when so; but nae if the moon is full and you've just eaten tripe. And doona pick your nose, ever, apparently."

He heard her sniffle of laughter and grinned, pushing himself up onto his elbows to have the pleasure of her face relaxed in a smile.

"Fine, we'll move on. Come on," she cajoled, stepping to the bed and offering her hands. She waggled her fingers. "Come on—up with you." She pulled him up and then released him. "Now. Dancing."

Padraig howled, turned on his heel, and collapsed back to the bed, facedown this time.

"Master Boyd—" Beryl began.

His voice was muffled by the mattress. "Nae! I willna do it, and you canna make me." He knew he was being childish and he didn't care.

"There will be dancing at the feasts. Perhaps you shall notice a lady you care to become acquainted with. As you now know, there are few proper ways a gentleman may interact with a lady unfamiliar to him."

Padraig stayed where he was, the only thoughts going through his mind that he would want to dance with no one save Beryl, and as she would not be in attendance on him at the feasts, he didn't care to go at all. It seemed a waste of time when he could be practicing his sword play with

Ulric and Lucan, or spending time with the lovely maid who had been his near-constant companion, when she was not indulging the Lady Hargrave.

"I'm hungry," he spoke into the mattress again, his voice comically muffled. But it gave him an idea, and so he sat up.

"Let's take nuncheon out of doors."

Her eyes widened. "What?"

"Nuncheon," Padraig repeated, warming to the idea as he gained his feet. "You ken, where one takes food and drink at midday. Nae reason we couldna place a bite in a basket to eat out of doors."

She blinked at him.

"Do ye nae ken nuncheon, lass?"

"Yes, of course I know what nuncheon is, Master Boyd," she scolded. "But nuncheon will not move you any farther along in your studies."

This time it was he who moved toward her and took up her hands, and he knew it unnerved her by the way she blushed and dropped her eyes.

"Please?" he cajoled. "Have a meal with me under the sky, Beryl. I've not been imprisoned inside walls for such a length in all my life—nearly a month, and most o' that's been rain. Today, the sun will shine on us."

She gave him a sideways look.

"Only an hour," he promised. "And then if you wish, I'll practice stepping on your toes all afternoon."

"It can't be all afternoon," Beryl warned. "I'm to help Lady Hargrave dress, and I do believe Marta and Rynn have your costumes ready for their final fitting as well. Perhaps you should take Searrach."

He raised his eyebrows at her. "I doona wish to take Searrach." He began walking backward, pulling her toward the door. "Come with me. Find Satan—he should have a day about as well."

"It's *Satin.*" Her face softened, and Padraig couldn't drink in enough of her features. He was winning her, he thought.

"*Satan,*" he whispered.

She sighed. "One hour, Master Boyd."

"You might also call me Padraig."

"Don't press your good fortune."

Padraig threw back his head and barked with laughter before grinning down at her and whispering conspiratorially, "To the kitchens!"

* * * *

In a quarter hour Padraig was leading Beryl down the slippery slope of the hill toward the narrow brook valley where he'd first held a sword in his hand. She'd tried to maintain what he was sure was a decorous distance from him, but the rain had made the ground soggy, and the dead grass gave through easily to mud beneath their feet, causing Beryl to grab for him out of instinct the first time her slippers slid through the wet, tangled mass. Padraig transferred the basket and oiled skin to his other hand and took firm hold of her slight biceps while Satin slinked slowly behind them.

The brook was high and swift with the late autumn rains, and Padraig spread the oilskin on a raised mound overlooking a melodic trill of water near a pair of boulders while Beryl laid the meal. The breeze played with the tendrils of hair that escaped from the dark twist around her head, like a crown or a halo, Padraig thought, and the hazy sunlight cast an ethereal glow about her face. The cat crept onto the oilskin as Beryl laid out the cheese and meat, although he only sniffed disdainfully at the crumb she pinched off for him before trotting on toward the rushing brook.

Padraig watched her delicate, precise movements with something akin to wonder.

"How'd you come to learn all this?" he asked without much forethought. The balmy weather, the sunshine, the company of the beautiful woman had all combined to make him rather relaxed and perhaps a bit more reckless than he should have been.

"All what, Master Boyd?" she asked airily.

"All the things you're teachin' me."

She looked up at him then. "They're generally taught to everyone raised in a noble home."

"You were raised in one, then."

"Well," she stammered, "yes. Of course. I...I spent quite a bit of time at the abbey, though. They are known as bastions of education, after all."

Padraig's eyes narrowed. She hadn't told him anything really.

"What about your home?" she parried, pulling a loaf of bread in half and handing him a piece. "Caedmaray."

He liked the sound of it on her tongue.

"It's certainly nae Darlyrede," Padraig allowed. "Nae lords nor soldiers. Just the sea and the sky." He chuckled. "And the sheep."

"It sounds quite primitive," Beryl allowed.

"Beautiful," Padraig countered. "Wild."

"How did Sir Lucan find you?"

Padraig chewed and looked down the valley toward the trees that only just hid the bend of the river. "He found my father. In Thurso, on the mainland. A man from our island—he'd borne Tommy a grudge since he came to Caedmaray. Last fall, they were on the mainland together getting supplies, and Dragan had heard rumor of a man wanted by the English king. He thought it might be my da, and so he left word with the sheriff. Lucan was waiting on Tommy at Thurso when the boat went over in the spring."

"And Thomas simply…left with Sir Lucan?"

Padraig nodded. "Aye. He's an old man, Beryl. Likely he was tired of running."

"He's certainly put up quite a chase since his capture for an old man who has tired of running," she quipped.

Padraig could only chuckle, for he knew she was right.

"Where were you?" she pressed. "When he was taken?"

"Home," Padraig said, and he wondered if Beryl could hear the regret in his voice. "One of our ewes fell ill, heavy with lambs, and I needed to stay with her." He tried to avoid the memory of the sheep's clouding eyes, her last hot breaths and whining sounds as she lay dying. Tried to block the images of his blade, taking the small creatures from its mother's dying body. It had been an omen of things to come, only he hadn't known it at the time.

Thankfully, Beryl's voice interrupted his macabre reminiscing. "How did you know what happened then? To your father?"

"Lucan came back to Caedmaray himself. In April."

"You spent the entire winter not knowing where your father was?"

"Aye."

They were quiet for several moments, and Beryl didn't press him, but for some reason, he wanted her to know.

"Lucan told me who my father really was—*is*. What he'd been accused of. He was kind to me, in his way." Padraig vividly remembered sitting outside his own fishing hut that day in the frigid April wind, mending the net in his lap as if his life depended upon its completion in that moment, while the strange, proper, black-clad English knight had detailed the thing to him in a crisp, English tongue. Padraig remembered his shock. His anger. His initial resentment toward his father.

"And then Sir Lucan told me that, because me da and mam had married, I was Tommy's only legitimate heir. That if anyone had a chance of winning Darlyrede from Vaughn Hargrave, 'twas I."

"I can't believe he would encourage you to come on your own into such a foreign, dangerous situation." She seemed almost angered on Padraig's behalf.

Padraig laughed. "Och, he didna. He told me to wait until he notified the king of my coming."

Beryl gave him that brief, rueful smile she held in reserve for when Padraig was doing something purposefully incorrect to serve his own amusement.

"All your life, you had no idea," she mused, "that your father was the third Baron Annesley."

"Nae in a mad dream," he said. "My father was Tommy Boyd, the hardiest Caedmaray man. He lived his life there as if he'd been born to it. Spoke the old tongue better than me grandda."

"What happened to the man who turned him in? Dragan, I think you called him?"

"Aye, Dragan. He died that winter of the sweating sickness," Padraig said, his jaw clenched. "I think he much have died happy, that he'd had his revenge on my da at last. Dragan'd been set on marrying me mother before Da came to Caedmaray."

"I'm sorry," Beryl said.

He looked over at her. "None of your doing, lass."

She was watching him closely now, almost as if she had something else to say, and so Padraig waited.

"Why did you come, though, Padraig? Really? Is it because you hope to inherit your father's title?"

Now Padraig did look away, to the bare company of trees standing sentinel across the rushing brook. He barely noticed the white mass that was Satin, making his way stealthily across the boulders to explore that wooded darkness.

He spoke aloud his own deepest fear. "Do you think I'm nae capable of it? Of Darlyrede?"

"That's not for me to say."

"My father has been wronged," Padraig murmured at last. "He is a good man—I wish you knew him. If he never returns to Northumberland, if he has nae wish to, he doesna deserve to be remembered as a *murderer*." He spat the absurdity from his lips. Then he looked at Beryl. "I'll do whatever I must to bring him justice."

She met his gaze evenly. "I understand."

"Perhaps I'm a fool," he said, suddenly self-conscious. He looked over at the ground near them and spied a bold red leaf tumbled there on the stiff breeze, leathery and moist from the rain. He picked it up and spun the stem between his fingers, watching the edges blur together. When he stopped he noticed the veiny pattern in the center: yellow-green, broken lines forming the symmetrical outline of a heart at its center.

He held it out toward Beryl suddenly.

Her delicate hand raised, hesitated, and then took hold of the leaf.

"But I believe that truth must always be spoken, even when it is of things that have long since passed," he said. "For in that truth lies hope for the future."

Beryl dropped her eyes to the miraculously random design in the center of the leaf, her perfect lips parted in wonder and surprise. When she looked back up, Padraig leaned his face toward hers.

She didn't pull away as his lips brushed her mouth, and so Padraig brought his hand to the side of her face.

But she stopped him then, her fingers wrapping around his wrist.

"Padraig, look," she whispered, her gaze focused on something over his shoulder.

He turned his head and saw the small figure of a child crouching at the edge of the wood, his little hand held out, as Satin crept toward him.

"One of Darlyrede's?" he asked.

"I don't think so—he's not dressed as one of the village children." She pulled away from him and stood, stepping around the oilskin toward the brook. "Hello, there! Hello! Is your mother with you?"

The boy's head raised, and Padraig could see the surprise on his little oval face beneath his red hair from where he sat. Then the child skittered back into the shadows and was gone, leaving Satin standing in the berm between brook and forest, his tail slashing at the brisk breeze.

"He's likely afraid of a hiding, being beyond the brook," Padraig said.

Beryl hummed, clearly unconvinced. "Any matter," she said briskly at last, "we should return. It has been a generous hour, Master Boyd. And although I would hold you to your promise of continued lessons, I fear that there are tasks I simply cannot put off." She began gathering up the remnants of their meal and placing them in the basket.

Padraig didn't want to go. He felt that, just for the short time they had sat together in this quiet place beyond Darlyrede's walls, everything else had ceased to matter. He reached out for the red leaf lying on the oilskin and stood, stepping toward Beryl and sliding the stem into the scallop of her hair.

"So you doona forget," he said.

Her eyes were star-filled as his fingertips grazed the side of her face, but only for an instant.

She reached down for the handle of the basket, the leaf a blaze of jagged color in her properly coiffed hair. "Don't *you* forget your fitting. Good day, Master Boyd. Satin!"

Padraig watched her climb up the hill in her gray skirts, her little white familiar following after her.

Aye. He might be winning her indeed.

Chapter 10

The greenery that usually decorated the great hall only in the weeks during Advent had been strung in preparation for the arrival of the hunt guests. Iris could tell as she walked through the fragrant space carrying Caris's freshly laundered underdress that no expense had been spared in making Darlyrede's public areas as grand in appearance as any that could be boasted by royalty, and it was obvious that Vaughn Hargrave wished to make a very clear impression on his guests of his affluence and rank. But why he would choose to throw such a fete at this vulnerable time of Padraig Boyd's claim to the hold baffled her—Iris would have thought it to the evil man's advantage to keep word of Thomas Annesley's legitimate heir secret until the king decided the legitimacy or no of his claim, and that was not likely to occur until well after the turn of the year.

It worried her too. Vaughn Hargrave did nothing lest it was to his advantage.

Her frown arched across her brow by the time she had mounted the stairs and arrived at the lady's apartments. Lord Hargrave was dangerously sly, and Iris knew that there was a reason for his actions. She only hoped she could figure it out before someone else went missing.

She heard a shrill voice issuing from the chamber. Iris took a deep breath and steeled herself into composure before tapping lightly on the door and then pushing it open.

"No! No! No!" Lady Hargrave was shouting as Iris entered. She briefly caught sight of the noblewoman flinging a wadded ball of cloth at one of the older maids. "I've told you, it's not the right one! Think you I don't know my own costumes?"

"Milady." Iris strode toward the little group gathered around Caris Hargrave, already holding out the underdress across both forearms as if in offering.

"Beryl, thank God." Caris's voice fell into a strangled whisper, and she clutched for the thick bedpost and leaned onto it as if her temper had cost her all of her strength. "The one with the ivory stitching?"

"Yes, milady." She held it higher toward the woman, who reached out one trembling finger to stroke the intricate and delicate hem.

"*I told you*." Caris turned her face only slightly toward the other women gathered. "You fools left it behind. My best underdress!" Her shoulders heaved as if she'd been running. "Get out," she demanded, and then turned away from the post to stumble to her dressing table, muttering, "useless," as she sank onto the cushioned seat.

"But, milady," the oldest maid offered hesitantly. "Your veil—"

"Beryl will arrange my coif for me." She waited for a response, her back to the chamber, her hairbrush in her hand. But when no one moved or replied, she slammed the tool on the tabletop. "*Get out, I said!*"

Iris looked sympathetically to the maids, but most would not meet her eyes as they passed her. She walked to the bed and laid the underdress carefully atop the coverlet as the door closed.

"What troubles you, milady?" Iris asked calmly, coming to stand behind the quaking woman. She reached past Lady Hargrave's shoulder and retrieved the brush, setting at once to smoothing the woman's hair. "Your gown has been found—it was only set aside from the rest of your costume because of its fineness. The beading of your kirtle would have snagged it."

Caris was panting shallowly through her mouth. "Useless," she whispered. And then she met Iris's gaze in the hazy-looking glass. "Forgive me, Beryl. I fear I am at odds with myself today."

Iris gave her a smile and continued brushing. "Surely it's not the guests arriving that has upset you so—you are known for your generosity as a hostess."

"But it is," Caris admitted suddenly, and the intensity of her tone caused Iris to pause the hairbrush in midstroke. "Oh, I'm a fool!" She covered her mouth with one pale hand and then closed her eyes as if against tears.

"Milady." Iris came around the stool to kneel at the woman's side. "You must tell me so that I might help you bear this burden."

Caris dropped her hand and turned to look down into Iris's face. "I fear I've done something in haste that I now very much regret, and because of it I have perhaps jeopardized your position at Darlyrede. With me."

Iris's heartbeat stuttered. "Milady?"

"'Tis vanity's consequence, is all I can say," the woman muttered, fidgeting with a fold of her dressing gown. "Pride. I wanted to show you off, I suppose."

"I don't understand."

Caris met her eyes again. "Lord and Lady Paget shall attend the hunt."

Iris blinked as the name wandered around in her mind, looking for its familiar resting place. Paget, Paget...

Lady Paget!

She swallowed with some difficulty. "I see. Lady Paget, my...former mistress. She is coming to Darlyrede...tonight?"

"She's already arrived." Caris dropped her eyes again with a pained expression. "I wanted to, of course, thank her for sending you to me. You have been an answer to my prayers, Beryl. Truly, you have. But I admit that part of me wanted her to see how happy and well you are. And now I fear that when she sees you again, she will steal you away. You loved each other, did you not?" She glanced at Iris from the corner of her eye.

Iris's heart no longer skipped but galloped in her chest. Perhaps the only person in the whole of England who could testify without doubt that Iris was not in fact Beryl was somewhere within Darlyrede House at this very moment. Iris could have already passed her in a corridor.

"Beryl?" Caris prompted. "Oh, I knew it. Already you dream of going away from here with her!"

"No!" Iris shook herself and grasped Lady Hargrave's arm. "Milady, no! I would never forsake you for Lady Paget. She is not my mistress. You are. I have no wish to leave Darlyrede House." Her mind was turning, racing, seeking a solution.

"She was very kind to you?"

"She...demanded I return to her in her letters, which you know I could not do."

True.

"Poor lamb," Caris cooed, reaching out a hand and stroking Iris's face.

"I should sit elsewhere at the feasts and keep myself from your side beyond these rooms. If she asks of me, you might...you might tell her I am ill. With the excitement of the hunt, she will soon forget about me."

"But she might see you about the hold, and what then?" Caris prompted. "I would rather you meet her at my side."

"She won't know me, surely," Iris insisted. "It has been more than a pair of years since she has seen me last."

"That is not so long as to forget a treasured servant. Nay, a friend," Caris insisted, pressing Iris's hand.

"Oh, but I have changed since France, milady," Iris said. "Greatly. She will not know me, I swear it. I will...I will disguise myself if needs be."

Caris Hargrave stared into Iris's face, her expression slowly relaxing into one of pleased surprise. "You truly wish to stay at Darlyrede, don't you, Beryl? You're not only saying that to stay in my good graces?"

Iris smiled. "Of course I want to stay. Who else would look after you as I do?"

Caris's eyes widened with almost childlike wonder. "Beryl, dare I believe that I have your love as well as your devotion?"

"Completely, milady," Iris said.

"Oh, my dear!" Caris wrapped her arms around Iris's shoulders. "Forgive me."

"There is naught to forgive." Iris smiled with her cheek pressed against the woman's thin shoulder.

"I shall send at once for some of Euphemia's old gowns to be brought out—you will be disguised so that none should know who you are, even if you must be pressed into the service of that Scottish savage." Caris pulled away. "And yet we cannot be reckless. You will still avoid being overlong in Lady Paget's presence, yes?"

"Milady, I swear, that is the very last thing I would seek."

True.

* * * *

Padraig Boyd stood in the center of his chamber, his arms once more held away from his sides as Marta and Rynn scrutinized him with narrowed eyes and hands grasping their chins.

Marta twirled a forefinger at him.

Padraig turned in a slow circle, and before he had come back around to face the women, the chamber broke out in applause. Padraig was grinning as he looked at the clutch of servants gathered.

"Why, you look like a proper lord, Master Boyd," Rynn said with a cheeky smile.

"Well done, Marta, Rynn." Lucan stepped to the fore of the gathering. "How does it feel, Padraig?"

"Bloody good," Padraig admitted with a nod. He was especially pleased that Marta had managed to incorporate Padraig's Scots heritage in his new costume, cutting a square of the best portion of his da's plaid and pleating it to be fastened to the breast of his tunic by the now oiled and polished wooden pin. He thought the burgundy color suited him, and his new boots made him feel properly outfitted to take on the whole of the English army himself, especially with the sword with which Ulric had gifted him.

"All right, everyone," Lucan began, but his announcement was cut off as the chamber door opened. Padraig didn't turn his head until he noticed Lucan's surprised expression.

Beryl entered the room and closed the door behind her, but it was not the Beryl Padraig had grown used to seeing every day in his chamber for the past two months, with her somber gray gown and her crisp white coif. This Beryl was wearing a fitted, peacock-blue kirtle with a saffron veil over loops of braids all around her head.

She stopped her approach halfway across the floor as her gaze met Padraig's, and he realized she was taking his measure just as fully as he was taking hers. He'd never imagined her like this—her clothing matching her demeanor—and he was suddenly hesitant to speak to her.

And yet it was expected of him. Beryl herself had taught him that much.

And so he gave her a bow. "Good evening, Beryl."

She dipped at once into a curtsy, inclining her head slightly. The gown seemed an extension of her grace, the veil a heralding banner of her exquisite presence.

"Good evening, Master Boyd. If it will not inconvenience you, I thought perhaps we might take the evening meal together. Lady Hargrave prefers me to sit elsewhere tonight."

Get it right, get it right, Padraig told himself.

"It would honor me to receive you at my table," he said, and her smile was all the answer he needed.

"Well done," she said quietly. "You've surprised me again."

"Wait 'til you see me with the salt cellar."

"Very good," Lucan interrupted, rather rudely in Padraig's opinion. "Beryl shall be continuing her instruction of Master Boyd at the meal. Grand idea, although it is rather ill-mannered of her to invite herself. Actually—Rynn, Peter, Marta; I think all of you who have worked so closely with Master Boyd these past days shall join him. You've no other duties for the feast, and Master Boyd has a table of stations to fill. And Cletus—where is Cletus?"

"Here," the sullen voice proclaimed from behind the screened corner where the chamber pot resided.

"Cletus, you shall be Master Boyd's taster. Anything he desires for his trencher shall be first put to your tongue."

"Aye, Sir Lucan."

"The rest of you are dismissed until your evening duties."

Padraig had heard the orders, had heard the other servants leaving the chamber, but he had been unable to tear his gaze from the vision standing in his chamber. She was so perfect—like a painted figure.

"You look lovely," Padraig said without hesitation.

Was that a blush?

"That's forward, Master Boyd. But thank you."

"The gown?"

"Prying," she answered in a singsong tone.

"It suits you," he said, and it sounded so pitifully inadequate to describe her beauty.

She hesitated. "Your costume as well," she said, and he thought there was genuine admiration in her voice. "Red is a strong color."

"If I werena a strong man, I wouldna be here." Did she perhaps think him handsome?

Lucan cleared his throat. "Beryl, a word, if you don't mind?"

Padraig frowned and turned to face Lucan. "I'd nae have you speak to my staff without my presence, Lucan. I mean you nae offense. You have done me a great service, and I thank you. But unless this is a private matter between you and Beryl, would that you speak your mind before me. Her welfare is my responsibility, is it nae?"

The knight's mouth quirked. "Master Boyd, I do find your recently acquired sense of responsibility rather annoying. But yes, you have every right to make that request." He looked to Beryl. "Would you explain the change of seating this evening, Beryl?"

"Forgive me, Sir Lucan, but I do think you've forgotten your manners. Master Boyd might also desire to be informed that Lord and Lady Paget of Elsmire Tower are to be in attendance at the hunt."

Padraig wasn't certain how exactly Lucan had broken etiquette, but Beryl had put him in his place just as surely as if she had been the lady of the hold. He thought perhaps Lucan's cool temper would flare, but he only gave her an indulgent smile—a lover's smile?—before turning his attention to Padraig.

"Lord Adolphus Paget is well known to be one of the king's patrons. His estate is one of the wealthiest of the borderlands, and yet his reputation is somewhat...unsavory, due to his habits and his many mistresses. Beryl was under the employ of Lady Paget at Elsmire Tower before her... stay in France."

There it was again—a mention of Beryl in France, just as Searrach had said. Did it mean that the gossip about her was true? What other reason would a young woman have for leaving her English mistress to remain behind in France for a time, and then taking the employ of another household when she returned?

And why did it matter so much to Padraig? Perhaps it was because he could not imagine the proper beauty in such a position—unless she had become pregnant against her will. In which case her circumstances would be understandable.

Just the idea that Beryl had been set upon by such a man was enough to cloud his thinking with rage. Had Lord Paget been her lover?

He met Beryl's gaze. "Did you run away from—what is it? Elsmire?"

"I did not."

"So Lady Paget knows you are here. And you have no wish to see her?"

"I do not, Master Boyd," she affirmed stiffly. It was a marked change in her demeanor from a moment earlier, and Padraig did not care for it. He liked to see Beryl smiling, or perhaps flustered and blushing under his attention.

So although he wanted to press her, and he thought that she would answer him if he did, he would not demand of her what she did not wish to willingly supply. For now, all that mattered was that she would be sitting at his side tonight.

"Well, then." Padraig closed the distance between them, gave her a bow, and then offered his arm. "Shall we?"

She laid her palm atop his forearm as they had practiced a hundred times in this very room, but standing in his fine suit of clothes, looking down at the woman dressed as she deserved to be, he stood even taller. As they walked from the chamber and made their way through the corridors, Padraig almost felt as though Darlyrede did belong to him—belonged to them. The lord of Darlyrede and his lady.

The intruder and his borrowed maid, who was perhaps in love with the knight who followed them to the hall.

He shook the unpleasant, bitter reminder from his mind. Tonight he was not the interloper and she was not the servant. This was his chance to show Beryl who he really was, who he could be, and perhaps make her think twice about who she would rather spend her time with.

Perhaps even her future.

Chapter 11

The great hall was already crammed with guests when Iris floated through the doorway on Padraig Boyd's arm. The smell of the rich foods that would soon be served wafted just under the great swags of greenery and ribbons, mingling together the crisp scent of the winter woods with roast venison and woodsmoke and spiced wine and heady cologne.

They made their way to Padraig's table, where Peter and Rynn and the others in Padraig's camp had caught sight of them and were rising from their seats. Padraig leaned his head closer to Iris's ear so as to be heard above the cacophony of voices and laughter and frolicking hounds, and the vibration of his deep voice so close to her skin caused gooseflesh to raise beneath the silk of the old gown.

"There must be two hundred people here," he said, warming her hair with his breath, and then he pulled out her chair for her.

Was he nervous? Iris certainly was. If he made a fool of himself, it could only be *Beryl's* fault. Had she remembered everything? Had she done enough to prepare him for tonight, for these people?

Iris sat at his side while across from them, around them, the servants lowered into their own seats. Iris could feel the sullen presence of Cletus as he stood against the wall at Padraig's back.

"Lady Hargrave said upward of a score of holds had been invited." Iris spread her napkin and then attempted to scan the crowd surreptitiously around the cupbearer as he attended to her chalice. She couldn't see very far into the wall of people in the center of the hall. "I suspect with their retinues, your approximation is accurate, Master Boyd."

She took a sip of wine, lowering her lashes as she felt the weight of the curious stares being cast in their direction. She could name several of the guests on sight, but thankfully, none of them knew her. Darlyrede's lesser servants would not be in attendance at such a lavish affair, and the kitchen staff was so harried that Iris didn't fear being outed. Even the ones who looked directly upon her didn't seem to recognize her in Euphemia Hargrave's old kirtle.

"I feel like a hare caught in a briar," Padraig continued in a mutter, and the nerves in his voice tugged unexpectedly at her heart. "They're all watchin' tae see which way I rin."

"Careful," Iris said in a quiet singsong voice. "Your Scots is showing."

"Och, one does beg your paardohn, my lady."

Iris couldn't help her giggle. "You would have sounded like Sir Lucan had it not been for your 'och,'"

"I love to hear your laughter, even if it is at my expense. 'Tis like a morning bird's song."

Iris turned her face toward him, still smiling. "Master Boyd, are you flattering me?"

His teeth flashed at her, and there was no trace of discomfort on his face now. He opened his mouth to reply but was cut off by the clear ringing of a bell.

Everyone in the hall stood—a hushed roar of wooden legs on stone, the rustling of finery—as Vaughn Hargrave led his wife to their seats at the lord's table. Lady Hargrave's gaze stuttered briefly over Iris at the table, but she did not give her away with sustained attention. The noblewoman's skin was cloud white save for the bright red patches high on her cheeks, and Iris grew ashamed. Here she was, playing at being a lady and enjoying the attention of the handsome man at her side while her charge suffered under the ever-watchful eye of that monster, Lord Hargrave.

Perhaps the lady was feeling similar sentiments about Iris's position.

Father Kettering cleared his throat. "Let us pray."

After the lengthy blessing—prolonged for the benefit of the priest's increased and noble audience, no doubt—Vaughn Hargrave held his palms toward the room with a generous smile, full of ease.

"Friends, honored guests, my lady wife, please, be seated." He looked on benevolently as the crowd once more found their places. "Thank you for answering my call to Darlyrede's final hunt of the season. Our lands have prospered, and it is my fondest wish to share our bounty with such good friends as have gathered here tonight."

There was a polite stomping of boots and several calls of encouragement.

"But," Hargrave continued, "there is a concurrent occasion for which I have summoned you all here to be witness. As you know, during our long, long time as neighbors; the many years—decades—during which our holds have flourished, my lady wife and I have suffered much loss. First, our dearest daughter, Cordelia, and then our beloved young niece, Euphemia. Perhaps you do not know—as several of you cannot claim quite the distinction of age as can I"—here the crowd twittered—"that Lady Hargrave and I first came to Darlyrede House some two score years ago, to care for the young son of our beloved friends, Lord Tenred, Baron Annesley, and his lady, Myra."

He smiled, and his thick eyebrows rose in encouragement. "Do you remember them? Yes, it was very long ago. And yet only yesterday it seems that we received the tragic news of their passing, and the bereft state of their only child, their son Thomas."

An awkward silence fell over the hall now, and Iris felt a chill race up her back. She dare not even glance at Padraig from the corner of her eye.

"Yes, him you likely *do* remember. Or, at least, you know of him," Hargrave conceded. "Thomas Annesley. Whom Lady Hargrave and I raised as our own son, and even gave our blessing that he should wed our beloved Cordelia. Darlyrede House was to be theirs, and indeed it should be they who give the welcome on this hunt eve.

"But alas, they cannot," Hargrave continued, his voice subdued now, his expression dour.

What is he doing? Iris asked herself. The crowd was alive with salacious glee. They'd all heard the stories, gossiped about the grand estate overhanging the river. From Iris's investigation, she knew they all envied it, feared it, and could not keep the name Darlyrede from their lips for long.

There had been no missing persons for months now. No vanishings. And the crowd was eager to know why they had really been gathered here.

So was Iris.

"As you all know, Thomas killed Cordelia on the eve of their wedding, and it was later discovered that he had done many other terrible deeds, befouling both our fair land and his parents' good names."

"Those are lies." Padraig stood in a rush, and his voice rang out clearly over the hushed crowd. "My father didnae kill anyone."

Oh, my God. Hargrave's plans were becoming clear to her now, and Iris wanted to take hold of Padraig's arm, beg him to sit, be silent.

But it was too late. Hargrave turned his sickeningly condescending smile toward the Scotsman as if he'd all but forgotten Padraig was there.

"Ladies and gentlemen, allow me to introduce Master Padraig Boyd, Thomas Annesley's alleged heir, and my special guest at Darlyrede House."

Any nod to polite quiet was forgotten by the crowd in that moment as guests leaned their heads together to exclaim, or craned their necks to look at the large man standing behind the lone table set apart from the rest of the room.

Hargrave was giving them what they all wanted: a victim in their very midst. They were going to witness with their own eyes, with Hargrave in plain sight, blameless. Iris's heart raced.

Padraig's voice rang through the chatter like a hammer on an anvil. "Did you think me to sit in silence while you so freely slandered my father, Hargrave? There's nae so much English in me as to roll over for that."

"No," Hargrave admitted quietly. "I did not think you would remain silent. Not in the least. And while I can understand your reluctance to accept the horrific truth of your errant sire—even respect that reluctance, to a degree—I must beg your forbearance to hear me out in full." He paused, and the pleading sorrow on his face was so thickly applied that Iris thought it might slide off and crash to the tabletop at any moment. "Please, Master Boyd. Allow me to finish. I assure you, you will have an opportunity to rebut what you will at the end. I am, after all, a fair man."

Iris could feel the anger radiating off Padraig. She had never experienced the quiet, deliberate Scotsman in such a way—she fancied the silk of her sleeve was rippling like the surface of a pond.

"Go on, then," Padraig demanded, but he did not sit.

"It has been my sole mission these past thirty years to find Thomas Annesley and bring him to justice for his heinous crimes. I do admit to you all that I became rather obsessed with the man in my passion to avenge my daughter's death, and to give peace to the many families in our own village as well as throughout Northumberland whose loved ones are missing."

Hargrave paused and artfully looked down at the tabletop as if shamed, and Iris had to concede that the man was a master at his craft.

"So much obsessed that I even went so far as to track down Thomas Annesley's bastard children, who he had sown throughout Scotland, intent on making them pay for the crimes of a man they'd *never even met*," he ended in a ragged whisper. He raised his eyes to the crowd again, his delivery perfect. "I regret that, now. And I confess before you all—before Sir Lucan, the king's own man, before God and before Father Kettering—that I heaped blame upon blameless heads."

Hargrave suddenly struck the tabletop with his fist, causing many gathered before him to startle. "No more! Padraig Boyd has come to Darlyrede House along with Sir Lucan Montague, to lay claim to Thomas

Annesley's title and estate as the fugitive's only legitimate heir. And I have welcomed him into my home."

The crowd broke out in exclamations again, and in their midst a thin man with an odd, potbelly stood, his black hair combed back from a high widow's peak that pointed to his thin beard.

The man's servant announced him. "Lord Adolphus Paget, Viscount Elsmire."

Iris tried to stifle her gasp, and her fingers itched for her quill and paper, even as her heart trilled in her chest, so close to danger herself now.

"Lord Hargrave, are you saying that this man from some godforsaken, primitive *Scots island*"—Lord Paget extended his arm toward Padraig—"claims openly not only to be that monster's son, but is demanding that he now somehow has a *right* to Darlyrede House, which you have built with your own hands?"

This is a farce, Iris realized. *He's memorized it as a verse from a manuscript. Lord Paget couldn't know where Padraig Boyd was from unless Hargrave had told him beforehand.*

"I've given Lord Hargrave leave to say what he would, *sir*," Padraig said in a cautionary voice, drawing the scrawny man's attention. "But as we've nae yet met, I'll thank you to keep your opinion a bit closer to the vest, if you ken my meaning."

A thrill of pride raced up Iris's spine. Perhaps it wasn't the way the nobility in the hall spoke, but she had to admit, Padraig Boyd's warning was very effective.

Hargrave made placating motions with his hands. "Lord Paget, if you please."

But Lord Paget apparently did not please. "If I ken your meaning?" He winced at Padraig. "Good lord. You can't possibly expect decent folk to accept that you have any right at all to even a crumb of bread from Lord Hargrave's table."

"Darlyrede House was stolen from my father. As his heir, it is my duty to reclaim it."

"Is that just so?" Paget challenged. "And you can prove your legitimacy? Present at your own conception, were you?" He twittered at his own joke.

"Aye," Padraig answered solemnly. "Shortly thereafter, I reckon."

There were a handful of sniffling snickers.

"Friends, Master Boyd, please," Hargrave intervened, the look of pleading on his face infuriating, considering it could only be he who had set this event in motion. "Allow me to finish."

Adolphus Paget gave a bow toward the lord's table. "Forgive me for the interruption, Lord Hargrave. I could not help but come to your defense." He sat.

Hargrave laid his hand upon his breast and gave him an understanding nod before addressing the crowd once more, his posture totally at ease after such a scene. "As I said, I have welcomed Master Boyd into my home until such a time that our king shall give his judgment as to whose right it is to claim the title of Baron Annesley. And so I vow before you all—friends, family, valued servants, and Master Boyd, himself: my household and I shall fully cooperate with any inquiry set forth by Henry or by his servant, Sir Lucan Montague. I am prepared to accept his ruling without question and without gall. If I am decided against… well, so be it. I shall assist with Darlyrede House's transition in any way I can."

He looked directly at Padraig now and raised his cup. "May the best man win." There was a bold glint in his eyes, cold, cunning. He swept his chalice toward the crowd. "To Darlyrede."

The answering huzzahs did much to mask the excited twittering of the guests, but Iris was so rattled that she was late picking up her cup and practically missed the toast to the estate's success. Lucan caught her eye for a fleeting moment, and she could see the solemn concern reflected in her brother's face.

At her side, Padraig sat and returned his chalice to the tabletop, where it was promptly attended to by the cupbearer. Music filled the hall then, as the string of servants began to snake through the maze of tables depositing the platters and chargers laden with food.

"Nae awkward at all," he muttered grimly.

"Perhaps, yes. But you handled yourself very well."

He turned his head to look into her eyes and, as usual, his gaze held more words than were released from his lips. "I had a good teacher."

"No," Iris argued quietly, fussing with her napkin while her stomach flipped at his direct, honest attention. If there was a single word that could be used to describe the man at her side, perhaps it was honest. And perhaps it prompted Iris's own transparency of thought. "As your tutor, I would have strongly advised against what you did. That was entirely Padraig Boyd a moment ago. And I think it was perfect."

His dark brows flinched toward each other in surprised curiosity. He leaned closer—perhaps only a fraction of an inch toward her—but Iris could sense him once more through the sensitive silk of her sleeve.

"Beryl—"

A platter clanged on the table between their places just then, startling them both from their concentration on each other and prompting them to sit upright as aproned servers swarmed about their table. The moment was gone, and it was likely just as well.

Iris blew a silent breath through her lips. She was forgetting herself. Which wasn't unreasonable, as she was a lady who was playing a maid, who was playing a governess, who was playing a lady. It had nothing at all to do with Padraig Boyd, she told herself.

"Hargrave's up to something," Iris whispered after a woman set an empty platter each before her and Padraig. "That was all just a performance."

Padraig huffed. "You suppose?" He picked up his eating knife, but Iris laid her hand on his wrist at once, staying him.

"What have I done now?"

"Naught," she said distractedly. "But Cletus is—"

"Aye," Padraig said, no little irritation in his voice. "I doona fancy having the slug slither across my dinner."

"Sir Lucan insists," Iris reminded him.

Padraig looked into her eyes and there was a sudden, hostile challenge there that Iris had never before glimpsed. "Do you always do what Sir Lucan demands?"

Three heartbeats passed. "No."

"You had me fooled, then. Would that you regarded my wishes as dearly."

Iris bristled, and she let her surprise blossom into perceived insult to cover the stew of feelings she could not immediately recognize. "Am I remiss in my duties to you, Master Boyd?"

"Nay," he said abruptly and looked to her again, his eyes keen as ever even as his voice softened once more. "But it's nae your duty I want more of."

Padraig turned his head away and motioned the sullen, toady man toward the table while Iris cut away a portion of meat, then spooned a bit of the pretty barley and mushroom onto a small plate. She tried to ignore the fact that her hands were shaking, rattling the silver against the plate.

Cletus reached between them and took the dish, giving a sigh and an eye roll before picking up the food sloppily between his fingers and scooping it into his mouth. He tossed the soiled plate back onto the table with a clatter and then returned to his position against the wall, still chewing.

"Is that Lady Paget?" Padraig asked, changing the subject abruptly. His eyes flicked toward a stick-thin woman with steel-gray hair who sat at Lord Paget's side.

"It must be," Iris mused, and then cringed inwardly. He had her so flustered, she was forgetting herself.

"You doona know your old mistress?"

"I didn't notice her before," Iris stammered, feeling her cheeks heat. Lie.

"Hmm. Perhaps sitting near me wasna the best of plans. She has been noticing *you*. I think she recognizes you."

Iris's gaze raised instinctively to the woman, and she found that, indeed, the older lady seemed to be watching Iris intently. She turned her attention to her own trencher, pushing the food about as if deciding what first to sample, but, in truth, between Hargrave's performance and Padraig Boyd's attention, her appetite had completely disappeared.

"After her husband's dreadful scene, she's likely only curious," Iris said. "Everyone is now."

"Maybe she thinks you're my wife," Padraig said smoothly and cut a perfect portion of venison with his knife. He admired it on the point, turning it this way and that. "You might encourage it."

Iris turned her head, feeling as though Padraig Boyd set out to shock her with every word from his mouth tonight.

He was still contemplating the venison. "That would remove suspicion from you, would it nae?" He turned his head to regard her casually. "Perhaps if I kissed you again before everyone here it would remove all doubt. I've thought of nothing else, since."

Iris tried to command her slack mouth to respond, but she couldn't seem to drag her eyes away from Padraig Boyd's shapely lips long enough to order her thoughts.

"There is no kissing at dinner," she stammered stupidly.

"I see," he said, nodding gravely. "Later, then."

A strangled wheeze beyond Padraig's wide back drew Iris's attention, and she saw a writhing dark shape in the wedge of shadow between the wall and the floor.

"Padraig," Iris gasped.

He dropped his knife with a clatter and bolted from his seat, Peter doing the same in the next instant. Both men went to where Cletus choked and thrashed on the stones, and a moment later, Lucan stood over them.

"We need help here," Padraig shouted toward the hall. "A man is ill." He met Iris's eyes.

Iris looked to the forgotten piece of meat still speared on Padraig's knife, the dripping coagulating from the cut like blood.

"What is it?" Lord Hargrave's voice rang out curiously over the din. "What's happened?" His tone conveyed a feigned interest in the scene, much as one might in a simplistic riddle being put to them by a child.

The servants helped Padraig and Lucan lift the twitching Cletus between them and began shuffling toward the exit of the hall. Iris gained her feet but then paused, fixing the rest of their dinner companions with a stern look.

"Don't eat or drink anything on this table," she warned in a low whisper, and then Iris hurried after Padraig.

* * * *

They went as far as the doorway that led to the courtyard before they were forced to place Cletus on the floor of the corridor beneath a torch. He had retched and fouled himself so that the close space smelled like a slaughterhouse, and now only the man's left arm twitched slightly. His gaze was fixed, unblinking, and only the faintest of wheezes came from him, the silence between his gasps growing longer, longer...

Swift footfalls approached from the blackness, and in a moment the fat priest, Kettering, appeared, still masticating a portion of his meal. Beryl arrived on his heels, and she brought a delicate hand to her face covering her nose and mouth at the stench.

Kettering approached. "Step aside, if you please, gentlemen." He lowered to one knee with a grunt and then leaned toward Cletus's face, peering into the man's unseeing eyes. He waved a hand before his face, snapped his fingers, then lowered his ear above the man's mouth.

Father Kettering crossed himself, muttering a string of Latin. He made the same sign in the air over Cletus and then rose to his feet with a groan. He turned to Padraig.

"He's dead."

Padraig felt as though he'd been butted in the stomach by a ram. He'd held no love for Cletus when he was alive, but the idea that the man had died within arm's reach of him was hardly comprehensible.

"What am I to do for him?" Padraig asked.

"Not much at this point, I'm afraid, besides bury him," Kettering allowed, his eyes repeatedly flicking to Padraig's chest. "The hunt will be breakfasting afield in the morn."

Lucan chimed in. "I do doubt Lord Hargrave would miss out on the festivities to attend the funeral of such a base servant."

Kettering frowned. "In any case, Cletus was Master Boyd's servant at the time of his death. Lord Hargrave shall not be pressed into attendance by propriety."

"Therefore it is my responsibility to see to his burial," Padraig acknowledged. The priest's expression of upset had deepened. "Surely you doona think the man's death is my fault?"

"What? No, I—" Kettering broke off, his eyes once more going to Padraig's chest. "I only—Master Boyd, where did you get that?" He pointed to the pin fashioned to the fan of plaid on Padraig's chest.

Padraig dropped his chin to look down, and he absently touched the wooden peg with a finger. "It was given to me by my da. He—"

Before Padraig could finish, the priest reached out and ripped the pin from his tunic, the fabric between the slits giving way with a tear.

"How dare you," Kettering gritted between his teeth, and then he shook his fist in Padraig's face, his fingers gripping the pin until the skin was white about his knuckles. "*How dare you?* Have you Blake's prayer book as well?"

Chapter 12

Padraig drew back his head. "I doona ken what you're talking about, Father. What prayer book?"

But Kettering only scowled at him with watering eyes before turning his attention to the male servants. "Bring the body to the chapel."

Padraig reached out for the wooden brooch. "I'll be having that back—"

Father Kettering flung his arm in a wide, surprisingly powerful arc, knocking Padraig's grasping hand away. "You'll not touch it again," he growled. Then he turned and strode through the doorway, disappearing into the darkness of the courtyard.

The stench was horrible, but the oppressive atmosphere left by the priest was worse. Padraig looked at Lucan and Beryl in turn as Peter and another pair of servants struggled to lift Cletus's limp, soiled corpse and then shuffled with it through the doorway. Beryl's face glowed as white as the moon beneath her veil and rich hair, her eyes big and full of shock and fear. If it hadn't been for Beryl laying her slender, cool hand on his arm at the table…

He reached out and took her elbow. "We canna speak freely here. My chamber is closest."

"The pair of you go on," Lucan said. "As much as it pains me, I have a duty to report back to Hargrave that Cletus has died. I'll away as soon as I am able and meet you there." Lucan looked to Beryl. "Stay with him."

"I need to go to my own chamber," Beryl argued, and although she did not address Padraig, he could see her agitated frown. "Lady Hargrave will call for me after the meal, and I must be there."

But the knight was already shaking his head. "No."

"*Sir Lucan*—" Beryl pressed.

"I'll keep her safe," Padraig interrupted, pulling her to his side. Although the sentiment behind his words was genuine, it pained Padraig to make the pledge to the knight under false pretenses. It was true that he had no intention of letting Beryl out of his sight after they had both come so close to death at an unknown hand. "I suspect everyone will be gathered in the hall for some time after such an event."

Beryl pulled free. "Neither of you understands," she insisted. "Lady Hargrave is fragile. She will be greatly disturbed by a death at the feast. She'll want me. And if she can't find me—"

"There will be disquiet, no doubt," Lucan acknowledged. "But I suspect that's what Hargrave wishes. I've the feeling he intends to somehow use the opportunity of Cletus's death against you, Padraig."

"He ate from *my* plate," Padraig said. "Whatever killed him was meant for me."

Lucan nodded, his noble face a grim mask. "And so I really must go." He again looked to the beautiful woman who had distanced herself equally between the two men in the corridor. "Please, stay with him."

She watched the knight return in the direction of the hall until the shadows had swallowed him, and then she turned and walked past Padraig. He caught up with her in two strides.

"I'll wait with you," she allowed. "But only after I go to my chamber. There is aught I must do."

"I'll accompany you."

"No."

"Aye."

She was silent until they stood before his door, and then Beryl stopped and spun to face him.

"I must see to Satin. If Lady Caris is in a state, I could be gone all night."

Padraig opened his mouth, but Beryl forged ahead.

"You can't come with me. I don't wish it."

"Sir Lucan said—"

"Do you always do what Sir Lucan says?" she tossed at him. "It shall take some time to change my costume, and it would do your reputation no favors to stand about in the corridor outside my door."

"I doona care for my reputation. You shouldna be alone."

"I'm not the one in danger, Padraig," she said sternly, but her cheeks flushed, and that was the second time she'd called him by his given name that evening.

"You would have eaten from the same platter."

Beryl's gaze did not waver. "It wasn't meant for me. I'll—"

The door at his back opened suddenly, and both he and Beryl turned wide eyes to it.

"You've returned sooner than I expected." Searrach was just visible through the slender opening, but what could be seen of her was shocking in the dim light of the corridor; she was very clearly nude.

"Couldna wait to get back to me, I see. Och, Beryl," she said in a dramatic gasp, and then moved herself behind the door. "I didna know you were there."

Padraig knew his mouth was agape and he looked between the two women.

Beryl's mouth was pressed into a thin line. "I wish you a good evening, Master Boyd." She turned and strode down the corridor on swift feet, escaping Padraig painlessly with the unlikely aid of the naked woman currently residing in his chamber.

"Dammit, Searrach, what are you doing here?"

But Searrach only opened the door wide with a matching smile, revealing the whole of her body.

"I'm your afters," she said, and then took her bottom lip between her teeth as she seized Padraig's hand, pulling him into the room and then slamming the door.

* * * *

Iris felt as if her entire head was afire by the time she pushed through her own chamber door and bolted it behind her. She went at once to the panel in the wall to retrieve her writing materials.

Her lips pressed together and her face continued to burn with humiliation, although she couldn't have explained why—*she* hadn't been caught naked in a corridor. She moved to her cot to unpack her supplies, wishing to set down the details in writing quickly, before they began to smudge together in her mind, although she realized that she would likely have more time than she'd anticipated now that Padraig Boyd was occupied with the Scotswoman.

Iris began to list the guests as she remembered seeing them in the hall, but her hand was shaking in an annoying fashion. She paused and raised her gaze from the page, took a deep breath and blew it out. Immediately, her mind's eye was filled with the image of Cletus, writhing on the stones.

"Argh!" She squeezed her eyes shut and shook her head, hoping the image would be dislodged. But when she opened them, only tears escaped, leaving space for so many other undesirable memories to rush in. Lady

Paget's study of her, Padraig's attentiveness, Lord Paget's embarrassing accusations, Father Kettering's bewildering outburst.

Searrach waiting for Padraig in his chamber. Naked.

Iris sniffed and swiped at her nose with the back of her wrist and then set to her notes again. This was no time for ridiculous self-indulgence. The facts wanted documenting.

The fact was, Cletus was dead. And it could have very easily been Padraig Boyd instead.

She forged ahead with an angry frown, detailing as best she could Lord Hargrave's speech, Adolphus Paget's tirade, the dishes Cletus had sampled from the platter on the table. Which servants had carried what dishes—she could remember very little clearly, it seemed; she'd been so distracted by Padraig Boyd.

It's nae your duty I want more of.

And all the while, Searrach had been awaiting his return.

Iris finished her notes and threw the quill to the floor in a fit of pique. She shoved the packet from her lap to the cot and gained her feet to pace the small chamber, as if she could escape her maddening thoughts.

Why did she care that he flattered her but slept with Searrach? He was obviously only playing with her. Practicing with her. Isn't that what Lucan wanted her for, any matter? To teach Padraig Boyd how to behave as a noble?

And wasn't that what noblemen did? Heap praise and petty flattery on those worthy of their station, while behind closed doors they sated their baser and terrible desires with women other than their wives?

Padraig Boyd is neither Adolphus Paget nor Vaughn Hargrave, she told herself.

No, but he is the son of Thomas Annesley.

Iris stopped in the middle of the chamber.

What had Father Kettering meant in the corridor? Why had he stolen Padraig's brooch with such antagonism? The priest had been nothing but mild mannered since Iris's arrival.

What if Lucan was wrong, though? Not only about Padraig Boyd but Thomas Annesley too?

Iris went back to her stack of papers, riffling through the bottom half until she found the information she sought. Euphemia Hargrave had disappeared from Darlyrede House the same year Lucan's and her parents had perished in the fire at Castle Dare. It had been Lucan's boyhood theory that if Thomas Annesley hadn't died in Scotland all those years ago, as everyone thought, he had returned to Northumberland to take unfounded revenge on the Montagues, wedding guests at Darlyrede House the night

Cordelia Hargrave had died. Lucan had vowed to track down Thomas Annesley and find out the truth.

What if Thomas Annesley *was* guilty and *had* passed down his terrible traits to Padraig Boyd? Perhaps Lucan had dedicated his life to handing back the domain of a monster to his spawn.

Then she remembered Padraig's face on the night of his arrival at Darlyrede, remembered his tender assistance in picking her up from the floor, remembered his pride at excelling at his lessons, the clear love in his voice when he'd spoken of beautiful, wild Caedmaray. Surely after so many months in the very lair of Vaughn Hargrave, Iris could recognize evil when it was so close to her night and day.

Iris grew still for a moment, a tickle in her mind, a spreading irritation that an instant later had her riffling back through the pages from her portfolio. Her eyes scanned the notes, her fingers flipped through the sheets; she looked back and forth between the two pages and then raised her unseeing gaze.

Cordelia Hargrave had only been sixteen years old when she'd been murdered.

Almost exactly the same age Euphemia had been when she'd disappeared from Darlyrede House—ten and five.

He hasn't touched you, has he? I don't like it when he touches my girls...

Iris shuffled back through the pages to the list of known persons who had disappeared from Darlyrede and the surrounding villages. She traced the line of names with her forefinger, men and women. There was no pattern for the masculine names, but for the women...yes, some were older and hailed from other towns, but—

"Ten and six," Iris whispered to herself, her gaze following her finger down the list. "Maid, ten and six; maid, ten and six; dairy, ten and five; kitchen, ten and six; maid, ten and four. All missing in winter. All from Darlyrede House."

Fourteen of them. One for each year Euphemia had been gone, save one.

* * * *

Padraig crossed his arms over his chest and regarded the raven-haired woman swaying before him, a sly smile on her face. Her forefinger twirled the velvet of his tunic. "Why are your clothes off? And how do you keep getting in here?"

"That's a lot of questions from a man standing before a naked woman," she teased, her stroking forefinger giving way to smoothing both palms up Padraig's biceps. "We can talk later. I need you." Her hands came around the back of his neck, pulling his head down.

Padraig shook her off and crossed the room, where he picked up her discarded gown from the back of a chair. "Get out." He tossed the gown at her, but it only landed in a pile at her feet.

She put her hands on her hips and gave him a rueful smile. "Are ye fashed your precious Beryl saw me?"

"Cletus is dead," Padraig said bluntly. "Sir Lucan will be joining me in a moment, so nae matter what task Hargrave has set you to, I suggest you get yer things on an' go."

"*Cletus* is dead?" she repeated.

He turned to the decanter on the table and poured himself a drink without answering her. But as he raised the cup to his lips, he paused. Someone had just tried to poison him in a hall full of guests; could he truly trust that the drink set in his chamber for his own consumption was safe? Goddammit. He hurled the cup and its contents into the hearth.

Searrach was still standing in the middle of the floor, her eyes wide. She hadn't flinched at his temper.

"Is the wine bad?"

"Aye. Nay." Padraig turned away, scrubbing a hand over his face. "I doona know."

He didn't hear her bare footfalls, but a moment later Searrach's arms slid around his middle from behind. He felt her lay her face against the middle of his back.

Padraig sighed and opened his mouth to command her once more to leave, but stopped as he noticed the faint scars around Searrach's wrists. Thin, faded pink over white. As if she'd been repeatedly bound.

Beryl had said the woman had been attacked before coming to Darlyrede months ago, but the markings looked recent.

Very recent.

"Searrach," he asked in a quiet voice. "How did you get the scars on your wrists?"

She was very still against him then; he couldn't even feel her breathing. "The wood 'round Darlyrede are full of robbers. Have you heard?"

"Aye," Padraig said. "Did they do that to you?"

She slid her arms from around his waist and withdrew. Padraig turned and watched her walk to the discarded gown. She slipped it over her head, not bothering with the ties so that it hung loose and sacklike on her frame.

Her expression was blank as she returned to his side, where she picked up the decanter and poured wine into the remaining chalice. She replaced the stopper and then picked up the cup deliberately.

"I doona want it," Padraig said.

But the woman raised the cup to her own lips and drank the contents in one go.

"Ah," she sighed, and then handed the chalice to him.

Padraig took the cup with a frown. "I know Hargrave sent you to spy on me."

"Is that what I'm to be doing?" She looked at him with eyes that were flat, like a dog who has been kicked for so long, it no longer expects kindness, no longer fears the abuse. She picked up the decanter and poured the rest of the wine into the cup Padraig still held.

He waited a moment and then brought the chalice to his lips. Like Searrach, he drained the contents in several long pulls.

Searrach looked into his eyes. "You might do well to wonder what secrets your precious Beryl is hiding. I'm nae the only one indebted to a Hargrave."

She left him in the silence of his chamber, the warmth of the wine in his stomach doing little to dispel the chill at the back of his mind.

* * * *

Iris stood from her seat at the wide window as the door to the chamber opened and Lady Hargrave entered. She was grateful for the interruption of her imagination running wild with thoughts of how Padraig was entertaining Searrach in his chamber. The lady paused in the doorway as her gaze fell upon Iris, and she brought a hand to her chest.

"Oh, Beryl," she breathed. Caris pushed the door shut and slid the bolt without ever taking her eyes from Iris. And then she hurried across the floor.

Iris met her more than halfway, her hands reaching out. Caris Hargrave ignored them, instead taking Iris into her arms and embracing her.

"Oh, my dear," she said near Iris's ear. "Are you all right?" She leaned back and framed Iris's face with her cool, slight palms, sliding her hands around as if feeling for fever.

"I am well, my lady," Iris assured her, a lovely, warm feeling blooming in her chest. It had been so long since anyone had cared for her welfare, and Iris hadn't realized how much she missed it. Perhaps her own mother would have done the same thing. "I came as soon as I had changed, so as not to be seen."

"Good girl," Caris praised. "But, my God. That terrible, dead man. You didn't touch him, did you?"

"No." Iris led Lady Hargrave to her usual post before the window, where the tray of milk and cheese was already laid. "Forgive me my prying, milady, but what is being said about Cletus's death?"

Caris sighed again, closing her eyes briefly, as if the strain of remembering was nearly too much for her to bear. "Padraig Boyd, of course, is under suspicion. That savage interloper would do anything to shame this house."

Iris hesitated, swallowed. "Do you think, perhaps, the meat was poisoned?"

Caris's eyes went wide. "Who could know? Oh, it's so distressing. At least the spectacle of it took away Lady Paget's attention from you."

"Did she notice me?"

"She did," Caris said gravely. "I had to assure her that you were no one. You could in no way have a hand in the dastardly goings-on."

Iris gasped. "She suspected *me*?"

"Oh, yes," Caris confirmed. "She saw you stay Padraig Boyd's hand."

Iris's stomach did a turn.

"But have no fear, my dear," Lady Hargrave said with a gentle smile. "You were right. She did not recognize the face of her maid even after such scrutiny. I don't think we're in so much danger of being found out."

Iris tried to calm her galloping heartbeat. "Milady," she began. "May I ask you something…of a personal nature?"

Caris blinked but did not answer.

Iris knelt down at the woman's side, clasping her shaking hands on her thighs. "Are you…afraid of Lord Hargrave?"

Caris Hargrave's face was a pale mask of serenity in the flickering glow of the candlelight, and Iris wondered how many years of practice the woman had needed to steel herself from emotional response. It was as if Iris hadn't spoken at all.

"Of course not, my dear." She paused for a moment. "Why would you think me to be fearful of my own husband?"

"Forgive me, my lady," Iris whispered. "But I think you know why."

Caris broke gazes with her to look out the window, and it was several long, tense moments before she spoke. "I feared you would hear rumors once you were away from my protection."

"I know you have tried to protect me," Iris rushed. "And that is the only reason I now speak of it. I fear for *you*, milady."

Caris turned her head to regard Iris once more, and now her eyes were wide with surprise. "For me?"

"Yes," Iris insisted. "If you should…continue to try to protect me."

"Ah," Caris said with a sad little smile. "I see. Oh, my dear." She sighed and then held out her hands, into which Iris placed hers. "You must listen to me very carefully, Beryl. And after I have said what I must say, you must promise me that we will never again speak of it."

"But, milady—"

"No," Caris interrupted. "I am still your lady, and I will have your word."

Iris clenched her jaw. "I promise."

"Thank you. I will hold you to that. Now, you have no experience with what it is like to be married. In fact I would dare say it is precisely because of men that you have ended up in your particular circumstances. And so you must allow me to advise you as I would advise my own daughter, were she here with me. Cordelia. Even Euphemia. So much alike. So much like you—ready to right the world."

Iris nodded once but said nothing, letting the woman have her reminiscences.

"When one takes the vows of marriage, it can be convenient to forget that the person you are bonding yourself to may not always be the person you'd hoped for. They may possess…peculiar tastes, of which their spouse might be…dismayed upon learning. Bad habits. Undesirable urges. Perhaps even things that are…awful." Caris paused, and her hands squeezed Iris's as her eyes pleaded. "Sinful things," she insisted.

"A spouse's role, however," Caris continued, "is not to judge. Only God can do that. And sometimes you are so enamored with...I don't know. Their boldness, perhaps. Their daring to tempt God's laws. Even natural laws. The horrible awesomeness, the recoil, it is an illness in itself for which there is no cure.

"And after so long," Caris Hargrave continued. "So many years, you realize that whatever has been done with your knowledge you also bear guilt for."

"No," Iris whispered.

"Yes," Caris replied fiercely. "A man and a woman cannot be married as long as Lord Hargrave and I and not bear responsibility for the other's bad deeds. We are one flesh in God, are we not?"

Iris felt a tear escape down her cheek. "What if he one day kills you too?"

Caris's voice was barely audible. "Don't you see? He would never do that. He would never show me such mercy."

Iris laid her head in Caris Hargrave's lap, her heart breaking for the fragile woman who held her. Who could withstand such horrors and still gain their feet each morning, knowing there would never be escape for them outside death?

And Iris realized then that, no matter Caris Hargrave's delicate body, even she had no idea of the lady's immense strength.

She only hoped the woman would hold on to such strength when Vaughn Hargrave was finally accused of all the murders he'd committed.

"Now," Caris said a little more briskly. "Let us discuss something more pleasant. We have had enough death and despair for one night, I think. You will accompany the hunt tomorrow?"

Iris raised her head with a sniff, resolved to give the lady whatever peace she could. "I suppose I must. What shall I do if I encounter Lady Paget?"

"Dear, resourceful Beryl." She stroked the side of her face with barely tracing fingertips. "If there is anything that has come out of this tragedy, it is that I am now completely sure you will think of something wonderful."

Chapter 13

The hunting party staged their breakfast outside the walls of Darlyrede House on a knoll overlooking the river. The air was crisp with the coming chill of winter, the leaves on the ground frosted sparkling white, crackling under the feet of the nobles who milled about to keep warm.

The atmosphere was festive, almost frenzied with the undercurrent of the unknown that had gripped the hold since the disastrous feast the night before. Cletus had been laid in the ground just after dawn, Padraig, Lucan, and a handful of servants the only mourners. And although Padraig wasn't necessarily mourning the man himself, he could not discount the fact that Cletus had indeed given his life in service to Padraig.

Father Kettering had only glared at Padraig and escaped the graveyard after the last amen. He would let the man be this morning, but Padraig was determined to have his father's pin back.

Now he stood in the midst of strangers on the hill, feeling both ignored and scrutinized amid the shouts of laughter, the baying of hounds, and the clanging of gear. An explosive report rang out over the river valley, causing Padraig to jump and turn as a roar of approval came from the group.

Vaughn Hargrave stood at the crest of the knoll, behind a fork rest on which a long arquebus was perched, smoke from the weapon hanging in the heavy air. The man met Padraig's gaze for the briefest moment, then his grin broadened.

"Don't worry," said a voice at his side. "He daren't bring it on the hunt with us. He's only firing to boast. And to scare the game into the valley. The veneur has sent lads ahead to contain them."

Padraig turned his head to regard a short, round man with thin, mousy brown hair. He was considerably older than Padraig and was dressed in the fashion of a wealthy lord.

"Edwin Hood," the man supplied as an afterthought. "Of Steadport Hall. Your first hunt?"

"The first one so formal. Padraig Boyd," Padraig responded. "Of Caedmaray."

"I know who you are. Oh, don't worry," the man advised a second time, apparently recognizing Padraig's guarded expression. "I'm not of the same camp as Paget. I simply wished to introduce myself as Hargrave hasn't seen fit to." He raised his voice conspicuously. "I couldn't very well wait around in hopes of Montague doing the propers, now could I?"

Lucan approached, a steaming mug in each hand, his typically solemn expression lightening as he regarded the rotund gentleman to Padraig's side.

"Lord Hood, it's been too long." Lucan handed a mug to Padraig.

"I say it has," Lord Hood replied. "It seems you have taken on quite the project in Master Boyd, Montague. I'm rather surprised at this alliance, I must confess."

"Little to be surprised for, my lord. Nothing more than my duty to the king."

Padraig sipped the mulled cider and looked between the two men, his instinct tingling at the undercurrent of information flowing somehow just beyond his comprehension. "The pair of you are long acquainted."

"Oh, aye." Lord Hood laughed. "The pride of English chivalry was yet a babe in swaddling clothes when first I knew him. The old Lord Montague and I were neighbors. How fares your sister, Lucan? Still cloistered away, I assume."

Padraig felt his brows raise and he turned his face toward the dark-haired knight, pinning him with an exaggeratedly curious expression.

"It's the best place for her," Lucan allowed, not meeting Padraig's eyes.

"Yes, yes. I do concur. With your blessed mother and father gone, it would not do to have you overseeing her care. She likely would have been educated to dust by now, her beauty wasted. Perhaps one day you'll find that it better suits you both to have her married."

"Perhaps," Lucan said.

"Well then, fellows," Lord Hood said, and although his words were lightly spoken, Padraig had the idea that Lord Hood sensed Lucan's discomfort with the topic of conversation. "I must be off to find my poor mount. If you've no objection, I'd ride alongside your party today. There is little chance of me taking any prize save a fine breeze, but it does an old man good to be associated with the victors of the day, and I'm willing to wager the pair of you have more cause than most to champion. At any rate, you'll be more interesting. I'll find you." Lord Hood waddled off in the direction of the marshal and the temporary corral, waving to this person and that as he went.

Padraig continued to stare at Lucan as he raised the cup to his lips. "What?" the knight said irritably and then sipped.

"You didna tell me you grew up near Darlyrede," Padraig accused.

"Didn't I?"

"Or that you had a sister."

Lucan shrugged. "It was not relevant."

"Did you know my father?"

"No." Lucan sighed as if put-out. "My parents did."

"Jesus, Lucan! That's nae relevant? Where did you live?"

"Castle Dare."

"And? Where's that?" Padraig demanded. He'd never known the loquacious man to be so short of speech. "How far from Darlyrede?"

Lucan was silent for a long pair of moments, then he gestured with his mug toward a far-off field in the distance, across the river, where the white dots of sheep could be seen like dandelion fluff.

"That outcrop of rock," Lucan said, "is where the hold stood. It was destroyed by fire, many years ago."

Padraig felt the earth move a little beneath his boots—Lucan Montague's family lands had been within sight of Darlyrede House. "And now Hargrave's sheep graze there." He spoke the revelation aloud, but it was more to himself than to Lucan.

Lucan nodded solemnly.

"If your father was the lord, that land belongs to you."

"I suppose it still does, yes. But something you will perhaps have opportunity to learn, Master Boyd, is that although one might be of noble birth, one cannot retain a holding with no keep, nor sufficient coin to build one."

Padraig narrowed his eyes. "Hargrave retains control of your family lands and yet you raze all of Scotland to persecute my father? To kidnap him away from his home to deliver him to London to be hanged?"

"I did not kidnap him. He came willingly." Lucan turned his head to look directly at Padraig. "The crimes I told you he was accused of—one of them was setting the blaze that killed my parents and destroyed Castle Dare. On the night Euphemia Hargrave disappeared."

Padraig felt as though he'd been kicked in the gut. "You think my father—you think Tommy Boyd is capable of that? You think he *murdered your family*? This isna about your duty to your king at all, is it?" he accused. "All yer pretty speeches about justice—it's all shite. This is personal. Why'd ye really bring me here?"

"Padraig—"

"Doona 'Padraig' me. I'm nae some simple Scot ye can hold up before ye while ye work yer own plan for revenge—whether 'tis again me da or Hargrave. I came here in good faith."

"And I have every intention of aiding you, as I said I would," Lucan insisted, lowering his voice in answer to Padraig's raised one.

"By settin' me in the midst of a plot to kill me?" Padraig demanded, unable to order his thoughts now that they'd been thrown into chaos by this new information. "I'm supposed to blindly trust you, and yet you doona tell me that you have a grudge against my own father?"

"I'll tell you whatever it is you feel you must know," Lucan said, turning his back to the crowd of nobility who grew increasingly interested in the altercation. "Just not here."

Padraig stared at the man. Until that morning, he would have considered the knight his friend. But now he was seeing Lucan Montague in a different light.

His attention was taken from Lucan, however, by the approach of a rider—a woman sitting sidesaddle, her skirts spread over the rump of the horse like a princess.

Beryl. Beryl in a crimson-colored gown and a black cape.

She reined her mount to a halt near them, a fine palfrey, and her presence upon it cast a regal halo about the pair. The mare tossed her gray head and blew out her nose as if in disapproval of Padraig.

Did every living thing in Northumberland think him unworthy?

"Beryl," Lucan said. "Good day."

"Good day, gentlemen," she said stiffly, but her gaze did not quite meet Padraig's.

"I must retrieve Agrios," Lucan said, and then left them.

Padraig could feel frustration flaring up in him like coals before a bellows, but he was prevented from saying anything further by a trumpet sounding near Hargrave. The hunt master was making an announcement, but Padraig couldn't concentrate on what the man was saying.

A page approached with a courser for Padraig. He took the reins and hoisted himself in the saddle. Once he was seated, Beryl walked her horse to stand next to his.

"Give the hounds a good lead," she said benignly, as if they were picking up an earlier conversation. "They'll need to tire out the game before anyone gets a chance at—"

"Where were you last night?" Padraig interrupted. "You told me you'd return to my chambers. But only an hour later, you were naewhere to be found in yours. Neither at midnight."

Beryl met his eyes at last. "I beg your pardon?"

"What is it with you and Montague? I trap either of you with an uncomfortable question and you drape courtesy before you like a shield," Padraig accused, trying not to feel too triumphant at her obvious unease.

"I was pressed into service by Lady Hargrave. I told you she—"

"Horse shite," Padraig interjected. "Caris was still in the hall with the other guests. I know—I looked."

"Well, I couldn't very well push in on you and your guest, now could I?" she shot back.

Padraig frowned. "Guest? You mean Searrach?"

"Is a nude woman in your rooms so frequent an encounter for you that you've already forgotten which woman it was?"

Padraig felt his neck heat. "Ye've nae fashed to push in to me chamber with yer prissy lessons any other time."

"What's happened to your speech?"

"My speech is bloody fine."

The trumpet sounded again, and the hounds were released with a cacophony of baying mixed in with the shouts of the hunters.

Beryl's expression was no longer placid and cool as she tossed him a glare and turned her horse away from Padraig and into the trotting flow of riders.

"Hah," Padraig shouted, kicking his mount forward after her.

The river of hunters flowed over the hill in a torrent, curving and winding up the next rise in unison, swirling to either side of an outcropping of rock as the tide recedes into the ocean. Her shining loops of hair bounced on the glistening cloak, the sunlight sparking copper and gold from its shining depths as Padraig followed her. Beryl made the awkward seat look graceful and effortless as she urged her small palfrey to pace just beyond Padraig's larger mount.

Padraig leaned forward to gain on her through the next valley, as was at her side as the hunt circled the wood and then reined to a halt, milling impatiently at the edge of the dark, cold forest.

"I sent her away," Padraig said to Beryl, who was again refusing to look at him.

"Who you choose to entertain is none of my concern, Master Boyd."

"Jesus, Beryl. Lucan and yerself could be related, the way you both try to turn the point o' the sword to suit ye."

Her head whipped around now, and her eyes were full of outrage. "I'm not trying to turn the point of anything, and I resent your tone, Master Boyd."

"Are you sleeping with him? Is that why neither of you can speak the whole of the truth of anything?" She continued to stare at him, increasing Padraig's sense of overstep. But he would not back down now. "You can tell me. It's nae as if the two of us are married. I doona care who you sleep with."

A trumpet blared from the blackness of the wood and was answered with a matching tone from a horn in the party. The group sprang into the trees, heading south. Beryl kicked her mount forward without comment, disappearing into the shadows.

Padraig followed.

They swerved between trees deeper into the wood, the echoing barks from the dogs rebounding off the trunks and confusing the direction. The group began to splinter as smaller parties decided their strategy, and Padraig heard a faint yelping from his right.

He pulled his mount to the southwest. Hearing the answering hoof falls behind him, he glanced over his shoulder to see that Beryl and Lucan followed, along with Lord Hood and another pair of riders, one of whom Padraig was surprised to recognize as the obnoxious Lord Paget.

The faint sounds of barks seemed to be coming from ahead, and so Padraig leaned forward once more, eager to be proven right. He wanted this success, in front of Beryl, in front of Lord Paget and the others. He wanted to be the one to bring back the kill, proving to everyone that this land, this wood, these animals, were his, a part of him and in his blood, no matter that there were so many who were determined that he should fail.

Mayhap he wished to prove it to himself most of all.

Over the next crest into an even darker hollow their party flowed, along a tiny ribbon of a stream into a small clearing.

A strangled shout from behind him prompted him to glance back again, just in time to see Adolphus Paget sailing from the back of his horse. Lord Hood gave a cry of dismay, and the party drew up on their reins.

Padraig too slowed his mount with a curse. Leave it to one of the nobles to lose his seat. If the man cost Padraig this hunt—

A piercing heat burst forth in his shoulder, and Padraig swayed in the saddle with a cry. He struggled with the jerking reins of his startled horse to feel his arm, his palm coming away red.

"What the bloody—?"

"Padraig!" Beryl shouted.

Another slicing pain lit across his ribs on his left side, and Padraig saw the offending arrow hit solidly in the tree ahead of him.

"Get down!" he shouted, sliding from his saddle and staggering out of danger of the stomping hooves. He slapped the courser's rear and sent it galloping into the wood and then pressed his hand to his side while he crouched low and ran toward Beryl, who had disengaged from her saddle and was sliding down from her horse. He caught her beneath her arms, gritting against the pain in his shoulder and ribs, and then grabbed her hand, pulling her down onto the dry leaves at the base of a wide oak.

Padraig saw Montague herding Lord Hood to safety behind another tree, but the other rider wheeled his horse and galloped hard to the east, and Adolphus Paget still lay in the open on the forest floor some distance away. The space between the trees was filled with only the rapidly dwindling rumbles of the escaping, panicked horses, and Paget's anguished groans. The birds had fallen silent.

"They're shooting at us!" Beryl cried in a horrified voice. "They must think us game—we have to tell them it is us! Padraig, you're bleeding!"

"Shh," he warned her, and then continued in a whisper. "'Tis nae accident, lass." He met Lucan's eyes and then nodded toward Paget. The knight answered with an understanding nod of his own.

"Stay here," Padraig said in a low voice. "Doona move. And keep quiet."

"Where are you—Padraig!" Beryl hissed, her clutching hands falling away as Padraig rose in a crouch and began running toward Paget. He and Lucan both stooped low on the cold ground near the nobleman's fine boots.

"Oh, God," Paget sobbed. An arrow protruded from his rounded belly, so at odds with his spindly frame. It resembled a banner staked upon a hilltop. "Oh, God."

"Grab his foot," Padraig said to Lucan as he took hold of the boot nearest him. "Pull!"

Padraig and Lucan began dragging Adolphus Paget toward the nearest tree when two swift thunks to either side of them caused them to stop. An identical pair of arrows quivered in close proximity of Lord Paget's narrow form.

"Stay right where you are," a man's voice warned from the shadows just out of Padraig's sight. The crunching of many footfalls could be heard advancing toward them, and suddenly it seemed as though the forest itself had come alive as shapes emerged from the gloomy shadows to ring the small clearing.

They were dressed in the colors of the bark, the dead leaves; the myriad shades of stone and earthen bank that rimmed the clearing, disguising them as well as any game Padraig had set out to chase. There must have been at least a score of them, all bearing bows with arrows knocked. Some wore leather hoods, concealing the entirety of their features save their eyes.

"Bloody bandits," Padraig heard Lord Hood growl behind him.

"Back away from his lordship," the voice said again, and this time Padraig could see that it came from a tall man who continued stepping forward. No hood concealed his red hair and beard, but the face of his slighter companion was fully masked. "Slowly," he added. "Any sudden movements and I'll be pleased to put one in the both of you. That's far enough," he advised.

Padraig and Lucan stood with their palms raised, halfway between the groaning Lord Paget and the trees where Beryl and Lord Hood crouched.

"What do you want from us?" Padraig demanded. "This is an allowed hunt on Darlyrede land."

"I know very well what you're about, mate," the man said with a chuckle. He carefully released the tension from his bowstring and laid the weapon on the ground as he knelt at Lord Paget's side and reached for the man's tooled leather purse. "Tsk-tsk. My, but that looks painful." He cut the straps holding the purse with a knife Padraig hadn't even seen emerge and opened the pouch as he rose.

He held it toward the smaller, masked villain. "Perhaps fifty," he said. "Not enough for what we've likely stirred up."

"It's more than enough," his companion rasped.

"You must release us," Beryl said from behind, and Padraig turned his head slightly to look at her. He hoped she could read the expression on his face. "Should he not receive attention immediately, he'll die. I demand you let us go."

The bandits paid her no heed at all, the masked thief gesturing to those remaining in the circle with a wave of the dangerous end of the bow.

A short, plump man with straight, dark hair worn in the old style cut around his forehead slung his bow over his shoulder and stepped from the perimeter. He opened the flap of the leather satchel he wore across his considerable girth, his long robe flapping with each step of his approach. His face appeared jolly and flushed as he drew near Padraig, not at all like the countenance of a bloodthirsty brigand.

"Good day, fine sir," the man said, beaming up at Padraig. He held the open satchel toward him. "Alms for the poor?"

Padraig frowned down at the strange man. It appeared as though he had shaved off his eyebrows.

"We're building a children's home," he confided with a wink and a proud grin.

"You are not!" Lord Hood shouted in disgust.

The man turned an offended expression toward Edwin Hood. "I say we are!"

"Thieves, the lot of you," the nobleman rejoined.

The robber looked back at Padraig and shook the bag for emphasis. "It's to have a cockhorse. I built it myself." He waggled the skin where his eyebrows should have been. "Real horse hair."

"I've nae coin," Padraig said. "And even if I did, I'd nae give it to you."

"No need to be ashamed of your poverty, my Scottish friend," the robber assured him. "I'll take your sword, in lieu. The poor little orphans need playthings as well, you know."

"That sword is property of the king's army," Lucan objected.

The masked bandit had aimed and fired the bow before Lucan could finish, the arrow striking through his boot, pinning his foot to the forest floor. Lucan let out a cry of agony and bent to clutch at the arrow, while Padraig knelt to his aid.

The round man swept in and pulled Padraig's sword from its sheath. "Stinginess is definitely not next to godliness," he sniffed in disapproval as he moved on to Lucan, cutting his fine black leather purse from his belt even as the knight grasped at the arrow piercing his foot.

Padraig quickly snapped the shaft of the arrow—it was thin and finely made and broke cleanly, thank God—and then grasped Lucan's calf just above the ankle and yanked his foot upward, dislodging it from its anchor as Lucan gave a guttural shout.

The faux friar bowed. "I thank you, sir. And the children thank you." He moved out of the periphery of Padraig's vision toward the trees behind them. "Alms for the poor, gentle sir? We're building a children's home. Ah, thank you. So generous."

"Help me," Lord Paget gasped, reaching up his hand toward the apparent leader of the group and his masked underling. But he could not support the weight of it, and so his arm fell back to the leaves as the man began to sob silently, descending into choking coughs. Blood speckled his lips and chin.

Padraig looked over his shoulder toward Beryl. He knew she had nothing to give the thief, and his anger increased as he watched her undo the pretty ribbon holding back her coils of hair and drop it in the man's open satchel.

"You're scum," Padraig accused. "None of us have done aught to deserve such injury."

The red-headed man smirked. "Were I you, I'd be cautious, throwing my lot in with the likes of this innocent." He nudged Adolphus Paget's shoulder roughly with the toe of his boot. "His riches are made from the sale of slaves. Young slaves. Girls, stolen away. Lads as well. Isn't that so, Adolphus?" He crouched down suddenly so as to look into the nobleman's anguished expression, upside down to him.

Lord Paget's only response was his rattling breaths.

Beryl's voice rang out. "What do you mean?" she insisted. "Stolen away?"

Bolstered against Padraig's arm, Lucan tensed further and sounded as though he spoke through his teeth. "Is that an excuse you use to ease your conscience? Your band has terrorized this land for years—it's unsafe for any traveler, not only those with coin."

The man retrieved his bow and rose, continuing to stare at them with his hard smirk. "We're only taking back what was taken from us." He used one long arm to indicate the band standing ready at the perimeter of the clearing. "All of us here have been robbed of something by these thieving nobles. As you well know, *Montague*."

"I've taken nothing from you," Padraig said, and again he was struck by the idea that Lucan was so well known in Northumberland—even unto thieves.

The masked accomplice suddenly touched the man's biceps to gain his attention and then gestured toward Padraig.

"That may be true, my Scots friend," the man allowed. "You're no servant, and yet you're part of Hargrave's hunting party." He looked Padraig up and down. "Not dressed *quite* well enough to be noble—certainly no appreciable fortune to your name. Perhaps you are better off one of us, no?"

"Don't answer him anything," Lucan advised grimly.

"I'd hope you'd learned by now that your advice brings only injury, good Sir Montague. Padraig, wasn't it?" the man suggested with a grin. "Hmm. Not a name common to Northumberland. Betrayed the Scots in you even if your speech hadn't." He stepped over Paget's body without a glance for the wounded man, until he was only one pace away from Padraig and Lucan. "Can you fight, I wonder, Padraig?"

"Give back my sword and you'll soon find out," Padraig challenged.

"Gorman," the masked accomplice warned in a low voice.

"Do you know what happened to Euphemia Hargrave?" Beryl's question rang out clear and anguished in the clearing, and it seemed as though everyone turned to regard the woman who was now standing against the tree, only the fingertips of one hand touching the bark as if tethered there by her fear, when she wanted to fly to the center of the clearing. She looked around, her eyes pleading as her undone hair flowed over her shoulders.

"Do any of you know? Was she taken? Did Lord Paget take her?" Her eyes were wild. "Please. Someone here must know something. Lady Hargrave wastes away in grief."

The masked accomplice seemed to be watching Beryl closely now, and that damned bow was still at the ready. Searrach's warning from the night before haunted Padraig.

I'm nae the only one indebted to a Hargrave.

This group had been lying in wait for them; there was no other explanation. The clearing was near no road, no outlying estate building or field. They'd been lured here, with the barking of dogs, which had suspiciously gone silent after the first arrow had flown.

Now the masked accomplice walked toward Beryl slowly, each deliberate step of fine boot sending forth a loud, crunching of leaves.

* * * *

Iris couldn't help her heaving exhalations of breath as the masked robber walked menacingly toward her, slowly, deliberately. The drawn bow, although aimed at the ground, struck deep fear in her heart. Both Padraig and Lucan had been shot, and Lord Paget had stopped moving, his jerky, watery gasps no longer menacing the clearing.

She backed against the tree fully once more.

"Please," she repeated, hearing the breathy shakiness of her voice, and yet unable to contain her fear as her eyes welled with terror. "I need to know."

"What is your connection to Euphemia Hargrave?" he rasped.

"I…nothing. I have no connection," Iris stammered. "I only serve the Lady Hargrave. I…care for her very much."

"Then you are a fool," the robber spat, then stepped closer, his voice lowering to a whisper. "Euphemia Hargrave is dead. She died the night she escaped from Darlyrede."

Iris's heart skipped a beat in her chest, and her voice caught on her breath as she asked the dreaded question. "How do you know?"

"Because," the thief whispered, "it was I who killed her."

Iris brought her hand to her mouth to stifle her sob. "How could you?" she finally managed to choke out, no longer caring about the consequences of her words. If the band was going to kill them all any matter, she would have her say. "She was just a girl! A child! She had done you no wrong, surely."

The bandit stared at her for a long moment, the blue eyes through the slits in the mask seeming to examine every aspect of her gown, her cloak. She was unable to read the intention in his eyes, and yet the bow hung relaxed.

"It was the most merciful thing I could do," he whispered. "Euphemia Hargrave...had suffered."

"What?" Iris's fright stilled like the water of a pond—slowly, gradually, even as a faint rumbling was heard. "What do you mean? Suffered how?"

"The priest knows wh—"

The clearing was lit up with fire and sound then, the forest floor exploding with light, smoke, shuddering crashes. Dirt and bark flew through the air, now filled with black, acrid smoke.

Iris dove to the leaves, and both heard and felt the many feet pounding by her. She covered her head with her arms.

It could be nothing other than Vaughn Hargrave's arquebus.

"Gorman!" the bandit before Iris called.

"Go! To the caves!"

Another boom echoed through the trees, and was followed by a piercing scream. Iris dared peek from her arm and saw one of the forest bandits—a black, ragged hole in his back—being dragged by his comrades deeper into the wood.

But then the clearing was filled with the sounds of horse hooves and a hand was on her shoulder.

"Beryl, Beryl," Padraig demanded. "Are you hurt?"

"I'm fine," she breathed, and let him gather her into his arms to help her to stand, and yet she did not release her clutching hold on his tunic. She looked around the clearing and saw Lord Hargrave leading the rescue party, his face a white, furious mask.

"Follow them!" he commanded to those riding at his side. "Find the vermin and kill them all! I want their heads mounted on stakes!" The riders lurched into action at once.

Hargrave got down from his horse and went immediately to kneel at the side of Adolphus Paget.

"Adolph," he shouted, grasping the man's pointed chin in his hands and turning the wide-eyed countenance toward him. He slapped the man's face twice and then grasped either side of his windpipe. "Adolph!" Hargrave rolled the man to his side with careful, practiced skill, but an instant later he let the body rock back to the stained ground without further action.

The forest again was eerily silent.

Iris realized she was clutching Padraig Boyd's slim, solid waist, the blood from his injured ribs sticky and drying against her. She looked up at him.

"Are any broken?"

"Naught to fash over," he said grimly. "But grazes. Lucan, though..."

Iris nodded and pushed away from the warm, solid comfort that was the Scotsman and ran to where her brother now sat on the ground.

"Help me get the boot off," he was saying before she was even kneeling properly. "The foot is swelling and I'd not cut it if it can be helped. They're Italian."

Padraig joined them in the next moment and helped to pull Lucan's pierced boot from his foot. He cried out as the slender leather slid away, and a trickle of blood spilled out in a stream.

"Goddamn him," Lucan gritted. "That bastard! I'll find him and kill him myself!"

"I do hope you're satisfied, Lucan," Hargrave said in a sanctimonious tone over all their heads. "Now you perhaps have a sense for what I've had to deal with in keeping Darlyrede safe from those... those common criminals. This is on your head, you know." He looked to the only man-at-arms who had remained. "Take Lord Paget's body on your horse to carry back to Father Kettering."

Hargrave then turned his gaze to Padraig. "That's the second death in as many days in your vicinity, Master Boyd. If I didn't know better, I would think someone had a grudge against you."

Chapter 14

Iris rode back to Darlyrede behind Padraig Boyd on his retrieved horse, at first trying to keep a distance between her torso and his wide back, clutching at the right side of his tunic. But the rolling gait of the horse and the shock of the morning soon became too much for the little strength she had left—both mentally and physically—and she at last gave in to the urge to lay the side of her face against his warm ribs and close her eyes as they made their way back to the courtyard.

If either of the arrows that had injured him had been inches inward, he could have suffered the same fate as Adolphus Paget. Iris couldn't imagine what her world would be like in this moment if Padraig Boyd had died, if she knew she would never again see his teasing smile, feel the warmth of his presence or the solid strength of his hand; debate the easy logic of his thoughts and the morals that guided him, his clear understanding of right and wrong. Iris's mind was a blank when she tried to gauge the suffering she would have felt at the loss of him.

Euphemia Hargrave had suffered.

Iris felt as though she'd been dropped into a dark chamber—shock causing all her senses to be exquisitely alert to the point of discomfort, and yet all the information they relayed to her made no sense in the blackness. Was the silence absolute in her head, or was she surrounded by a deafening roar? She didn't know which way to turn to escape; was it blistering heat or icy cold that seared her nerves? Was the ceiling just overhead or was she standing at the brink of a bottomless abyss, hungry for her to take that first, fatal step into the nothingness that would swallow her forever?

Would Iris be delivering salvation to Caris Hargrave with the information she now possessed, or the penultimate blow that would at last break the fragile woman?

He would never show me such mercy.

For some reason that she could not order in the chaos of her thoughts, the memory of what Lady Hargrave had said to Iris haunted her—specifically, the mention of the word "mercy" in regard to why her husband would never kill her.

It was the reason the thief in the forest had cited for taking Euphemia Hargrave's life.

It was the most merciful thing I could do.

They arrived just then, and Rolf appeared at their side to help Iris from the back of Padraig's horse before he himself swung stiffly down. A page took charge of the mount, and she and Padraig wordlessly made their way toward the section of inner wall that housed the chapel and Father Kettering's parsonage, following the form of Lucan, supported by a king's soldier beneath each of his arms.

They ducked through the doorway in time to see Lucan being lowered onto a cot, and the priest swirling through the throng of oblates and soldiers, handing out supplies and issuing crisp orders.

"I must fetch wrappings for Lord Paget. Clean Sir Lucan's wound," Father Kettering commanded. "But leave it unbandaged for now." His eyes fell upon Padraig, and Iris tensed at the way the priest's mouth thinned as he looked pointedly at the bloodstains on Padraig's clothing. "Master Boyd's as well. Lord, I'll need more comfrey," he muttered.

The priest pushed past them on his way toward the door.

"I'll be back," Iris muttered, avoiding Padraig's gaze as she impulsively turned away and went after the priest. "Father Kettering," she called, trotting to catch up with him in the courtyard. "Father, I must speak with you."

"Forgive me, Beryl, but I am harried."

"It's about Lady Hargrave."

The priest stopped in his tracks with a concerned frown. "She's not injured, is she? I didn't think she was to accompany the hunt."

"No, she didn't," Iris assured him.

Kettering started forward once more. "Another time, then."

Iris reached out to seize his sleeve. "I'm afraid it can't wait."

The priest sighed. "What is it? I have wounded men to attend to, and one corpse to prepare to journey back to his own hold. If I am too delayed, I may have two to arrange."

Iris glanced around them for prying ears. "Euphemia Hargrave is dead," she whispered.

Kettering stared at her, the recently acquired hard look in his eyes falling away at last and he was once more the kind man Iris had come to know during her time at Darlyrede. "What?"

"I met her killer. One of the band of thieves that haunts Darlyrede's wood. The same ones who attacked our party this morning. He admitted it to me."

"Lord have mercy." Kettering crossed himself quickly before returning his full attention to Iris. "Certainly that should bring some manner of peace to Lord and Lady Hargrave, but I don't understand what this has to do with me. There are no remains, I assume?"

"I don't know," Iris admitted. "It was only a moment. But he—the thief—said something before Lord Hargrave interrupted the robbery. He said that he killed Euphemia because she had suffered at Darlyrede. And then he said, 'The priest knows.'"

The heightened color that rose at the seriousness of the immediate tasks before him swiftly drained from Father Kettering's face.

Iris's heart fluttered in her chest. "What did he mean, Father?"

Kettering was already shaking his head, little nervous movements, his eyes wide, his gaze shifting around the courtyard. "I can't understand what he might mean," he muttered almost to himself. "Surely he couldn't know. Unless she..."

"What?" Iris demanded in a whisper, stepping so close to the priest that they were nearly nose to nose. She angled her head so that he was forced to meet her gaze once more. "What couldn't he know? You must tell me so that I can decide what—if anything—I should tell Lady Hargrave."

"You must tell her that her niece is dead," Kettering chastised with a lowering of his brows. "To not do so would be cruel."

"Then you must tell me what you think caused Euphemia such suffering," Iris demanded.

"I couldn't possibly," he insisted with a horrified look. "It's guarded by the sanctity of the confessional. You of all people should know that."

"Euphemia is dead," Iris said through her teeth. "She is with God now. The sanctity of her confession no longer matters."

His eyes were hard again. "It does to me, young woman. The seal admits no exceptions."

Iris stood straighter. "Fine. If you will not tell me, I have no choice but to try to find the man again and get my explanation." She turned away, her heart pounding.

"Beryl, wait," Kettering called, and she felt him grab her arm. His eyes were pleading when she turned to him. "You can't possibly think to go out there on your own. One has already confessed to the murder of Euphemia Hargrave. Lord Paget is dead; Sir Lucan and Master Boyd are injured. What will they do to you?"

"Then tell me," Iris demanded.

"I will not break the seal of Euphemia's confession," he insisted. "But," he interjected with a jerk on her arm when Iris would have pulled away, "I can tell you the rumors that she heard before she disappeared. That we all heard. And what I saw for myself."

* * * *

It was some time before Father Kettering returned to the surgery, and Padraig lay on the cot glaring at the ceiling while the oblates assigned to his care cleaned the jagged arrow wounds to his shoulder and ribs. He ignored Lucan Montague, who groaned and hissed intermittently as his pierced foot was attended to.

Adolphus Paget's body was brought through the aisle and placed on a table at the far end. The oblates draped him with a sheet.

That could be me, Padraig realized. *Or Lucan Montague.*

Or Beryl.

Kettering came to his side before Lucan's, his earlier stilted aloofness with him now replaced by a distracted air and what appeared to be new lines of concern about the priest's eyes and mouth. He placed a basket of pungent herbs on the floor.

"Where is Beryl?" he asked as Kettering bent to inspect the wound on Padraig's ribs.

"She went to lie down," he muttered. "She's been through an ordeal."

"I ken. I was there," Padraig reminded him. "Ow!" he exclaimed as the priest pressed into the cut.

Kettering straightened and wiped his hands on the towel hanging on his cincture. "You'll be fine while I attend to Sir Lucan. I will plaster your wounds when I've finished with him."

Padraig reached out and grabbed the priest's arm, staying him when he would have turned away. "I want my father's pin back."

Kettering shook him off without a response and then picked up the basket and went at once to the end of Lucan's cot.

"Soak the foot through three changes of water," Kettering announced with a sigh, "and then we shall see it bandaged. You must not walk on it, Sir Lucan. I'll need to check it hourly, that it does not fester. At the first sign—"

"No. No, no, no," Lucan interrupted, coming onto his elbows. "You'll not amputate my foot."

Kettering fixed him with a look. "I'll not watch you die."

"Padraig," Lucan called crisply. "Assist me."

Padraig turned his head with a quirked brow. "I think you should listen to him, Lucan."

"I require you to get your Scots arse over here and assist me in liberating my person from this crypt before God's butcher turns my foot into mince."

Padraig couldn't help his bark of laughter. It was the first time he had heard Lucan Montague lose his composure, and his resultant language was too humorous to ignore.

"Let him soak it and bandage it, Lucan," Padraig reasoned. "He's nae cleaver in his hand now, doos he?"

"Thank you, Master Boyd," the priest said stiffly, but he didn't quite meet his eye.

"I'll help you keep Sir Lucan under control," Padraig said easily. "If, while you tend him, you tell me why you think my da's pin belongs to you."

Now Kettering did turn his eyes to Padraig's.

But it was Lucan who came to the priest's rescue, turning his head to regard Padraig. "Did Tommy tell you how he came to be in possession of the pin?"

Padraig shook his head. "Nay. Only that it and the man who'd given it to him had once saved his life."

Kettering's temper was just barely in check; Padraig could see it by the color returning to his cheeks. The priest went to the hearth to dip ladlesful of steaming water into a metal dish. When he returned to the bedside he seemed to be under a bit more restraint.

"Thomas Annesley wasn't given it. He stole it."

Padraig opened his mouth to argue that his father was no thief, but Lucan again inserted himself in the argument.

"I don't think he stole it," Lucan said quietly as Kettering helped him into a seated position on the side of the bed. "Thomas Annesley told me the tale of the night he ran from Darlyrede House. The night he met your father, Kettering."

Padraig felt his head draw back. "Your father was also at Darlyrede?"

"No," the priest said in a clipped voice. He set the pan on the floor and added cooler water from a ewer near the bed. "He was only passing on the road with his friend, Blake, that night."

"Yes, Blake," Lucan agreed. He hissed for a moment as Kettering guided his foot into the water. "Thomas claimed he was direly wounded in his escape from Darlyrede, and that your father stopped on the road to help him. Thomas's injuries were so severe that your father gave him his hat pin upon which to bite so that he could seat Thomas on his own horse."

Kettering looked into Lucan's face for a solemn moment. "Yes," he agreed quietly. "That is something he would have done, even not knowing who Thomas Annesley was."

"But when Thomas heard that the two men unwittingly planned to return him to the very place from which he was so desperate to escape, he became more frightened, and he used the pin to spur the horse onward, thwarting their good intentions to help him."

"Ah-ah," Kettering said, his thoughtful expression fleeing before the frown that cascaded over his feature. "Even was the story you were told true up until that point, Sir Lucan, you—or Thomas Annesley—have left out vital information." Kettering looked directly at Padraig now.

"My father and his friend were found dead on the road only a half mile from Darlyrede House the next morning. Thomas Annesley had robbed them both of their horses and their possessions—the pin, Blake's prayer book, what little coin they carried—and then he killed them before escaping."

Padraig felt his stomach in his throat. Yet another crime of which Padraig's father was accused that Lucan had concealed the details of. He was shaking on the inside now. It made sense why Kettering had asked about the prayer book in the corridor when Cletus died, and Padraig couldn't help but remember all the times Tommy had prayed over their meals, prayed over their flock, or prayed over Padraig's own mother as she lay dying.

As if Kettering had read his thoughts, he asked quietly, "Do you have the book, Master Boyd?"

"I already told you—nay," Padraig said in a choked voice. "Da never had one that I saw in all the years of my life. I swear to you."

"It's simply not possible that Thomas Annesley killed those men on the Darlyrede Road," Lucan interjected. "By the time he'd gained Scotland, he was nearly dead himself. He'd been shot and nearly bled to death." Lucan paused a moment, letting the idea of that settle about the room like the first smoke of a new fire, waiting for the scent and the sting of it to be realized, accepted.

Padraig understood right away. "How could an unarmed man so gravely injured overpower, rob, and then kill two grown men outfitted for travel?"

Lucan nodded. "Precisely."

"Then who did?" Kettering demanded.

Lucan paused for a long, long moment, and then simply shook his head. "I cannot say for certain. I'm sorry."

Kettering walked toward Padraig's cot and sat down at the foot of it with a sigh. The priest stared at his hands, bloodied from his work on Lucan's foot. He lifted the towel lying across his lap and wiped at his stained fingers absently.

"It *was* a hat pin," Kettering said. "At least, that's what it became. It had originally been a shard of a battle shield from Agincourt, where my father had been a soldier when he was little more than a boy himself." The priest paused, shook his head. "The English never should have won. The fighting was so fierce, they were so outnumbered. My father had been wounded and thrown to the field—he said he could see nothing for the hooves and mud and bodies. He knew he was going to die. He crawled beneath the long battle shield of a fallen French soldier, and he prayed without ceasing through the night, begging God to spare him."

Kettering looked up toward the end of the room where the wall met the ceiling, but Padraig didn't think he was seeing anything in the chamber. "When the fighting was over and he finally crawled from beneath that shield, it was in pieces. Splintered, my father said, by the sheer number of arrows that had pierced it, the horses that had trampled him. He took a splinter of the shield and vowed there, on that field, that he would devote the rest of his life to serving God, in thanks for sparing him.

"Once he had returned home, he began his studies for the priesthood while he healed, and he carved the splinter into the pin. He was never without it. When I was a boy he often recounted his night on the battlefield—likened it to the garden of Gethsemane, he said, only God had seen fit to pass the cup from him. His faith was so great—it's why I became a priest myself. I never dreamed after surviving such horrors that he would be shot down in the middle of a road in his own land."

"Shot?" Padraig repeated.

Kettering nodded. "He and Blake each received a bolt in the chest, to that I can personally attest. When news reached me of his and his companion's death…I was devastated. I came to Darlyrede and I buried my own father. That is how I know so intimately how he died. I buried Cordelia Hargrave as well—Thomas Annesley's betrothed. Lord Hargrave saw to it afterward that my mother and siblings were cared for, and he offered me charge of the chapel. And here I have remained."

The chamber was silent, filled with Kettering's grief, Padraig's confusion, and the enigmatic thoughts of Lucan Montague. Padraig could not think of anything to say—Kettering had been his enemy before, Lucan his friend. Had their roles reversed?

The priest sighed and stood up. "I'll change the water now." He went around the far side of the other cot and wiped Lucan's foot with the towel at his waist before picking up the basin. He carried it out of the door leading to the bailey.

"I know you're angry, Padraig," Lucan said quickly in a low voice. "But if I had explained all the connections between the accusations against your father, you wouldn't have trusted me to help you."

"You're right, I wouldna've."

"And I can't blame you. I made a pledge to bring Thomas Annesley to justice, aye. For the crimes he committed. And especially for the murder of my parents."

Lucan glanced toward the doorway through where Kettering was returning and finished in a rushed whisper. "But perhaps now you understand why I no longer think he is guilty of any of it. In fact I know he's not."

"The difference between us, Lucan," Padraig murmured, "is that I've always known it."

* * * *

Iris shuffled the pages back into her portfolio just as she heard the scratching on her window. She admitted Satin, somehow mustering the energy for a smile.

"I don't have anything for you yet," she warned when he went straight for the hidden niche in the wall. She gently scooped the cat out of the way and then placed her portfolio inside before reattaching the panel, and then set about at last changing the gown stained with Padraig Boyd's blood.

She held the material in her hands and stared at the dark splotches, brown against the crimson fabric. Stroking her thumbs against the stiff stains at once returned her to the sober mood that Satin's arrival had briefly dispelled. All the secrets, all the lies, all the years of darkness within these walls—what would be the outcome? The final verdict? Had Padraig Boyd come all this way, risked his life and his freedom for naught?

And what would their future be, in the aftermath?

Iris placed the gown on the back of the chair, then bent down to scratch Satin's chin and scoop him up. "Back out you go," she said, rising and walking to the window. "I'm going to go check on Lucan. I'll bring you *un petit gouter* later."

"Meow."

"Well, you can't go with me, I'm sorry." She unlatched the window and placed the cat on the deep stone ledge, encouraging him through the opening when he balked.

She banked the fire that was just finally starting to warm the chamber in earnest and slipped into the corridor.

Padraig Boyd was waiting for her in the shadows, leaning his tall, wide frame against the stone wall. He straightened as she pulled the door closed behind her.

Iris glanced up and down the corridor. "Padraig, what are you doing here?"

He walked toward her at once and took Iris into his arms, lowering his mouth to hers and kissing her. She stood dumbly in his arms for a moment, but with her next inhalation, smelling his scent, feeling the roughness of his upper lip against her own skin, his strong arms about her, she relented. Her arms skimmed up his shoulders, mindful of the bulky bandage beneath his shirt, until her fingers were sliding through his hair, holding his head to hers.

His kiss, his embrace, was like shelter to her after so long—decades, it seemed—being on her own, with no one to care for her but herself. Here, now, was this strong man, this good man, who wanted her.

He wanted her, yes, but perhaps that was only because he didn't truly know who she was.

The thought caused Iris to pull away. "Padraig," she whispered. "I'm sorry about last night. But we can't carry on like this."

"Tell me you're nae in love with Lucan."

"I'm not at all in love with Lucan."

He lowered his head again, as if to continue the kiss, but Iris turned her head and pulled out of his embrace, feeling as though she was dragging the weight of a boulder with her.

"What?" he said. "What is it?"

"I mean it. We can't do this," Iris said. "There's too much at stake for both of us."

"I say we must do this, for the verra same reason." Padraig stepped toward her again, but this time he only took her hand. "Beryl, either of us could have died today. It's clear there are people who will go to whatever lengths they must to see me gone from Darlyrede, dead or alive."

"I know," Iris said, her conscience twisting every time he called her by that name—the name of the maid who was dead. The name of the girl who no longer existed, who had never existed in the role Iris was playing. "It's dangerous for us both. It's why we must not allow ourselves to be distracted."

"Are you telling me I don't already distract you? That we doona distract each other?"

Iris looked away.

"Is it your past?" Padraig pressed.

She turned her face to look at him again. "Yes."

True.

"I doona care," Padraig said with a gentle smile. "I already know, and I doona care."

Iris swallowed. "You know what?"

"I know about the abbey, and why you were there," he said.

Her heart pounded in her chest. "I don't think you do."

"Nay, I do," he insisted. "And I doona care about your station. Whether I win Darlyrede House or nae, nae matter the pretty manners you've taught me, I'm still the same man I was when I first arrived here. And nae matter what happens, I want you to know that I intend to make you mine. I wish to take care of you."

Iris felt her eyes welling with tears. "This isn't Caedmaray, Padraig. It doesn't work that way here. And you don't know me as you think you do."

"I know you in the only way that matters," he insisted yet again. "I know your heart."

She pulled her hands away. "I have to speak to Lucan."

Padraig frowned. "Why? Asking his permission, are you?"

Iris shook her head and then looked both ways down the corridor. "No. The masked man in the wood, he told me he killed Euphemia Hargrave. I need to tell Lucan alone."

"I doona understand," Padraig said. "You doona wish me present when you're discussing things that concern Darlyrede?"

"I have to ask him about your father," Iris said. "And I don't want to further upset you. I need you to have faith that—"

Padraig's brows raised. "Am I some wee bairn now, that needs your sheltering?"

"No," she insisted. "But I know how you loved him and—"

"Love him," Padraig corrected. "I still love him. He's nae dead."

"You are so quick to defend him," Iris reasoned. "I just need—"

"What does any of this have to do with you any matter?" he demanded. "You serve Caris Hargrave, and you were to train me up to be a proper Englishman. What does anything my father did or didna do have to do with you?" He looked at her closely for a long moment. "Searrach warned me that you were keeping a secret. I'm wondering now if she wasna right. If I'm playing right into your hands. Have you been lying to me?"

Oh, God help me, Iris prayed silently.

Tell the truth as often as you can, she reminded herself.

"Yes," she whispered.

"Yes?" he repeated incredulously. "Yes, you've been lying to me?"

She nodded briefly.

Padraig's handsome face was a mask of confusion. "About what?"

Iris took a deep breath. "Come with me to see Lucan."

Padraig's frown deepened.

Iris couldn't stand the pain that his wary confusion was causing her. Whether Lucan liked it or not, Padraig was going to learn the truth about her that night. He might hate her afterward, she knew.

And so Iris did the only thing she could think of in that moment. She reached out for him and kissed him again, pressing her lips against his with all the hope she felt in her heart while the tears pressed painfully against her eyelids. Hope that Padraig would listen and understand. Hope that he would forgive her. Perhaps even still consider loving her when it was over.

She pulled away and leaned her forehead against his. "No matter what happens after tonight," she whispered, "I've never lied about how I feel about you."

This time it was Padraig who stepped away from her. "Let's get it over with, then."

Chapter 15

Iris followed Padraig through the corridors of Darlyrede House to the courtyard, and then once more toward the chapel. The atmosphere was tense—news of the assault in the clearing had spread quickly, and everyone they passed fixed them with curious stares, whispering to their companions. Indeed, the very stones of the keep seemed to be murmuring.

It was only through sheer determination that Iris managed to place one foot in front of the other, nearly skipping to keep up with Padraig's long strides. Her entire body felt jumpy, as if she'd been struck by lightning, in anticipation of what was to occur.

Lucan was still lying on the same cot when they entered the darkened antechamber of Father Kettering's domain. He had one forearm across his eyes, and his left foot was propped up, wrapped in thick bandages. He raised his arm slightly to see who had entered and then took it away altogether, rising to one elbow while Iris barred the door behind her.

"What is it?" he asked, at once alert. His expectant gaze went to Padraig's and then followed Iris as she went to the doorway leading to the chapel proper and secured the barrier.

"We're going to tell him," Iris said, stopping at her brother's bedside and turning to face the Scotsman, clasping her hands together tightly to stop her nervous fidgeting. "Now."

She saw Lucan collapse back to the cot in her periphery. He sighed. "We don't yet know—"

"We do," Iris interrupted. "At least, I do. Lucan, Thomas Annesley lied to you."

"What?" Lucan said.

Padraig spoke in the same moment. "Lied to him about what?"

Iris looked at each man in turn and then settled on Padraig. "Your father told Lucan that the reason it was unthinkable that he could kill Cordelia Hargrave was that she carried his child. They were to be married the next day, and the unborn babe would have been Thomas Annesley's heir—the security of his and Cordelia's future at Darlyrede. No one save he and Cordelia knew for certain about the child, although there were rumors."

"What?" Padraig breathed incredulously.

"*Beryl*," Lucan warned pointedly. "You assume too much on rumor."

"I assume nothing," Iris returned crisply. "It was you who relayed the information to me, Lucan. I'm certain you recall."

Padraig regarded her warily now, and Iris was caught between saying what she must as quickly as possible to get it over with and ordering her words so that the sting of them was lessened.

She decided on efficiency.

"The thief in the wood bragged to me today that he killed Euphemia Hargrave the night she disappeared, as mercy for the suffering she had endured. When we all returned to Darlyrede this afternoon, Father Kettering confirmed that, prior to her disappearance, young Lady Euphemia had become obsessed with the idea of Thomas Annesley and Cordelia Hargrave, nearly to the point of madness. She was consumed by the rumors of Cordelia's secret pregnancy and vile murder. She would not accept Father Kettering's refutation of the rumors—that Cordelia Hargrave had definitely not been with child."

Padraig's eyebrows raised slightly. "Kettering said it was he who buried Cordelia," he acknowledged. "But perhaps she wasna so far gone that he—"

"No," Lucan interrupted. "No, Padraig. Thomas said she was nearing the end of her time—a month, mayhap, at most. It would have been impossible that Kettering could have overlooked a pregnancy that advanced."

"But my father has nae reason to lie about that," Padraig said with a confused frown. "If anything, it would have brought more charges against him."

Iris nodded. "You're right—and so neither does it make sense that, if Cordelia had indeed been pregnant, Lord and Lady Hargrave would not have shouted it from Darlyrede's walls. They would have lost not only their daughter but their grandchild. And the Hargraves have done naught but disregard the rumors since the very beginning."

"Wait," Padraig said, "I would expect Sir Lucan to have divulged this information to me, having been charged by the Crown to bring my father to so-called justice, but why would *you* care to know anything about it,

Beryl? You've told me you're nae sleeping with him, so it's nae mere lovers' confidences."

"My God," Lucan muttered distastefully.

Iris took a quick, deep breath. "I came to Darlyrede House to work for Lady Hargrave some eight months ago. This you already know."

"Aye," Padraig said warily. "From an abbey in France. You'd been sent there to have a child out of wedlock."

"That is not *completely* true," she acknowledged. "I was living at the abbey, yes, but I had been there for many years as a guest, on a stipend from my parents' estate. Beryl was indeed an English maid of the Pagets', who bore her child at the abbey. But she died. And I assumed her identity in order to gain passage back to England and to help find out the truth about the fire that killed my parents and destroyed my home."

"You should have stayed there, as I told you," Lucan said grimly.

"Because you were doing so well on your own, chasing your tail back and forth across Scotland," Iris snapped. "I've compiled information that will likely help incriminate Lord Hargrave."

Padraig could have been carved from stone, he was so still. His eyes shifted to Lucan, then back to Iris. "You're the sister. The sister Lord Hood mentioned."

Iris nodded once. "My name is Iris Montague, Padraig."

"You're nae maid."

"No. I'm not."

"It's why Lucan grabbed you the night we arrived," Padraig reasoned out loud. "He didna expect you to be here."

Lucan muttered, "A rather subtle understatement."

"It's how you knew so well to tutor me," Padraig continued, and Iris could tell he was reliving each of their moments together. "You were born into a noble family. Neighbors to the estate stolen from my own father. Castle Dare was your home too."

"That's right," Iris said.

"You both were *using* me."

Lucan scoffed, "What?"

"No, Padraig," Iris said. "But we couldn't tell you—"

"You couldnae tell me ennathin' until you'd determined what worth I was to you," he said. "Without me winning back Darlyrede House, there's nae chance in hell you'd get back even a blade of grass from Castle Dare. Unless Hargrave had promised to—"

Padraig stilled suddenly, his head drawing back, and Iris could see the devastation in his handsome face in the instant the pieces fell into place for him. He looked at Lucan.

"You've been working for Vaughn Hargrave the entire time."

* * * *

Lucan met his gaze without wavering. "Not the entire time," he said.

And even though Padraig had recognized the idea as truth as soon as it had entered his mind, hearing Lucan confirm it was like a blade to his heart.

"I trusted you," Padraig said with a disbelieving wince. "I came all this way—I trusted you both."

"You can still trust us," Beryl—nay, *Iris*—said, stepping toward him with a hand out, as if to touch him, comfort him.

Padraig backed out of her reach and looked to Lucan once more. "That's why you were searching out my father's other children," he realized aloud. "My brothers. Nae so you could give them the opportunity to clear Tommy's name, but to make sure there would be nae nasty surprises to reclaiming your own estate. You wanted my father out of the way just as much as Hargrave did."

"That's not at all true, Padraig," Lucan argued. "I don't believe Thomas committed any of the crimes he was accused of. Not one. Upon my honor, it is my intention to present my evidence to the king to exonerate your father."

"And, lucky for you, here's poor, dumb Padraig, who has a legal right to Darlyrede. Your golden goose, am I?"

"Padraig, please." Iris stepped toward him yet again, her beautiful face splotchy with unshed tears.

But Padraig fought the pull of her, knowing it was all a lie. Everything she said was a lie.

"I was happy," Padraig insisted. "Me mam and da—we didna have two pennies to press together, but we had each other, and we were happy. Now look at us all," he demanded. "Me da is again being chased across the land, a price on his head. Me mam's dead. I've been shot, brained, had me food poisoned, been humiliated, led to believe I had the loyalty and affection of friends who, in truth, only wanted me for what I could gain them. *You used me*," he repeated.

He looked between them several times, ignoring the silent tear that raced in a silvery line down Iris's cheek.

"To hell with ye both," he sneered and then turned away, stalking to the door. He threw the bolt and flung open the door, sending it crashing into the stone wall, and then strode across the courtyard toward the doorway that led to the corridor just outside the great hall.

I've never lied about how I feel about you.

He ignored the memory of her words. Everything she'd ever done, said, was suspect now. Lucan too. He thought of the lives they'd ruined with their spying and treachery as he strode through the wide entry chamber into which he'd fought his way that first night at Darlyrede, and he paused in the center of it, paying no heed to the nobles, the servants who stopped what they were doing to stare openly as Padraig, in his dirty, bloody clothes, looked about the tall, paneled walls.

Portraits. All these people he had never even known existed before Lucan Montague had arrived on Caedmaray. He walked up to the largest one, a painting of a hopelessly pale and despairing-looking girl, her faded blond hair and translucent skin seeming to blend in with the ivory cloth of the backdrop draped in long, graceful swags behind her. Her blue eyes seemed to see nothing, her thin, pale mouth turned down. Her right hand was laid upon the back of a gilded chair, her left hand clutching a single, pale lily, held down against her thigh as if she had not even the strength to pose with a proper bouquet. Indeed, she did look defeated for one so young.

The last portrait of Lady Euphemia Hargrave…she was ten and five…

And now she was dead.

Padraig turned away toward the hall, where he could hear Vaughn Hargrave shouting at his first in command.

"Then you shall go back and search again!" the nobleman insisted, standing before the hearth while the kindly Lord Hood leaned heavily on the lord's table nearby. "Do you not understand? They have killed Lord Paget! If you come back without at least one of them, *I will kill you myself!*"

The man-at-arms was stony-faced through this tirade. He gave Hargrave a stiff bow. "As you wish, my lord." He turned and strode past Padraig without a glance.

"Oh, now what do you want?" Hargrave sneered in exasperation. "I've enough to deal with without—"

"I've come to tell you I'm leaving," Padraig interrupted.

Hargrave stilled, looked at Padraig suspiciously out of the corner of his eye. "Leaving?"

"Aye. Leaving Darlyrede House. You can have the lot of it. I doona want it."

"Is that so?" Hargrave said in a tone of surprised interest. "Did you hear that, Edwin?" he said to the slouching lord who had raised his head to fix Padraig with a look of unabashed surprise. "Proved too much for you, after all, I suppose. I thought it might. It takes a strong man to keep Darlyrede in check. Your father was never that man, and neither are you. *Weak. Stock*," Hargrave enunciated. "And speaking of weak stock, are you taking your friend Montague with you?"

"He's nae my friend," Padraig said, feeling a pinch in his chest at the words. "But I think you knew that long before I."

"Ah," Hargrave mused. "Yes, I suppose I did. It seems that everyone in my house is at last coming to their senses."

Padraig steeled himself for the request he was about to make. "I'd have a horse for the journey."

Lord Hargrave's eyes widened again. "By all means, take two, if only that I should be rid of you sooner."

Padraig had never hated another human being as much as he hated Vaughn Hargrave in that moment. His hands shook so that he clenched them into fists to stay the tremors from taking over his entire body.

The nobleman looked at him pointedly. "Well? Goodbye. I shall be sure to give your regards to the king."

Padraig lifted his chin and turned away, his pride screaming out as he felt the stares of everyone in the hall. He could imagine their thoughts, slimy and dark and cold, brushing up against him as he passed.

Interloper.

Peasant.

Fraud.

Coward.

He was no longer lost in the maze of corridors that made up the interior of the castle and came to his door in moments. He found the old satchel he had carried to Darlyrede those many weeks ago—it seemed years—and he was embarrassed by its condition, filthy and patched. This place had made him embarrassed of what had once been his own contented life—negating his happy past in exchange for the lure of something noble and grand. But it had been nothing more than a glittering façade, hiding an oozing, putrescent core.

He opened the flap of his bag; there was nothing in it now, save the letters Lucan Montague had given him. Padraig unfolded the now-worn-soft messages, read each through once more with new eyes, wiser eyes, as he walked toward the hearth. One letter given on Caedmaray, luring him to this place of death and deceit; one letter the night he'd arrived at Darlyrede, dangling the hope of the king's favor before his ignorant nose.

He tossed the pages and the ribbon to the flames.

Padraig located his father's ragged shawl and folded it inside the satchel, along with the stoppered flasks of wine on the table. It was fully winter now, and the journey would be even harsher heading north, but this time he was well-nourished, well-clothed, and would be astride. He ducked his head through the strap of his satchel and then put on his thick cloak. He'd been a fool here long enough.

He was going home.

His door opened then, and Searrach slipped inside. She closed the door and leaned back against it. Her dark eyes flicked over his costume.

"You're leavin'."

"Aye."

She came toward him then, holding out a piece of parchment that he took from her.

"What is it?"

"Lord Hargrave wants you to put your name to it," she said as he skimmed the words. "Before you go."

Padraig turned back to the table, and in the next moment he was scrawling his signature across the bottom of the page.

"Did I nae tell you?" she said in a voice that was not unkind.

Padraig tossed the quill onto the page, where it skittered and sputtered ink, like a spurt of black blood across the words. "You did," he acknowledged, and his heart was so heavy it felt like cold lead in his chest. He looked to Searrach and thought he glimpsed compassion in her dark eyes.

She knew the pain of Darlyrede too.

"Neither one of us belongs here." He saw her throat convulse as she swallowed, and then she whispered, "Take me with you."

And Padraig's hurt and disillusionment, his betrayal, was so deep, so blindingly painful in that moment that he nodded.

Chapter 16

Iris left Lucan in the chapel annex, ignoring his harshly whispered demands to return. She swiped angrily at the tears that ran in rivers down her cheeks, each one like a silent condemnation that she only now realized the truth of.

Padraig had been right all along. Even Iris herself hadn't understood how indebted to Hargrave her brother had become, hadn't understood the depths of what he'd agreed to. But now that Padraig had revealed the truth to her, Iris couldn't believe that she'd failed to see it herself. How else had Lucan Montague, a young orphan boy forgotten in France, managed to secure a position of authority under the king of England? Was there no place safe, no office sacred enough, to be out of Hargrave's reach?

But now Iris knew the truth. And Padraig knew the truth. And Lucan knew the truth.

There was just one more person who must be put through pain today, and Iris knew that duty could fall only to her.

She made her way up the long, wide flights of stairs to Lady Hargrave's wing, and was surprised to find Rolf and another house guard standing to either side of the corridor.

"Mistress Beryl," Rolf said. "You're early."

"The events of the day seem to warrant it, Rolf. Is Lady Hargrave in her chamber?"

"She is," the man answered. "You should know that Lord Hargrave has commanded that the family wing be closed to visitors until the thieves in the forest are apprehended."

"I see," Iris said. "I'll go down for the tray myself later, then."

"No need," Rolf said. "It's already been placed, miss."

"Thank you." She passed between the two men but then stopped. "Rolf?"

"Yes, miss?"

"If you should happen to see Master Boyd, will you tell him I would very much like to speak with him after my duties to her ladyship are finished for the evening?"

"Yes, miss."

Iris turned and strode down the corridor, her slippers making no sound on the thick rug that ran down the center. Iris passed Euphemia Hargrave's chamber and stopped at Caris's door, considering this thing that had never seemed important to her before, although she had made note of it in the journals. This was the only carpeted corridor in all of Darlyrede. It pained Iris's heart to think of the lady's fragility requiring such a thing.

If Lord Hargrave ever struck her, the woman would crumple like a pillow of ash on the hearth.

Iris rapped softly on the door. "Milady?" she called out, and then engaged the latch, pushing the door open. "Milady?"

The plush, opulent room was empty, but the door leading to the connecting chamber stood open, and it was from there that Iris heard her call answered.

"Beryl, is it you?"

Iris closed the door behind her and went through to find the lady already seated in her usual position at the window seat, although it wasn't yet dusk. And just as Rolf had reported, the tray had been delivered.

"You've experienced many trials lately, have you not?" the woman said with her sad smile. "Oh, Beryl, what would I do without your stalwart strength? Do go on and place the candles for us—it will be dark soon enough."

Iris crossed the rug to the chest where the supply of beeswax tapers were kept. In her mind, she knew it was no longer necessary to keep a vigil for the girl who was in fact dead but was putting off that dreadful moment for just a bit longer, and Iris was glad for the reprieve. Her own heart needed some time to recover before dealing out the next blow.

Tonight would be a memorial rather than a vigil; fifteen tiny flames for each year of Euphemia Hargrave's young life.

And Iris would never light them again.

Once the room was golden and soft, the gray light through the window deepening to steel, Iris approached Lady Caris again.

"You've heard what happened during the hunt today," she said.

Caris nodded up at her with a smile, and reached out to take Iris's hand. "I have. And how you stood up to those awful criminals, for my sake."

She squeezed Iris's fingers, but it was little more than a flinching pressure. "You were very brave to do so. Foolish, I must add."

Iris shook her head and went down to her knees before the woman. "Perhaps it was foolish, milady," she allowed. "But I would do it again a hundred times over. For I gained the information you have been so desperate for."

A faint frown appeared between Caris's fine brows.

"The man I confronted," she began and then then had to pause, swallow, take a breath. "He admitted it was he who met Euphemia the night she disappeared from Darlyrede House. She died at his hand."

Caris's expression never changed, and save for the single blink of her eyes, it was as though she had become a marble statue.

"Milady?" Iris asked softly. "Do you wish to lie down?"

Lady Caris's lips parted, but she did not speak.

Iris edged closer, rubbing the woman's upper arm. "Breathe, milady."

She heard the intake of air, swift and sudden, as if Caris had been held underwater these past moments, these past years. Perhaps she had felt as if she was drowning, Iris acknowledged.

"She's...dead," Caris said quietly.

Iris nodded. "Yes."

"How?"

"I don't know, milady."

Her eyes were wide but dry as she nodded absently again. "It's over. At last."

Iris gathered the woman to her, embracing her gently through the shock. "Does Lord Hargrave know?" Caris asked as her head lay on Iris's shoulder.

"I've not told him," she said. "But he is having the wood searched for the criminals now. If he finds them, I have little doubt what will be the outcome, even if he doesn't yet know that one of them is Euphemia's killer."

"He will leave no stone unturned." Caris pulled away then, and something outside the window caught her eye and she turned her head nodding toward the wavy, bubbly glass. "There go two more searchers now."

Iris only gave the most cursory glance out the window; she didn't care what Hargrave's men-at-arms did to the monsters who inhabited the wood. "I'm sorry to be the one to have to deliver such news to you, my lady."

"Oh, Beryl, I'd have wished it from no other." She looked with bittersweet longing to the twinkling lights about the room, the tray sitting on the bed, the foodstuffs and cup perfect, just as it had been every night since Iris had arrived at Darlyrede.

Then she looked back into Iris's eyes. "I wish you were she," she said. "Forgive me."

Iris felt tears well in her eyes. "There is naught to forgive."

"Perhaps, just for tonight, we could pretend," she said in a small, pleading voice. She reached out to smooth back Iris's hair behind her ear. "Before my lord comes for me, let us drink and eat of the last meal I will ever have prepared for my sweet, lost Euphemia. And then, if the morrow comes, we shall decide what we shall do next."

Iris nodded, not willing to tell the woman that she planned for the morrow to find her without station in Darlyrede's current incarnation; she would stand firmly, openly, on Padraig Boyd's side, both before and after the king had passed his judgment, whatever it might be.

That would be too much shock for the woman, and Iris would not betray her so.

She gained her feet, and Caris took her hand once more as they walked together to the bed. The lady pushed the tray to the center of the perfectly arranged mattress, and the women sat upon its edge, facing each other. Caris reached out for the ewer and the cup with a peaceful smile and poured a generous portion before handing the cup to Iris. Then she broke off a piece of the thin loaf and held it out.

"You must be famished, my dear, running about the wood all day like a peasant." Her smile was indulgent, perhaps a mother speaking to her spirited daughter.

"Thank you." Iris took it and tried to keep a bright smile on her face, although she felt almost guilty participating in the farce. Perhaps it would help the lady achieve peace, but Iris had a sick feeling in her stomach as she bit into the soft bread and chewed.

A dead girl's meal, she couldn't help hearing in her head.

The bread was dry and difficult to swallow, so she lifted the cup and drank of the tepid milk, even as she heard the door in the next room open.

"My lady?"

Iris forced her throat to swallow as her eyes widened, and the noblewoman's face lost all traces of contentment, to be replaced with blatant anxiety.

"He was not to come so soon," she whispered, as if in apologetic explanation.

"Lady wife?" Lord Hargrave called again. "Are you in there?"

"Stay here," Caris whispered and pressed her arm before scrambling from the bed and walking around the chamber and through the doorway. "I'm here, my lord." She pulled the door closed behind her.

Iris put the bread back on the platter and stood with the cup, tiptoeing around the end of the bed toward the closed door. She could hear the muffled conversation through the thick slab, harsh and clipped. Iris felt her head start to swim and realized that she had been holding her breath. The deeper voice of Lord Hargrave seemed to be growing louder, closer to the door.

She was suddenly very afraid, though she could not have said why, and turned to the door that opened into the corridor. Iris engaged the handle, yanked, but the door stayed firmly shut.

She remembered her notes, the curious lock on the exterior of the door.

Iris hurried back to sit on the side of the bed and then began to worry why Hargrave had chosen this night to visit Caris's chamber. In all the months of Iris's employment, he had never called upon his wife's apartments during the twilight hours while Beryl was present.

He was not to come so soon...

She drank the last of the milk to soothe her parched throat and set down the empty cup, pushing the tray from her. She looked about the room, but she could see nothing to be used in defense of herself. Not a heavy bowl, nor an iron poker for the fire; not an eating knife on the tray—nothing heavy, hard, or sharp in the whole of the room.

She stood up, not willing to be caught off her feet, but then another wave of dizziness overcame her and she sat again. Her nerves would be her ruin this day. She breathed in and out slowly through her nose.

The chamber door opened, and Iris heard Lady Caris shout "No!" in a strangled voice as Lord Vaughn Hargrave walked into the room with a curious smile on his face.

"Well, look who is here," he said, his smile not warming the cold glint in his eyes.

Iris's head began to swim, and each of the fifteen tiny flames turned into little explosions of light, sparkling on the air like the sun glinting off water. She could no longer see clearly, but she heard his muffled footsteps drawing closer on the thick carpet, and so she held out a warding hand.

"No," she thought she managed to choke out, but the voice she heard sounded too far away, so perhaps it was Lady Hargrave who had spoken again.

And then everything was black and silent.

* * * *

If Padraig had been sensible, he realized, he would have waited until morning to depart from Darlyrede instead of setting off with Searrach just as the sun was dipping below the far-off, rolling foothills, washing all the color from the landscape and replacing it with a gray chill that clouded his breath. The air was still and growing tighter, colder, as if the solid blanket of clouds overhead was stretched taut with the snow it held.

But he could not stay there another night; nay, another hour. He couldn't risk seeing Beryl's face again. No—Iris's face. The face of the woman he'd thought he loved. The face he'd thought he wanted to see every day for the rest of his life. She had hurt Padraig in a way that he hadn't known it was possible for him to be hurt.

And so now he headed north on the road that ran before Darlyrede as a failure, seeing the distant monoliths as dark, wide shadows on the moor around this side of the estate, a suspicious, perhaps unstable Scottish maid behind him. He thought of the stories he had heard today of his father's escape from Darlyrede House, Kettering's father's gruesome end. Padraig looked around him, wondering what Tommy Boyd had suffered on this same road thirty years ago—and every day since, likely. Padraig himself was only a handful of years older than his father had been the night he'd fled, and the idea of it sobered Padraig. He'd pondered so many times since he'd learned of Darlyrede's existence why Thomas Annesley had not fought for his home. But riding now through the cold, dark night without even a sliver of moon to light the way, after having had his life endangered these many weeks—Padraig was beginning to understand.

He tried to imagine how he would feel if it had been Beryl killed today in the wood.

Not Beryl, he reminded himself again. *Iris.*

If it had been Iris and not Lord Paget, dead and bleeding on the forest floor. And Hargrave and all his money and his power and his reputation waiting, ready to destroy Padraig before the king.

Thomas Annesley had been gravely injured that night years ago, more injured than Padraig now was. And yet he had managed to escape, to find his way eventually to Caedmaray and Jessie. Padraig thought longingly of the little cottage waiting for him on the island in the spring. He'd sell Hargrave's horses in Thurso to pay for board and supplies to carry back when the boats started to run.

He could be happy there again.

Probably.

But with Searrach? a voice inside his head asked him.

He didn't know why he had agreed to take her with him. He didn't want her physically and he didn't trust her. But the familiar sound of her accent, the remembrance of the scars on her wrists…perhaps it was nothing more than the idea that she had asked to go, and in that moment of weakness, giving his permission had made him feel in control of his future. Perhaps he had thought to soothe the sting of Iris and Lucan's betrayal by departing Darlyrede House with a woman Padraig knew Iris was jealous of. Whatever the reason for it at the time, Padraig now regretted the hasty decision.

He thought they had at last left Darlyrede lands as they neared the dark abyss of a stand of evergreen trees and the snow at last began to fall, fast and thick. They could not ride through a snowstorm in the dark—it was cruel to the horses, and Padraig wasn't certain they wouldn't lose their way if the already dim track became covered over. And so he turned his mount's head toward the stand of fir, Searrach following unquestioningly behind him.

She was already dismounted by the time Padraig's own feet found the ground, and after looping the reins of her horse around a tree branch, she began searching beneath the spreading boughs for kindling and dry branches—she had obviously camped on the road before. Neither of the travelers spoke as Padraig broke off a portion of the lowest branches of a wide fir, sweeping away the needles at the base of the tree down to dry ground and then stacking the fresh boughs to afford some protection from the frozen dirt. Soon, a small fire crackled at the edge of their little evergreen cave, and Padraig and Searrach sat side by side, sharing the wine in his satchel and the food in hers. The snow fell around them, over them, quieting the world and seeming to grant them a little bubble of peace.

"What's your island called again?" she asked in a low voice, and the sound was so unexpected after the last hour of quiet that Padraig felt his heart stutter at the interruption.

"Caedmaray." He used one of the little bones from the chicken they'd eaten to pick at his teeth.

"Caedmaray," Searrach repeated. "Is it grand?"

Padraig tossed the bone into the fire. "Nay."

"I'm sure it's grand," she said softly.

The realization that Padraig had made a mistake in allowing Searrach to accompany him grew ever larger in his already burdened mind.

"There'll be no crossing until the spring." When she didn't comment, he offered, "What is your town?"

"Town Blair," she said, staring into the fire with wide eyes, and the reflection of the fire in their glassy depths gave him an uneasy feeling, as if Searrach's mind burned and her eyes were windows to the raging furnace of her thoughts. "I know your brother. You could be his twin, but that your hair is lighter."

Padraig stilled. "My brother?"

She nodded but didn't look at him, still seemingly mesmerized by the fire that mirrored her secret musings. "Lach-lan-Blair. Lachlan. Lach-lan." Her mouth turned down suddenly, and her next words were whispered. "Your eyes are just like his."

The color of them.

Padraig too frowned, wondering at the truth of the woman's ramblings. Indeed, Lucan Montague had reported that Padraig had a half brother named Lachlan Blair residing in the Highlands, but how had Searrach managed to make her way alone so far south to Darlyrede House? And why did the idea that this woman, so close to Vaughn Hargrave, had known Padraig's brother cause the muscles along Padraig's spine to stiffen?

People seemed to appear and vanish at will, and everyone—everything—was connected in some grotesque fashion. Padraig's thoughts went back to the portrait of Euphemia Hargrave in the entry hall.

Lady Euphemia had become obsessed with the idea of Thomas Annesley and Cordelia Hargrave nearly to the point of madness...

Thomas Annesley is accused of returning to Northumberland and setting the blaze that killed my parents and destroyed Castle Dare. The same night Euphemia Hargrave disappeared...

Must be the English of you all. Your eyes...

Searrach, Lucan, Iris, Hargrave, Castle Dare...everything—*everything*—seemed to be connected by gossamer threads that were invisible at first glance. The only outlier seemed to be Euphemia Hargrave, who had turned up at Darlyrede apparently from nowhere—a motherless infant who'd had no other to care for her in the world save for Lady Caris Hargrave—and then vanished fifteen years later.

Padraig thought of the lambs he'd taken from their dying mother in the spring, and then he stilled.

It was madness, the ideas that were circling in his mind then, like carrion birds waiting for the opportunity to swoop down and devour the carcass of Padraig's reality.

But Tommy Boyd was no liar. He was no murderer, and he was no liar.

Could Euphemia Hargrave... have been Cordelia and Thomas's baby? If it was true, the sad girl in the portrait had been Tommy's firstborn child, and Padraig's own sister.

He could see nothing in his mind now but the eyes in the portrait in the entry hall—unhappy, hopeless, frightened.

Even if the insane idea was true, there was no way Padraig could prove it. Euphemia Hargrave was dead, and Padraig knew too little of that long-ago time in Northumberland, had no facts, no station to call on to demand the truth.

But Lucan Montague did. Iris did.

The sudden touch of Searrach's cold hand creeping around the back of his neck shook him from his reverie, and he realized that the woman had slunk closer to him, pressing against his arm, reaching up her face to nuzzle his hair.

"Do you think me beautiful, Padraig?"

"Searrach," he began.

Her lips tracked along his ear, his cheekbone. "Your skin is cold," she whispered. "Let me keep you warm."

"Nay," he said, half turning and placing his hands on her arms to halt her progress. "It's not like that between us. It will never be like that."

"It will," she countered easily. "You're taking me to Caedmaray. I'll be your woman there. I'll take care of you."

"Nay," he repeated, more firmly this time even as she struggled against his restraining touch to move closer to him. Padraig released her and stood, looking at her from over the fire. Her face was bright with yellow light, turning her already dark eyes black. "I'm going back to Darlyrede."

She stared at him with those black eyes for a long moment. "I canna go back there," she said. "Nae even for you, Padraig. Lord Hargrave will kill me."

"Then doona," Padraig said. "But I must."

"He'll kill *you*," Searrach insisted. "Are you so blind that you canna see what he's been doing? He nearly succeeded while you were there." She got up suddenly and walked toward him. "I've saved your life a dozen times already. And now you owe me mine, by taking me from here."

"What do you mean, you've saved my life?"

"I made excuses. I took the punishment. Those scars you saw…" Her mind seemed to wander for the briefest instant, but then her brows lowered. "So now you will take me from here. Back to Scotland."

Padraig shook his head. "I'll nae force you to return to Darlyrede. Take the horse, go on if you would. But if anyone else figures out what I think I have, people could be in great danger."

"Figures out what you have?" Searrach's eyes narrowed and she fixed him with a derisive look. "You mean about your precious Beryl?"

Padraig didn't respond. Something in Searrach's eyes—perhaps it was madness—reminded him that he'd always known to be wary of the woman, and just now there had been a quiet whisper of something more sinister behind the words she'd spoken. And so Padraig held his tongue, sensing that she could no longer keep the darkness to herself.

And he was right.

Searrach walked toward him slowly. "He already knows," she whispered through a smile. The snow fell on her dark hair, turning it white in the flickering light. "He knew before you. And so did I."

"What are you talking about?" Padraig managed to croak.

She walked closer to him, another pair of steps. "Your precious Beryl was supposed to have been a servant—a very special servant—of Lady Paget's. Only," she was just a hand's breadth from him now—"Lord Paget didn't know her. Wherever she's come from, it's nae from Elsmire Tower. He told his good friend, Lord Hargrave, just after their arrival."

Padraig was as still as the stone monoliths rising out of the earth around Darlyrede.

"Lord Hargrave told you this, did he?" Padraig asked at last. "It doesna seem like the sort of information he'd share with a servant."

"He's shared lots with me," Searrach said. "I'll nae forget any of it. And now neither will Beryl. Or whatever her name is. My lord was quite put out when he found out she'd been lying all this time, in such close quarters with his sickly, pathetic wife."

Searrach reached out and grasped a fistful of his cloak. "There is naught you can do to save her now. You must believe me. She's gone. Vanished, like all the others. We must leave this place."

He pulled away from her with a jerk, and after a confused blink, her brows drew downward and she gave a furious shriek.

"You'll nae leave me here!"

Padraig caught her wrists as she struck out at him, not feeling the pain from the pulling of his wound on his ribs, but the sensation of warmth took over his flank. He wrested her to the ground and then stepped away, leaving her in the flattened snow.

"I'm sorry, Searrach. I've no wish for harm to come to you. Take shelter here for the night," he said as he retrieved his mount from where it was tied and led the animal in a circle away from the fire. "Then, in the morning, if you haven't changed your mind, take the horse and go while you can."

"You can't save her! She's already gone!" Searrach insisted in a hysterical screech. "Come back!"

But Padraig did what his young father hadn't had the strength to do those thirty years past. He mounted and turned the horse sharply back in the direction of Darlyrede. It reared with an affronted scream and then bolted into the storm, carrying Padraig back to that house of the damned and the bigger storm that waited for him there.

Chapter 17

Iris first became aware of flickering light beyond her eyelids, and then cold seeping into her aching bones. She wondered if she had somehow managed to escape Lord Hargrave and wandered out of doors before she fainted, for she was lying on her back on what must be frozen ground. It was so very cold…

Her eyelids felt weighted as they fluttered open, and she saw what she thought was the black sky above her, sparkling with starlight and a nearby fire. Was she in the courtyard? But no, her vision began to clear, and she realized it was a ceiling she stared at, pulsating with dazzling torchlight. Her head ached so, she raised a hand to try to shield her eyes.

But her arm stopped not even halfway to its intended destination, the dull clang of a chain sounding out. She jerked her arm in an attempt to free it while her eyes sought out the reason for her impeded movement.

She was restrained.

Her other arm too was hampered by a cuff of iron about her wrist, attached to a clinking chain. She kicked her feet, digging in her heels in an attempt to gain a seated position, but they were clamped to whatever sort of slab on which she lay. Iris stilled, trying not to gasp for breath in the frigid air, the pain in her head like searing icicles through her brain with each strangled inhalation.

Where was she? What had happened to her?

The last thing she could recall was Vaughn Hargrave breeching the sanctity of Euphemia's chamber.

What had happened to Lady Caris?

"Hello?" she called out, the words scratching along her parched throat like a sledge through dry summer fields. "Can anyone hear me?" Her voice recalled back to her, indicating that the dark ceiling was not very far above her.

Iris turned her head to locate the source of the light, and saw oddly striped flickering on a faraway wall. Several blinks of her eyes revealed that it wasn't the flame itself that was striped, but that she was viewing the torch through a set of iron bars.

She was in a cell.

"Help!" she cried out toward the door. "Help me! Is someone there? Help!"

The only answer was the crackle of the torch that didn't so much as flutter. No breeze. The cold air around her smelled metallic, like sharpened steel or...or blood, somehow.

Where was she? How had she come to be here?

Iris turned her face back up to the ceiling with a strangled sob. She drew in a deep breath.

"Help!" she screamed. "*Help!*"

* * * *

Padraig saw the men-at-arms when he was yet some distance from Darlyrede's grand entry, the snow turning them into hazy, dreamlike figures beneath the miniature suns above their heads. There had been no guards at the door when he'd left.

Padraig's gaze traveled up at the façade of the estate, the glowing windows high above the moat.

"Iris," he whispered, her name being manifest on the icy air for an instant before disappearing into the night.

He thought it likely that the guards would admit him, and nearly spurred his horse forward, but then reconsidered. It was safer for everyone if Hargrave believed Padraig had left Darlyrede and was gone; if the men-at-arms had been stationed there to alert the lord of Padraig's return, it could set into motion things not yet begun. Better to let Hargrave continue to think Padraig had shaken Darlyrede's dust from his boots.

And yet, how then was he to get inside the fortress and find Iris and Lucan?

The question was answered for him in the next moment, as the guard to the left gave out a sudden cry and then crumpled to the ground. His comrade drew his sword, shouting something unintelligible at that distance into the quietly falling snow. But Padraig saw the arrow find its mark in the opening beneath the man's helm, and then that soldier too collapsed.

Padraig held his breath as slinking shadows separated themselves from the storm, creeping stealthily toward the entry—more than a score of them, from what he could tell, carrying bows. Some of them appeared to be wearing helmets or...

"Masks," he breathed in the shelter of the trees.

The last pair of robbers paused before disappearing into the hold, taking time to ensure that each of the fallen guards was dead, and then relieve them of their weapons. In a blink, they had rolled the two men into the moat and then closed the tall doors after them.

Padraig let out the breath he'd been holding. The stakes had just gone up in this mission to warn Iris and Lucan Montague. Padraig wasn't certain what the thieves intended for Darlyrede House, but their mission had already proved deadly, and would only likely become more so the deeper into the hold the band managed to penetrate.

He swung down from his mount and left it in the shelter of the trees before running as fast as he could across the open expanse of ground before the hold. There were likely only so many moments he could count on the distraction of the bandits, and he took advantage of every spare bit of strength he possessed, ignoring the strain in his ribs and shoulder as he pulled up, breathing hard, before the doors. He grasped the handle and eased the door open the slightest crack, peering through the slit and listening.

The entry was empty, but somewhere deeper inside the castle—the hall, he thought—Padraig heard shouts, a single scream.

He slipped through the door and ran at a crouch toward the sounds of commotion. He flattened himself against the stones as the hall doors came into sight, closing before his eyes. In the next moment the sound of the heavy beam being slid into place sealed the fate of those within the hall. Padraig approached carefully, peering through the crack while holding his breath. Lucan, Hargrave, and Lady Caris—but where was Iris?

Padraig turned away from the door and ran back through the entry toward the right-hand corridor, leading deeper into the castle. As he passed beneath the portraits towering over his head, he had the eerie sensation that Euphemia Hargrave was watching his every move.

* * * *

Lucan sat at the lord's table, his throbbing foot propped on the tufted stool Lord Hargrave had so courteously provided. Although in truth he wished to be anywhere but in Darlyrede's hall, Hargrave had so pressed

Lucan to attend, and the man seemed in such a pleasant humor and behaved so accommodatingly—the seat at the lord's table, the servants to wait upon his every wish—Lucan knew that something potentially calamitous was stirring.

A handful of the more cautious noble guests had departed Darlyrede posthaste at the news of Lord Paget's death, and yet far more of the attendees had remained, their thirst for gossip proving stronger than any fear for their safety. Lucan sat at Hargrave's right, and he noted crossly that Iris was nowhere to be seen. And while he hoped that she was with Padraig, somehow convincing him of their sincerity, it was more likely that Lady Caris had made more demands than usual upon his sister's time and sympathy, while Padraig had simply deigned it unnecessary to attend the feast.

Padraig was angry. And hurt. And Lucan understood that he bore responsibility for those injuries.

Lord Hargrave, however, appeared as though there was nothing at all wrong in the world. In fact Lucan couldn't remember a time in which the man had appeared more contented, and with each passing moment, each smile, each shout of laughter, Lucan's unease increased.

Father Kettering entered the hall then, and cast a pointed, questioning look toward his injured foot.

All right?

Lucan nodded. He was well enough, he supposed, for having been shot clean through his boot and then exposing himself as a would-have-been traitor to Thomas Annesley.

Where have you gone to now, Thomas? Lucan thought crossly to himself.

But then Vaughn Hargrave stood, clearing his throat genially and looking about the hall with a broad, sparkling smile.

"Good evening," he said crisply. "Let us first have the blessing." He nodded toward Father Kettering, who obliged with an unusually brief but seemingly heartfelt prayer. After Kettering's final "amen," Hargrave picked up his chalice.

"And now, let us remember our friend, Lord Adolphus Paget, who lost his life in a senseless act of cowardice and treachery. I vow that I will do everything in my power to rid our lands of this pestilence once and for all, and avenge the death of so great and honorable a man."

Lucan had to steel his face against a reactive expression. Everyone gathered knew Adolphus Paget to be a greedy, boot-licking lecher.

Hargrave raised his chalice. "To Lord Paget."

Lucan lifted his cup along with the others as the hall answered the toast, but he only pretended at drinking and set the wine back on the table untouched, the memory of the bastard who'd shot him still clear in his mind.

His riches are made from the sale of slaves ...

"And now," Hargrave continued, "let us proceed with happier news. I am pleased to announce that the man who had come to Darlyrede House to challenge my right to it has departed without reservation."

A collective gasp raced through the hall, and Lucan turned his head quickly to look up at the man standing at the side of his chair.

"Yes, I was quite surprised too," Hargrave conceded. "But after some thought it only made sense; Padraig Boyd was perhaps the source of much treachery within the hold these past months, and it is my thought that— even if the Scotsman wasn't directly involved, of which I am not entirely convinced—the death of Lord Paget at least pricked at his conscience. He knew he would be held accountable before the king, and far from being granted our beloved Darlyrede, Padraig Boyd would have wound up losing his life for the crimes he'd orchestrated and the accusations he'd prepared against me. And so"—here Hargrave gave a slight shrug and gestured with his chalice.

"It was the wisest thing for him to do, really. And although he has put his signature to a document releasing all claims to his supposed father's title, I think it likely that he will be pursued by the Crown's soldiers in his flight, as he's absconded from Darlyrede with a pair of servants. Whether the women went willingly or nay, I cannot say at this point."

Lucan felt a cold chill creep along his spine at these words, and he was once again very aware of Iris's absence from the hall.

Hargrave turned to Lucan then, his face bright with optimism. "I am certain it shall be none other than Sir Lucan who pursues him, as Boyd has left with the Scottish maid Searrach and our own Beryl." Hargrave paused with a concerned frown on his face. "You know, I'm sure, how treasured the girl was to Lady Hargrave. She's simply inconsolable, aren't you, my dear?"

Caris Hargrave stared unresponsively over the heads of the guests.

Vaughn Hargrave continued as if nothing at all were amiss. "But if anyone can track him down, I'm quite certain it shall be one of Northumberland's own."

Hargrave's smile never wavered as he regarded Lucan with something akin to pride, and though perhaps he was only imagining it, Lucan thought he could see a fury behind that noble façade, made all the more dangerous by its indiscernibility.

Lucan was well aware how Padraig felt about his sister, and he also knew that Iris had been shocked at his own admission this afternoon. Could the pair of them have reconciled and left together? Without so much as a word to Lucan?

If so, why would they agree to take Searrach with them?

And where was Iris's packet of damning information?

Lucan caught sight of Rolf then, standing against the wall behind the lord's table, his expression one of unabashed surprise. Rolf then looked to Lucan, the alarm on his face clear.

There was more to this tale than Hargrave was revealing, and Lucan had the urge to get up from the table and leave the hall in that moment. But he remained where he was as Hargrave was now giving the floor over to him with a gracious wave of his palm.

"Forgive me if I do not rise," Lucan addressed the hall and gestured toward his injured foot, which set a ripple of good-natured, sympathetic chuckles through the guests. "Of course I will do whatever duty calls me to, to assist the Crown in its continued investigation."

"Such loyalty," Hargrave said, a hushed admiration in his tone, but there it was again, Lucan was sure—the danger. "Allow me to say on behalf of all, we have the utmost faith in your abilities." He placed one palm over his heart and again raised his chalice. "To Sir Lucan!"

The crowd answered back, and Lucan acknowledged their honor with a nod of his head, although inside his guts were twisting.

The hall doors burst inward then, and the sounds of angry shouts bounced off the stone walls as a flood of leather-clad invaders swarmed into the room.

"Sit down! Sit down!" they shouted as some of the men rose.

A scream rang out, and Lucan saw a guest collapse to the bench, an arrow pinning the hem of his tunic to the seat.

"*I said, sit down!*" the red-bearded man shouted again with finality. Lucan recognized him: Gorman.

Around the perimeter of the room, the few Darlyrede men-at-arms lining the walls swiveled their weapons, as if unsure whom to make their target.

Incompetent, Lucan thought with bitterness. While the kings'-trained men linger, unaware, banned to their courtyard barracks.

"Don't do it, mates," Gorman warned the men ringing the room. "If you do, the deaths of at least a score of these good people are on your heads. Drop your weapons and none of them will be hurt."

The men-at-arms hesitated.

"Do what he says," Lucan commanded.

"No, *do not* do what he says," Hargrave demanded, no trace of fear in his voice. "What in the bloody hell is the meaning of this? How dare you!"

Two of the brigands hung back to either side of the hall doorway as the last masked member of the band entered the room, his arrow knocked, his boots clicking ominously on the stones as he walked down the center aisle toward the lord's dais. The bandits closed the door behind him and reached at once for the long beam to bar the entrance from the inside, as if they'd been inside the hall a hundred times and knew the exact protocol to secure the room. Lucan glanced to either side of the wide hall and saw the single-passage portals already guarded by the forest criminals; no one was getting in or out of the room in the immediate future.

The masked man stopped his advance midway down the aisle, positioning his lean form, the very focus of both the hall and its occupants, but all the while the eyeholes in the leather mask remained trained on the dais, on Hargrave, and on Lucan. The slender boots. The short cape.

This was the man who'd shot him in the wood.

"Where is Padraig Boyd?" the criminal demanded.

* * * *

Padraig halted before Iris's door and looked quickly in both directions before rapping softly upon it. The door opened easily, and he slipped inside.

The chamber was quiet, dark and cool. Iris hadn't been here in some time, if, indeed, she had come here at all after their words in the chapel. This caused Padraig's brow to furrow; she wasn't in the hall for the evening meal, but Lucan had been given an obvious place of honor at the right hand of his deadly benefactor.

She must be taking refuge in the lady's chamber, he realized, and it gave him a modicum of relief as he lit the short candle on Iris's small table. Both Lucan and Hargrave had their hands full at the moment with the thieves from the forest, and that suited Padraig just fine.

A scratching at the window distracted him from his thoughts, and Padraig remembered Iris's pet. He went to the stone opening and released the latch, allowing a snowy Satin to pour himself through the gap and leap silently to the floor to twist himself about Padraig's legs.

"I'm nae she," he warned the creature. "But I wish she were here too, you ken."

"Meow," Satin offered plaintively.

"I've got naught for you," Padraig muttered in reply, even as the cat padded quickly across the floor to the wall and began rubbing the top sides of its forehead against the wood panel. "Mad beast."

"Meow." The cat glided back and forth against the wall pointedly, his head rubbing against the seam where the panels were nailed close together. He stopped and sat on his haunches, his tail swishing impatiently. "Meow."

Padraig's frown turned curious and he advanced toward the wall, crouching down as the cat gained his feet once more to stretch his front paws up on the paneling, paddling silently against the wood. The seam there was wide—wider than the other close-fit panels—and Padraig could feel a cold breath of air emanating from within the wall.

"Meow."

He looked down at Satin, who was once more sitting patiently, although he had fixed Padraig with a pointed look.

Padraig curled his fingertips into the seam and pulled, and to his surprise, the panel fell away with a clatter. In a blink, Satin was nosing about the opening, instigating a metallic, ringing clang.

"Aye?" he said half to himself. He pulled out the little dish and set it aside, noticing the thick leather packet tucked into the shadows. While Satin nudged the empty bowl about, rattling it across the floor in an impatient fashion, Padraig withdrew the thick wallet.

He moved to the narrow cot along the wall and sat down, at once unwinding the thin leather strings holding the packet closed. He opened the stiff leather to behold a veritable fortune of parchment and vellum, each page scrawled over in neat, black writing. Padraig flipped through the topmost pages, his surprise increasing to shock with each sheet revealed. Lists. Inventories. Dates upon dates, going back at least a score of years. Some of the pages were cracked and dog-eared; some were so faded, Padraig had to hold them up toward the meager light to guess at the ghostly information that had paled over the years as the page itself had darkened.

This was not some lady's simple diary full of mundane trivialities—this was Iris's work, he realized, and the depth of it shook Padraig to his boots.

He flipped through several more pages, his gaze skimming the words until a lumpy object between the next two sheaves gave him pause.

It was a leaf, now faded and dry and brittle, its pointed tips fragile like butterflies' wings. Padraig recognized it as the one he'd tucked into Iris's hair when he had still known her as Beryl, and the memory of that sweet day pricked at his heart, even as he read the entries on the page.

Is called Padraig Boyd, from the Scottish isle of Caedmaray...
Crude, ill-mannered...

Funny, kind...
Devoted to his father...
Masterful with a sword...

Padraig looked up from the page then, letting the silence of the room settle on him like a cold blanket. Satin had abandoned his noisy efforts to make a meal appear in his empty dish, and now he leaped onto the cot, stepping daintily across the pages on Padraig's lap until his white head was in charging distance of Padraig's chin. Padraig reached up and stroked the underside of the cat's jaw mindlessly as his eyes stared at the cold hearth and his mind was filled with memories of Iris.

Aye, she had played him false. But looking at this sampling of evidence she had amassed, considering the grave personal danger she'd risked every single day while living at Darlyrede, Padraig realized what a pigheaded fool he'd been. She'd wanted to tell him the truth, but by the time she knew she could trust him, the situation at Darlyrede had become so much more deadly for them all.

Iris had used her incredible ingenuity to come alone to Darlyrede from France and slip into the cogs of the household so intimately as to become invisible. Likely the information Padraig held in his hand, even if it did not exonerate his father, would incriminate Vaughn Hargrave and his cronies in a host of heinous deeds. Padraig had also come of his own volition into this dangerous situation, aye. But he was a man, and had counted on Lucan Montague's aid. He had intended on fighting for the prize that was Darlyrede House.

What had Iris stood to gain from all her risk and effort?

Nothing, Padraig realized. She would never have her parents returned to her, or her childhood home. Even if Castle Dare were rebuilt, it would take years, and it would be Lucan's by rights. She had risked her very life for nothing more than the truth—the truth for her brother and their parents, and for Caris Hargrave, and for Padraig.

And Padraig had punished her for it.

I've never lied about how I feel about you.

Padraig realized it was true. And he also realized that after his foolish pride had faded away, the whole truth about who Iris really was and what she stood for only made Padraig love her more.

He stilled then. Aye, he did love her. He could no longer deny it. And rather than be frightened by the further realization as the scales fell from his eyes, they settled around him like his da's old plaid—fitting and comfortable and absolutely correct. He was not fighting for Tommy Boyd to regain Darlyrede House, or even to win it for himself. Perhaps he never had.

Padraig was fighting for the very idea of Northumberland.

For home. For Lord and Lady Hood and Lucan and—yes, hopefully—for himself and Iris. For his brothers, yet strangers to him, and for the future of all their families. Thomas Annesley had been a frightened, injured, devastated young man with no family, no friends, the night he escaped from Darlyrede, and in Padraig's mind, he reached back through the decades to speak to that young man.

We're here, now, Tommy. Let us help you.

The reign of terror visited upon this land—both from Vaughn Hargrave and the bandits currently infesting the hall—would stop, if it was the last thing Padraig did.

But first, he needed an army.

Chapter 18

Iris screamed until her throat was raw, and now even the shallowest breath of damp, cold air seared her throat like fire as she lay shivering on the table. She realized now that no one could possibly hear her. The sizzling of the torch had grown louder as her ears strained for the smallest sound, but that hissing was broken only by the random, faint percussion of water dripping in some darkened corner.

Iris thought she had at last discovered where all the missing girls had gone.

All this time she had assumed that Hargrave had stolen away with his victims to another location, or kept them prisoner in his own rooms, but she realized now that it would have been impossible to remove her from Lady Caris's wing without the guards at the stairs seeing them, Rolf in particular. To keep her mind from breaking altogether with madness and fear, she sought to recall with the greatest detail the maps she had drawn in her notes. She must be somewhere beneath the west wing, under the oldest part of the hold. The far, dark end of the corridor, then—the entrance to this subterranean hell must be located there. Perhaps in one of the rooms on the opposite side of the passage—a secret door, perhaps, like the one in Iris's own chamber, where the maps themselves were hidden.

She stifled a sudden sob. She should have given the portfolio to Lucan when he'd asked for it. No one would ever find it—or her—now. All her work, all the evidence, hidden away until, by the time it was discovered—years from now likely—none of it would matter any longer. Everyone would be long dead and the grief caused by Vaughn Hargrave would be nothing more than terrible, frightening fables.

She thought of Lady Hargrave and squeezed her eyes shut. She remembered the last hazy words she'd heard the noblewoman speak, how she'd sought to protect Iris from the monster that was her husband. How she had always sought to protect her, keep her close and away from the unpleasantness that swirled just beneath the glittering façade that was Darlyrede House. She thought of the locks on the doors to hers and Euphemia's rooms, Caris's bittersweet relief at learning that Euphemia was dead. She must have suspected her husband in the disappearances; she must have known all this time, at least partially, of his sick appetites. And still she had tried to save Iris.

What had Lord Hargrave done to silence her this time? The pain of not knowing was almost too much for Iris to bear.

A short squeak of hinges echoed in the stone vault like a scream and Iris felt her blood turn to ice. She waited for the sound of footsteps, her ears strained until she thought her skull would explode. But there was no sound, no shadow in front of the torchlight to indicate anyone had entered.

Iris's heart seized in her chest as a weight dropped onto her abdomen, and her fear was so great that for a moment she thought she had fainted again.

Satin had leaped onto her body from the floor and was now staggering to keep his balance on Iris's heaving stomach.

"Satin," she croaked as he carefully stepped up her chest toward her face. "How did you find me?" The cat butted and rubbed his head against her chin, and then in his careful, deliberate way, lay down, tucking his paws beneath his chest and looking about the room with slow-blinking disdain. His heavy warmth soaked into her skin like sunshine.

She remembered Padraig's skepticism of the animal. *I prefer a dog meself.*

"Fetch Padraig, Satin," she whispered, and then gave a harsh, delusional giggle as he ignored the request to instead lick at the inside of his elbow.

Iris closed her eyes as the chuckle died away, and thin tears leaked from the corners and ran down the sides of her face into the cups of her ears.

"Good boy. Lovely boy." Her whisper was a mere creak now. "Don't leave me. Don't leave…"

* * * *

Padraig accompanied Ulric at the fore of the wave of men who crept up the eastern corridor, staying just beyond the torchlight, where one of the thieves from the wood stood as guard, facing the hall beyond. He was impressed by the manner in which so many of the king's men moved soundlessly into place.

They stood in silence several more moments, giving the other half of the company ample time to circle the courtyard and approach from the kitchen passage. Ulric looked back at the soldiers directly behind him and Padraig and gave a series of hand gestures that were quickly relayed to the readied company.

Padraig understood the plan, and he flexed his fingers around the hilt of the sword Ulric had found for him, waiting, eager. Iris's portfolio was secured in his satchel at his back, and although he'd allowed Satin to escape the chamber, Padraig doubted the cat's presence would be noticed in comparison to what he and Ulric and the king's soldiers were about to instigate.

The air was tense, heavy with the anticipation of battle, as Ulric held his open hand in the air and began to move forward, the company following on whispering feet.

Padraig felt alive with anger, with purpose, with determination, as part of the advancing troop. Tonight, good would overcome evil.

Ulric curled his hand into a fist and the company halted, perhaps three paces behind the villain guarding the mouth of the corridor. Padraig could see the glittering candles on the table, the pale, shocked faces of the nobles shining in the light. He looked to Ulric in the same moment that the captain turned to him, a question in his eyes.

Ready, lord?

Padraig gave a single nod.

Ulric slashed his arm down through the air with a shout, and the soldiers surged forward with battle cries, matched by echoing shouts from the company entering the hall from the opposite corridor. The captain himself took down the guard at the mouth of the passage, incapacitating him with one deadly thrust. Padraig darted from the corridor to the right and brought up his sword just in time to parry a slashing blow from a short blade. His wounded shoulder burned, but Padraig did not care—he barely felt it beneath the rush of battle fever coming over him.

A whisper of hot air rushed by his cheek, brushing his hair: an arrow.

Padraig dismissed the averted danger and brought up his sword again, swinging through a block and slashing at the underside of his opponent's arm, causing the man to cry out and the sword to fall to the ground. Padraig shoved the man over, where he collapsed against the wall. Padraig kicked his sword out of reach as he turned, ready to strike again.

Arrows were flying through the hall now, slicing through the screams of the people ducking beneath the tables, servants diving for the relative safety of the floor as the king's soldiers stormed the room. Some warriors climbed atop tables to gain the center aisle, some ploughing along the perimeter, buffeting aside Darlyrede's own men.

One of the woodland bandits rushed past him in an attempt to escape, but Padraig seized him and swung him toward a pair of the king's soldiers who were holding a clutch of the invaders at sword's point. Padraig looked around again, ready, wanting someone else to fight.

But it was over. The king's seasoned men had secured the hall in moments, leaving the dead where they lay and holding the prisoners, including the red-bearded leader. Only a single, masked villain remained standing in the center of the aisle, his bow yet in his hand but the quiver on his back empty, a trio of the king's soldiers circling him at sword's point.

And then Padraig realized the ruse that had been thrust upon them all in the wood—the distraction. Gorman, the bearded man from the wood, was not the leader of the gang of criminals at all; it was this smaller, trim man with the quiet, raspy voice. The man who had shot Lucan. A man who was perhaps forced to wear a mask because otherwise he would be recognized.

Padraig would know who he was.

He stepped upon the nearest bench, to the tabletop, then down the other bench to the floor, his gaze fixed on the masked radical. The king's soldier stepped aside, allowing Padraig to pass.

"Drop the bow," Padraig commanded the man. "Now."

After only an instant's hesitation, the leather-clad arm tossed the weapon aside with a motion of surrender. It skittered to the stones some distance away.

Padraig sheathed his sword and strode forward again until he was standing before the man, who was even smaller than Padraig had guessed from afar. Surely this could be no mere adolescent who had caused such chaos? He reached out and grabbed the top of the leather mask at the crown and yanked.

"Ow!" A gloved hand shot up to rub at where Padraig had grasped the disguise, and as the mask was swept away a long, blond plait unfurled like a tolling rope. Accusing blue eyes Padraig recognized burned into his own. Only these eyes were no longer flat, despondent, defeated. These eyes snapped with life, crinkles at the corners brought on by age, the lashes longer, thicker.

"My God," Padraig breathed.

"Ah. Just who I was looking for," the woman said with a wry smile. "A moment, though, if you please." She turned nonchalantly on one bootheel to face the lord's dais.

Vaughn Hargrave's face went the color of curdled cream and Caris gave a choked cry.

"Hello, Uncle Vaughn," Euphemia Hargrave said lightly. "Or should I say Grandfather?"

* * * *

Searrach slid off the horse before it had come to a halt, and the beast, perhaps sensing the madness of the woman who had commanded it, reared and turned at once, speeding off into the muffled darkness as the snow fell as fast and thick as down from a burst cushion.

She didn't care that it left her; she would no longer require the use of it.

Two guards lay tangled together in the moat to the left of the entry, but Searrach paid them no heed as she pulled the door open and slipped inside. They were the lucky ones. She crossed the entry, hearing the shouting commotion coming from the direction of the hall. It sounded as though everyone at Darlyrede was gathered inside.

Good.

She quickly found the corridor that led to the east wing, and then the doorway that spilled her out into the dark courtyard. The snow had driven even the basest servant to shelter and there was naught to be seen in the open space of cottages and workshops within the wall. Only the white blanket of accumulating snow, set to a golden glow by the single torch outside the quiet soldiers' quarters at the far end of the bailey. Searrach was drawn to the source of that light as surely as any moth—there would be no interference from the king's men. She wrestled the torch free of its holder and ducked inside the barracks.

The cots, the blankets, the clothes all made easy fuel. As she backed out of the doorway, the single shuttered window and doorway showed an almost cozy glow within, and Searrach stopped and watched it. But even its lovely warmth brought no smile to her blank expression. She turned around and walked toward the chapel, the torch in her hand sizzling through the delicate crust of snow as she carried it along, held down by her calf.

No aid either, from their imaginary god.

Moments later, the smell of smoke followed her from that holy structure and into the curtain wall corridor in the west wing, up the slight incline toward the hall. She heard the maids in the kitchen exclaiming to each other as she passed, but their panic did not trouble Searrach. They would investigate where she had already been, and by then it would be too late.

She passed a tapestry hanging on the stone wall and touched her torch to a bottom corner of it on a whim. The ancient threads curled with flame at once. Searrach walked on, while behind her, shouts of alarm were like musical whispers in the back of her mind.

The far end of the passage to the hall was blocked by a king's man, and so she carried on to the entry. She put the torch on the marble floor while she strained to push the heavy settle against the main double doors of the hall. As she turned to retrieve her weapon, she caught sight of the portraits soaring up to the ceiling. Beautiful likenesses of a beautiful, old, noble family that at its heart was as rotten as the insect-infested core of a dead tree. Traitors and liars and murderers and torturers.

A sob caught in her chest, interrupting her numbness for the briefest moment. They were all as dead as she was now.

Searrach strained upward to reach the portrait closest to her, then the next, struggling to pile the heavy works of art she could touch, one by one, on and against the settle blocking the hall doors. She stood back and looked at them for a moment: Lord Hargrave, Caris, Euphemia, Cordelia, and others Searrach did not and whose names she would never know. All dead. Like her da. Like her dreams.

The din within the hall went suddenly quiet. Black smoke was billowing up the throat of the west corridor and now toward her; surely it had begun wafting into the hall by the kitchen corridor. No more time for musing.

Searrach set the cushion of the settle well ablaze and then retraced her initial steps into the east wing to wait, touching a tapestry here and there—a chair, a portrait—with fire as she went. She heard the pounding against the hall door behind her like the faint sound of the sea.

* * * *

"Euphemia?" Caris Hargrave's question was like a whistle of breeze through reeds.

The blond woman swept an arm before her middle and gave a gallant bow while, behind her, Padraig felt frozen in place. This woman before him, wearing tall boots and trousers and a cape; the woman who had shot Lucan, who had killed Lord Paget in the wood; this leader of the band of highwaymen who had terrorized the Darlyrede Road for years—this woman was the girl from the portraits in the hall.

"It is indeed I, Grandmother," the woman said. "Although I am not Euphemia Hargrave, and I never was. That was simply the name you gave me after you cut me from my mother's body. I prefer Effie now. *Effie Annesley.*"

Padraig's heart skipped a beat. *Euphemia Hargrave was alive!*

"Euphemia, where have you been?" Lord Hargrave demanded gruffly. His face had lost its fish-belly cast, and was now rapidly deepening to scarlet. "Lady Hargrave and I have searched for you for years. We thought you dead."

"Had I not gotten away when I did, I'm certain I would be dead by now," Effie quipped. "And I'm certain you both very much wish I *was* dead. Neither of you monsters are worthy of being called family. The people I've been living with these past fifteen years are the only family I have known, and now—" She half-turned and met Padraig's gaze. "Now, my blood family will return to Darlyrede. And you—"

She faced forward once more. "You both will pay for what you've done."

"I'm very disappointed in you, Euphemia," Hargrave said, his face now a terrible purple color. "All these years I had no idea it was you who had caused such anguish on Darlyrede's lands." Hargrave glanced about at the frozen, terrified faces of the nobles in the hall. "Did you all hear her?

"And now you are somehow convinced that this—this *stranger* is your true family? A man spawned by our own Cordelia's killer? I am ashamed. And it will in fact be you who pays for your crimes." He looked to his men-at-arms, still standing about the perimeter of the hall with an air of confusion. "Seize her. You heard her—she is the leader of these bandits. These murderers. They killed Lord Paget, and countless others have been robbed of their wealth."

Effie threw back her head and laughed loudly. "It's absurd that you think anyone here believes I am behind the grotesque crimes committed against the people of this land. Am I supposed to be frightened by your threats? Intimidated? You stupid, stupid man. I'm not afraid of you anymore. Why do you think I've come back now, after all these years? Why didn't I flee south? Or to Scotland, like my father? To another country like *brave* Sir Lucan, at your side just there?" The way she spoke of the knight insinuated that she did not in fact hold him in high regard.

She turned suddenly to face Padraig once more. "Why did I risk my life to stay within a stone's throw of this hell on earth, brother? I think if anyone can tell them, it is you."

As Padraig looked into her eyes and he saw Tommy Boyd's stubborn determination there, Padraig realized. Thomas Annesley had been injured, alone when he'd fled Darlyrede the night Cordelia was murdered, and for most of their lives neither Padraig nor his brothers had had any idea of their father's history, their own connectedness.

Euphemia alone had escaped with the terrible knowledge of Darlyrede's evil past. And she had waited.

"Because you knew he would come back," Padraig thought aloud. "You knew we would all come back."

Euphemia nodded. "I knew you would come back," she repeated softly, and there was hard triumph in her eyes. She faced the dais once more. "And so here you are," she announced loudly and extended her arms, the fingers of both hands clasped together into one fist, addressing the soldiers still standing surrounding her. "I'll no longer evade the king's men. Let them take me into their custody. I'll happily remain under their guard to be brought before the king. Sir Lucan, perhaps you would like to do the honors?"

Clever woman, Padraig realized, amazed at Euphemia's forethought. Under the protection of the king's men—and Lucan Montague—Hargrave could not touch her. And everything she knew about Vaughn Hargrave would be laid bare before the king himself.

Padraig's thoughts at once returned to Iris's leather packet of notes and maps, still safe in the bag at his hip. The nobleman on the dais—his wife at his side, seeming to be stricken with panic and gasping for air—was finished.

They'd won.

The soldiers now looked to Lucan, who was staring down at Euphemia with an unusually dark expression on his ordinarily unimpressed visage.

"You shot me," he blurted out.

Euphemia's hands turned, palms up toward Lucan. "I admit, I shouldn't have done that. It was a clean shot, though. I'm sure you'll be fine. You *seem* fine. I've seen much worse."

"You're sure I'll be—?" Lucan winced and shook his head and then nodded toward his captain. "Take her into custody. If not for her own protection, then the protection of everyone else." Then he looked to Padraig. "Where are Searrach and...Beryl?"

"Searrach was afraid to return. Beryl didna—"

"Fire!" A woman's echoing shout came from behind a guard standing watch at the entrance to the corridor leading to the kitchens. "Fire in the north wall!"

The hall was at once in an uproar as guests gained their feet and began fleeing, but black smoke could already be seen roiling from the tops of each doorway along the ceiling. The guards went at once to the bar holding the double doors to the hall closed. They slid it free of the brackets, but the onslaught of the crowd pressing against them prevented the doors from swinging inward.

"Back up," Padraig shouted, fighting his way through them, pulling them by their arms. "Back up or they canna open the doors. Back up, you fools!" He gained the sides of the guards and took hold of one of the oddly warm handles. "*Move!*" he shouted as they strained at the doors.

The crack between the doors widened, and some of the guests inserted their fingers, pulling at the gap even as more black smoke slithered through the opening. Padraig let go at once as he realized what lay beyond, but it was too late—the crowd strained backward and the doors flew open. Fire and smoke rained down from a towering inferno in the entry, collapsing on the guests elbowing their way to be the first to escape the hall.

"Let the lord through!" Padraig heard Hargrave shouting. "Let me through, you useless peasants!"

The nobles and servants scattered again as those touched by flame screamed and writhed on the floor, their hair, their clothes singed or burning. Padraig leaped to the nearest tapestry hanging on the wall and flung one end to Ulric, who stepped toward him. They fell upon the burning people, smothering the flames while the hall continued to fill with smoke and the people screamed and rushed around the benches and trestles, over them. The sound of tables collapsing, splintering, filled in the gaps made by the crackling flames.

Lucan appeared then at Padraig's side, holding one end of a bench; Peter held up the other. "The corridors are already filled with smoke; we have to clear a way before we're all trampled to death."

"Can you push?" Padraig said. "Your foot—"

"I must," Lucan protested.

"I'll do it," Gorman said, appearing at Lucan's elbow. The red-bearded man from the forest took the heavy bench from the knight's hands and then looked at Padraig. "Let's get them out."

Padraig nodded and took up Peter's end, crouching as best he could with Gorman behind the narrow height of wood.

"Go," Padraig shouted.

They blasted into the pyre blocking the doorway with a crash and a shower of sparks. Padraig felt hot embers on his face and neck, burning through his shirt as he followed the bench through into the center of the entry hall. He straightened and slapped at the smoldering patches on his clothing, brushed at his hair as the rank smell hung about his face. He coughed, gasped into his elbow at the acrid smoke. The guests ran, limped, staggered, screaming around them like a panicked sea, and someone threw the main doors wide.

Padraig felt his arm seized and looked through watering eyes to find Lucan's intense gaze.

"Where is Iris?"

"She didna come with me," Padraig said. "I've nae seen her since the chapel." He looked around at the roiling sea of escaping people, and realized that Gorman had vanished.

Rolf skidded up to them then. "Beryl came to Lady Hargrave's wing just as you were leaving, Master Boyd, but she did not accompany the lady down to sup. Lord Hargrave left the wing sometime after his wife had departed."

All three men looked up toward the ascending flights of stairs just in time to see the slight form of Caris Hargrave pulling herself along the railing into the black smoke hovering at the tall ceiling, stopping at the top to gasp and cough against the balustrade.

"She must still be there," Padraig said. And then he looked back to Rolf. "Find Lord Hargrave and anyone else who might still be in the hall. Then get out."

"I lost Lord Hargrave in the crush—he's likely to have escaped. But we must try to slow the blaze," Rolf objected. "There'll be naught left for you to win."

"It's only stones." Padraig gripped the man's shoulder, very aware that Lucan stood at his side, watching, listening. "Only stones, Rolf. A house can be rebuilt. But you canna be replaced, you ken? Nor Marta nor Rynn nor Peter."

Rolf nodded, and his shoulders squared. "Aye, Master Boyd." And then he was gone.

Padraig turned to Lucan, who was looking through the doors into the smoky hall into which Rolf had disappeared.

"She's gone too," Lucan said.

Padraig froze. "Who?"

"Euphemia." He met Padraig's eyes.

"She'll be back," Padraig predicted. "I canna see that woman giving in now." He clapped Lucan's arm as he passed toward the stairs.

He took the risers three at a time, gaining in moments the uppermost level where the smoke was thickening like angry, choking storm clouds. He realized that Lucan had struggled up behind him on his wounded foot, but Padraig pressed his mouth and nose into his elbow and ran ahead through the corridor to the first door on the left and pushed through.

"Iris!" he called. It no longer mattered that her secret would be known. Padraig intended that only the truth be spoken between them, about them, from this time forward. And he intended to protect Iris from whatever storm lay ahead of them both. "Iris! Lady Hargrave!"

He heard Lucan enter behind him and shut the door, keeping as much smoke in the corridor beyond for as long as possible.

"They're not here," Padraig advised as he ran through the adjoining doorway. "Iris!"

The lady's chamber was also empty, the banked fire and single, low lamp revealing the lush appointments in an ironic, flickering glow even as the air grew quietly hazy with stinging smoke.

"What else is up here?" Padraig asked Lucan, who was wincing and leaning hard on one arm against the frame of the connecting doorway.

"Nothing. A pair of apartments, but they're never used."

Padraig grabbed the lamp, and then he and Lucan ducked back into the smoke-filled corridor. One of the chamber doors stood open and they pushed inside, but Lucan had been right: The only things there were ghostly draped furnishings.

"Perhaps she returned to her chamber while everyone was gathering in the hall," Lucan suggested.

"She could have left this wing, aye," Padraig said. "But it wasna for her chamber—I went there first. And Caris Hargrave climbed the stairs before us—where did *she* go?"

Lucan's frown intensified and he limped in a circle, his eyes examining the floor, the ceiling. "She couldn't have just vanished. And why would she have come at all unless she was certain Iris was still somewhere here?"

Padraig remembered the satchel resting on his hip, and its contents. He shoved the lamp at Lucan and scrambled to pull the leather bag to his front. He withdrew the portfolio and held it up as evidence.

"Mayhap this will tell us."

"My God, you found it," Lucan said. He set the lamp on a draped table and took the packet, opening it and pulling out the thick sheaf of pages. He split the stack and handed half to Padraig.

"Maps," the knight said. "Iris told me she thought there was another way into the wing, but I didn't listen to her."

"Here," Padraig said, pulling out a trio of pages. "Look." He held them close to the light, and Lucan skimmed the lines with his fingers.

Lucan tapped one page. "Here…here are the lady's rooms. And so… yes, here we are now." He flipped up the page to look at the one beneath.

"And here," Padraig said, tracing the shapes. "The floor below. It doesn't quite meet the curtain wall, but there's naught in the space between. So this chamber—" He looked up at the wall to the west, noticing at once that the paneling seeming asymmetrical in the dim, rippling light.

"Perhaps it's an escape passage," Lucan suggested. "Many of the old holds kept them in case of attack."

But Padraig was only half-listening—the wall section was not asymmetrical. One of the panels had a gap along the trim.

"It's there," he said to Lucan. He was stuffing the pages back into his satchel as he dashed to the wall. He felt the cool breeze wafting from beyond, smelled its freshness in opposition to the close, smoky air in the chamber they occupied. He pulled open the panel without a sound and could sense the descending darkness before him.

"It canna be an escape to the curtain wall," Padraig said half over his shoulder in a low voice. "The passage would be filled with smoke, and the air is fresh. You didna know this was here?" he added accusingly.

Lucan seemed taken aback. "Not at all. But Darlyrede House is old, and has been added on to so many—" His explanation ended abruptly. "It leads to the old dungeon. It must bypass the wall entirely."

Padraig gave a single, curt nod. "Aye. O' course it does." An instant later he was ducking out of his satchel and handing it to Lucan. "Take this and go back down."

"I will not," he said. "The fire will surely spread and there could now be two women trapped down there."

"You'll only slow me down. If Iris is down there," Padraig said emphatically, "I'll nae be coming up without her. You have my word, Lucan. But if we doona make it out, her work canna have been in vain." He glanced pointedly at his old leather satchel. "Iris's notes may very well support everything Euphemia Hargrave has to say. Now go while you can."

Lucan seemed to hesitate a moment longer. "I'm trusting you with her life." He offered his hand.

Padraig seized it. "I ken ye are. You've both saved mine enough times."

Padraig turned and ducked down into the darkness.

Chapter 19

Satin's eyes opened from slits, his ears swiveled forward, his breathing paused. Then the sound of the hinge squealed through the silence again, and the cat leaped from Iris's chest into the shadows of the murky cell.

Iris tried to quell the sob in her chest if only to save her throat the agony. She had never been so scared. There was a metallic clatter from beyond the bend in the corridor, an almost delicate clink. She wanted to close her eyes, but she could seem to do nothing else but turn her head and stare at the torchlight through the doorway.

And then there it was: as shadow. A human shadow, appearing suddenly on the wall, looking back the way it had come, as if watching for someone following. It grew larger, larger, until it was in the doorway, a wheeze of labored breath, and the light revealed—

Iris released her sob with a pained gasp. "Milady! Thank God," she croaked. "Hurry! If he catches you here, he'll kill us both!" Her voice sliced her throat like a knife.

"Shh, shh. I'm sorry. There is no escape for us," she wheezed through her smile, her red-rimmed eyes bright with unshed tears. She brought her hand beneath Iris's head and lifted it, setting the rim of a chalice against her lower lip. The whoosh of air around the woman smelled strongly of smoke. "Here, drink this for your comfort."

Iris nearly choked on the tepid, milky substance, but Caris kept tipping the cup, flooding Iris's throat with the drink until she must swallow or drown. It tasted somehow green, but it was smooth and cool and seemed to fill in the deep, bloody fissures Iris imagined lined her throat.

Lady Hargrave's grip failed as a spasm overcame her, and the cup nearly tumbled away into the darkness as she coughed and choked against the slab, each breath sounding like a strained whistle.

As if she was dying.

"Milady!"

After what seemed an eternity, Caris straightened slightly over her and brought her pale, shaking hand to stroke the hair back from Iris's forehead, her cheek, and she realized the drink had done more good than she'd expected; her throat was almost numb.

"Milady, hurry," she rasped.

"I will…release you, Iris. Only…do be patient…a moment," she chastised with a rasp. "Do."

Iris stared up at her in confusion, her mind seeming to catch on something the woman said. And then she realized that Lady Hargrave had addressed her as Iris. Her face must have given it away, for the woman's smile deepened knowingly.

"Yes, I know. It pains me…to admit that I did not realize the truth on my own, especially after…you spoke of your brother." The woman's words broke off as she struggled to catch her breath. "I was so enamored of you. So…trusting. Lady Paget was your undoing…after all."

Caris gasped, and Iris didn't know how any air at all was getting into the woman's lungs at the tight whisper of sound. "There is no use…denying it. What happened to…Beryl? I must know." She pulled a kerchief from her sleeve and held it to her mouth, and again Iris was struck by the strong smell of smoke.

It could not only be Satin's recent presence that had brought on such difficulties for the woman.

Iris swallowed with some strain herself now, she realized. The numbness in her throat had increased.

"She died. After the birth of her child."

Caris's eyes narrowed over the kerchief.

"I had nothing to do with her death," Iris breathed. "I swear. I did everything I could to help her. But I was desperate to gain Northumberland, and her death was the perfect opportunity to return."

Lady Hargrave lowered the kerchief, gasping weakly. "To return…to me?"

Iris was confused. "To return to the land of my family. I didn't yet know you, my lady."

"You did," Caris rebutted, her chest heaving pointlessly. "You… don't remember."

"Perhaps I don't," Iris acknowledged. "I find that I am muddled just now. I—my lady, I've only tried to protect you. But we must go."

"Protect me from what...sweet Iris?"

"From Lord Hargrave," Iris insisted, her voice sounding hollow and echoey. "I know about the people he's murdered. The young girls he's taken."

Caris nodded weakly. "Do you? I've already told you...Lord Hargrave would never harm me." She leaned close to Iris's face, her breath bitter and faint against Iris's mouth. The woman's nose was running unchecked. "When your parents...died, I wanted to take you. Lucan. Mostly you. I have...fond weakness...orphans."

Iris felt her mouth going slack, but it wasn't from surprise; her entire face seemed to be going numb, creeping down her neck to the top of her chest.

The drink. The drink in Euphemia's chamber.

A dead girl's meal...

"My lord forbade it. Too suspect. I let you go...pretty child. All...dark hair." Her forearm moved as though she were stroking Iris's head again, but Iris couldn't feel the woman's touch as Caris seemed to collapse more heavily against the table. "Euphemia fled to...fire...at Castle Dare. To find...Thomas...she thought. She left me...for him." The words ended on a wheeze. Caris paused, looking deep into Iris's eyes as she struggled to draw breath. "Her father."

"Iss true?" Iris slurred. "Cordelia?"

"Cordelia." Her words were little more than breathy squeaks. Caris lifted the heavy-looking cup and drank from it, choking as she tried to swallow, spraying Iris's face with a fine mist of the green-smelling liquid.

In a moment the woman could gasp again. "Cordelia didn't... understand. She discovered...my husband's interest in...the human body. She didn't... understand. Wouldn't...listen. He is brilliant. Lord Hargrave knows more... about...what a person can withstand and recover from...as do...the greatest surgeons...in the East. The organs...their functions. He should...been a master teacher. But he was chastised...hated...hunted for his work."

Caris raised the cup once more, and this time managed to swallow whatever liquid remained in the cup. When she looked again at Iris, her eyes streamed, the circles beneath them purpling. She gulped each breath now, as a fish coming to the surface of a pond.

"We knew...Cordelia was pregnant, stupid girl. If she would have stayed...silent, she could have...married weak little Thomas. But no. No, Cordelia was going to...tell about the stupid servant girl. Many girls...but all one girl. All the same. All eager to... seduce the lord and gain...his favor. He let them think…they'd won him. Stolen him away to…a secret place. Here." Her words ended on a screech of breath.

"Cordelia freed her," Iris whispered as she herself realized.

Caris nodded and leaned even closer, kissing Iris gently on her slack lips. "But the girl…couldn't run. Mercy. What happened to Cordelia was…an accident. She fell. I had to…stop her screaming. She would have…suffered. Then I realized…my responsibility. Take care of…my girls before…they ended up here. I don't like it when…he touches them—they're…never the same afterward. Pieces…missing."

Iris's voice was barely audible. "Cordelia's baby?"

Caris coughed into Iris's face, and her tongue darted out, trying in vain to wet her lips. "I'd forgotten. But…my lord…is a skilled surgeon." She leaned even closer. "Life…emerged…from *death-h-h*."

Iris moaned in horror, too weak to do anything more.

"I loved them," Caris insisted, her voice nothing but a wheeze now, the sagging bodice of her gown revealing skin over heaving ribs, a living skeleton. "All my girls. And you. Could not…let them suffer so."

Caris reached down to Iris's hands, and she heard a faint rattling through the dizzy spinning of her head. Her forearms rocked free as the manacles around her wrists were released. Then her ankles.

"There," Caris wheezed. "Go. Run."

Iris tried to sit up as she swung her legs over the side of the table, but it was as though she no longer had command of her torso. The world spun as she tumbled to the cold stone floor, banging her suddenly heavy head and scraping her face on the supports as she fell. She strained to lift her head on her weak neck, looking at Lady Caris's blurry slippers, tried to get her hands beneath her.

Her head jerked back and Caris squatted over her, grasping the top of her head by her hair. She saw the flash of the blade in the torchlight, but was thankful that she could not feel it against her throat.

"Just like them," Caris wheezed. "You want to…leave me. I won't let you…sweet Iris. You would…burn."

Lady Caris suddenly wobbled on her feet, falling over to one elbow. Iris's head jerked with the motion, and a white mass swept across her face. Satin.

Lady Caris's scream was a rusty puff. "Get it…away!" Her words were broken, rocky. She kicked out at Satin and he yowled pitifully as he skittered across the stones against Iris.

No! Iris's mouth formed the word, but no sound came out. Her own lungs felt tight, frozen, in her chest.

"Away," the woman gasped. "Can't..." The blade rattled to the floor as Caris clawed at her throat, dragged her bodice down from her chest. Her mouth continued to move, but no sound at all issued forth.

Iris's view was blocked as Satin walked between the women once more. He butted Iris's cheekbone, her chin too, perhaps, then sat down. Iris saw the dark streak on his fur. Her blood.

Satin, she mouthed.

Her eyes were closing. And she was no longer cold.

* * * *

Padraig knew he'd been right the deeper he descended through the bends of the dark stone passage. The steps were impossibly old, worn smooth and slanted beneath the soles of his boots, the walls jagged under his left palm as he stepped carefully, his sword in his right hand. The stairs curved to the left in a semiregular pattern, and after what seemed like a quarter hour of creeping over the stones, a faint glow flickered up the passage.

Light. Someone was down there.

It took all Padraig's will not to shout for Iris. If she was there she was likely not alone, and for all Padraig knew there could be another way into the subterranean depths. And so he crept on, at last coming out of the narrow channel into a low-ceilinged, wide room, it's damp-striped walls ringed with benches and shelves, each of which were laden with crockery of all sizes, corked bottles in varying colors, leather-wrapped jugs sealed with wax.

And where no containers stood, tools and utensils and implements of unknown and terrible purpose hung on tidy hooks, all the supplies fitted together so perfectly as to have created a mosaic of sorts. All the tools were dark, stained...

And Padraig noticed the old, wide-shafted boots resting on the floor near the seam of wall—boots discolored with thick, dark grime that could only be grisly in origin. And above the boots, a pair of long, leather aprons, perhaps one time of light color but now splashed with what appeared to be drying blood.

Padraig's heart stuttered in his chest. Had Hargrave already solved the problem of Iris Montague?

Was Padraig—and Caris Hargrave—too late to save her?

Padraig forced himself on toward the torchlight beckoning from a turn of corridor beyond the iron gate that stood open at the far end of the gruesome supply room. There was still no sound of anything living in the dungeon, and Padraig wondered with anguish how anyone could survive down here for long under the terminal weight of dread emanating from the very stones.

Padraig crept forward, clenching his jaw against the emotion that prickled behind his eyes.

Please, God, spare her. Spare her for her kindness, even to those who doona deserve it. Spare her for her courageous heart. Spare her for her clever mind. The people of Northumberland will need her hope and her fortitude now more than ever.

Spare her also for me, so that I may spend the rest of my life caring for her, and seeking to be as good and honorable as she.

Padraig came around the corner, and for a moment his eyes couldn't differentiate between the shadows beneath the tall, wide table and the shapes on the floor. But then the shape closest to him jerked, and a breathy squeal emanated from it.

It was Caris Hargrave, her face a terrible gray, her eyes bulged, her lips turned blue, as her own fingers dug into her throat like claws.

And beyond her, facedown, lay the still, crumpled shape of Iris, a white, fluffy pile near her dark hair. Satin.

The cat yowled pitifully.

"Nae." Padraig sheathed his sword and stepped over the noblewoman to drop to one knee at Iris's side.

"Iris," he called. He lifted her upper body and turned her in his arms, holding her against his chest. "Iris, look at me, lass."

Her eyes weren't closed evenly, he noticed, and her lips were slack. Her dark hair was like an inky river around her pale face and he smoothed it back with a shaking hand to lean his ear close to her mouth. He cursed the pounding blood that roared in his head and drowned out any sound—he could neither hear nor feel breath.

"Nay. Nay."

Padraig gathered her high up in his arms and then stood, stepping once more over the noblewoman. The cat mewed, and its lithe, fluffy limbs scissored past Padraig, sending him like a streak out of the chamber and toward the stairs.

Padraig carried Iris up the interminable spiral, feeling the heat increase, the choking smell of smoke thicken as they climbed, and he wondered that he wasn't delivering them both into an inferno. He bumped his shoulder into the panel at the top of the black stairs, and the lamp he'd left on the table was only the tiniest twinkle of starlight in a black sky. The room was nearly filled with smoke, and so he knew that the passage beyond would be impassable to them.

Satin was nowhere to be seen, and he sent up a breath of prayer that Iris's beloved pet would be spared.

He stood just beyond the door of the hidden passage, Iris still limp in his arms, struggling against the fear that wanted to overtake him. Their only two options were to retreat once more to the stone dungeon to pray that the burning keep did not collapse and smother them, or the window.

Padraig couldn't imagine spending his final moments in that ancient den of torture, and so he strode through the ever-thickening smoke to the single, narrow window in one of the oldest chambers of Darlyrede. He lowered Iris to the floor and then rose up to push at the thick wooden frame. It rattled, bowed, but then Padraig stopped, coughing, his lungs already burning.

Once the window was open, the room would become like a chimney for smoke and flames—once begun, he could not hesitate.

Padraig dropped down to his knee and shook Iris.

"Iris," he shouted. "Iris, you must wake up. Wake up! Iris!"

She gave a raspy moan in her throat—the slightest sound—but it was like a choir of angels to Padraig's heart.

"Can you hear me, lass? You've got to stand on your feet—we have to go through the window."

"Padraig," she whispered. "My legs feel strange." She began to cough.

Padraig pressed his lips together with a curt sigh.

Have faith.

"Listen to me, lass," he said in a rush, his own throat raw with smoke. "I'm going to break out the window and lower you down. I doona know how far it is, you ken?"

"Lady Caris..."

"I couldna carry you both," he said, guilt heavy on his heart. "I had to choose."

"She poisoned me," Iris whispered. "She killed Cordelia. She was going to kill me too."

Padraig couldn't let the shock of her words overtake him in the moment, and so he ignored the horrifying declaration. "Shh—you must try to stand, ken? Up you go." He lifted her around her ribs and leaned her up against the wall near the window. Iris slid at first, but Padraig propped her higher, and her knees seemed to lock. "Hold just there. You must stay up, Iris. You must."

He turned to the window once more, ripping down the long, heavy drape in two swift pulls, working by feel alone as the room was completely black now. Iris coughed and choked in the darkness; Padraig's own eyes ran with tears.

He wrapped his hand in one end of the drapery and punched through the thick glazing. A breeze of hot air whooshed past his face as he swept at the sides of the frame, clearing away the jagged shards. He stuck his head out into the cold night and shouted with surprised relief—the narrow window was over the curtain wall, not three stories above the bailey as he'd feared, but perhaps only twelve feet above the stone wall walk. The fallen snow flickered against the reflected glow of the burning keep against the backdrop of night.

"Padraig?" Iris choked.

He ducked back inside, and where the room had before been black, a terrible heat now painted the absence of color, as if hell itself had bloomed around them. Padraig felt Iris grasping for him in their shared blindness. They had perhaps only moments left before the flames reached them.

"It's the wall beneath you," he rasped, his throat parched and raw as he looped the length of drapery around her back and beneath her arms. "Nae far. Bend your knees and roll when you drop." Padraig turned her toward the window and lifted her to the sill, helped her to fit her legs through the opening. He held the ends of the drape in one of his hands and Iris's wrist in the other while she slid through, the little sounds of scraping glass on stone beneath her causing him to wince. "Did you hear? Roll."

"Yes," she choked. "Don't leave me, Padraig."

"Get far out of the way. Far as you can," he said as he let her slide out further, stretching his arms, his back to their limits to retain his hold on her for as long as he could. He took firm hold of the ends of the drapery and raised up on his toes. "Go!"

Padraig thought he had never known such fear in his life as when he felt Iris's sliding reverberate through the thick material, and then her short scream cut through the smoke boiling around him out the window. He thought he heard the soft, crumpling thud of her landing, but he couldn't see the wall any more for the heavy billows climbing the keep from the lower levels. He let loose of the limp drapery and it was swallowed up by the black smoke.

"Stay back," he choked as he gained the window ledge. He turned onto his stomach and slid over the edge, his sweaty, sooty fingers already slipping, the flesh of his palms scraping away as he fell free of the window.

He'd tried to keep his legs loose as he fell, so whether he had turned in the billowing smoke or instinctively reached out with his feet to meet solid ground, the end result was a sharp pain in his lower left leg before he fell onto his side on the stones with a cry.

But there was no time to concern himself with so slight an injury. Iris was at his shoulder then, her hands brushing over him. Iris, alive and speaking to him, urging him to his feet.

"Are you all right?" she asked as he pulled her aright. Her legs were still weak, for she sagged against him.

"Fine," he said, turning to her and gathering her against him, wrapping both arms so completely around her shoulders that she was truly enveloped by his embrace. He would never let her go, he thought. But they both flinched and ducked as a pair of flaming window frames plummeted from the uppermost floor with a terrible explosion of glass and smoke.

"Let's get away from here," Padraig said and, limping, half-carried her to the edge of the wall.

A large crowd of people were looking up at the façade of Darlyrede House, the bright light flickering over them, indicating to Padraig that the fire was so much thicker on the front of the hold. Their faces were solemn, round with horror as they watched—soldier, servant, nobility alike. Padraig waved an arm and shouted.

"Lucan!"

It was Rolf, though, who heard Padraig and turned his head to notice them standing on the high wall, Rolf who grabbed the arm of Ulric. They ran to a tall ladder lying in the trampled snow behind the crowd and trotted to the base of the wall where they leaned it against the stones.

Iris reached the ground in moments, Lucan arriving in time to receive her. It took Padraig a bit longer, for while he knew the shock had taken much of the pain of his injured leg, putting any weight at all upon it was akin to torture.

He and Iris, Lucan, Rolf, and Ulric joined the silent crowd watching Darlyrede House burn, while liberated animals roamed the lawn in confused freedom. Marta cried silent tears, wiping at her face occasionally with her apron. Peter and Rynn clung to each other.

Iris broke the solemn silence with a wary question. "Where is Lord Hargrave?"

Padraig looked to Rolf, who only shook his head, his mouth set in a grim line within the dark frame of his beard.

* * * *

Searrach staggered through the blazing pillars of the great hall from the eastern corridor, the grand space so bright, so hot now with flames. The rippling, hungry sheets of fire crawled across the ceiling, turning the cavernous room into a chamber of hell, its roar that of a multitude of insatiable demons released from the very walls of Darlyrede House by the flames and now crying out for their victims.

Even so, she heard the weak yelp coming from the rear of the hall, from the floor before which the lord's dais now crackled with wicked fire, resembling some hellish altar. She walked toward the sound and soon saw Vaughn Hargrave lying amid the wreckage of the flight of people, the broken table legs and planks of benches. His torso was twisted, his legs lying oddly thin and awkward on the stones, as if he'd dragged them behind him. He was bloodied and black with soot, his usually coiffed hair falling over the side of his face, revealing the bald spot Searrach had never known existed.

He looked old. But he was old, she supposed. He only looked his age, now—his skin sagged on his face, his eyes nestled in a pool of recently acquired wrinkles, deepened by soot.

He saw her, and his bloodshot eyes widened. "Searrach. Searrach, my dear girl," he gasped. "Help me. My back—"

Searrach only stared at him and shook her head.

"Please," he sobbed in his warbly, old man's voice.

She was fascinated by what he had become, this man who had hurt her, tortured her so. He was just a man now. No demon, as she'd thought. He'd been able to hurt her because she had offered herself up to his depravity in vain hopes of a future. But the only future he had brought her to was a painful death in this strange land. She walked toward him, wanting to better see the agony on his face.

"Please," he repeated as she drew near. "We can escape this together, you and I."

"I'm nothing to you," she reminded him, kneeling near his head.

"No, no, that's not true at all," he rushed. "It was our plan all along, remember?"

She leaned down. "I'm going to watch you die."

"No," he said on a quavering breath. "We can escape if you help me."

Searrach shook her head. "I doona want to escape. I've naught to escape to."

Hargrave gave an animal cry of rage and frustration. "Help me!" Then he quivered with fear, the stench of it rolling off him, and Searrach leaned even closer to smell it fully, wondering if this moment was what he craved from his victims. Searrach would not have thought it pleasing before, but now…

"Help," he repeated in a whisper.

"I am helping," Searrach replied, equally as quietly, as above their heads the unmistakable sound of a beam cracking exploded through the roar of the flames. "I'm just nae helping *you*."

Hargrave's hands shot out then, and his fingers tightened around Searrach's throat, pulling her down to him with all his remaining strength. She remembered then how strong he had always been, unusually so for his age. And so although his legs may have been rendered useless, his iron fingers tightened around her throat.

Searrach stared into his eyes as she grasped at his wrists, but she knew she had not the strength to free herself, and so she satisfied herself with the knowledge that she was succeeding where so many before her had failed.

Lachlan Blair.

Lucan Montague.

Thomas Annesley.

Padraig Boyd.

Countless men had sought to put an end to Vaughn Hargrave's terrible reign. But it was she—a poor, beaten Highland lass who had naïvely allowed herself to be used in such heinous ways by this monster—Searrach, who was here now. Alone. She was the representative of all those other girls, all the forgotten people Hargrave had used and tortured and then discarded as rubbish. No matter the things she had done in the past, no matter her own mistakes, Vaughn Hargrave would never hurt another soul, and she could be proud of that at least.

Her vision was dimming now, and she worried that she would be dead before she saw the proper end of him.

But then another crack sounded above their heads—a loud creaking and moaning of timbers. A shower of sparks rained down like fae fire with a triumphant roar, and then a shuddering crash filled the hall as the entire ceiling collapsed.

Chapter 20

The sun came up slowly over Northumberland, as if it was loath to see the carnage its rays would reveal.

Iris sat against the same tree under which Padraig had deposited her hours before, the effects of the poison lingering after the energy her fear had given her was spent. Padraig still limped through the crowd on a makeshift crutch, speaking to soldiers, to servants, to the king's men, to Lucan. She watched him with a bittersweet pain in her heart, a combination of pride in his caring for the people of Darlyrede and sorrow for what was left of his birthright.

Darlyrede House was a blackened, smoldering shell in the gray light of dawn. The center of the tall keep seemed to have been cleaved down the center, as if with a mighty blow from some mythical ax. The crown had been broken; the building within still seethed. Somewhere beneath the fuming rubble, Vaughn and Caris Hargrave lay dead.

Lucan limped over to collapse to a seat at her side once more. She hadn't seen him since after she and Padraig had escaped the fire, when they'd all exchanged information about what had happened during that horrific night.

"How are you feeling now?" he asked.

"Heartbroken," she answered at once, without thinking that he was likely referring to her physical health. She turned her head to look at her brother. "I loved her, Lucan. I defended her. Nearly forsook Padraig for her. And all that time, she intended to kill me." Her throat constricted again and the tears wanted to come, but her body had nothing more to give.

"Caris Hargrave was mad," Lucan said in his matter-of-fact manner. "Being married to Vaughn Hargrave for so many years perhaps contributed to her insanity, but nothing you did or didn't do could have changed what she truly was. You had no idea what she was capable of."

"I don't know that her choices were because of Lord Hargrave," she mused. "We'll never know, now. But I do think they found the perfect match in each other."

"Well-paired, certainly," Lucan mused darkly. "But far from perfect. Now, you and Padraig Boyd…"

She turned her head to look at him. "Lucan, I love that man."

Lucan grinned. "Pleased at last that you're no longer bothering trying to deny it. I feel rather indebted to him myself. I only wonder what will happen with"—he waved his hand in his decidedly Lucan fashion about the lawn—"all this once the king receives word."

"He'll have to give it over to Padraig, won't he?" she asked with a frown. "Hargrave is dead. There is no one else entitled to it."

Lucan shrugged. "I don't dare speculate. If he finds Thomas Annesley guilty, he could confiscate the entire barony for the Crown. Send our good Master Boyd back to Caedmaray empty-handed."

Iris remained silent.

Lucan gave her a moment to sit with the idea. "Would that change your feelings for him? If he were to be nothing more than a simple fisherman for the rest of his life?"

She looked sharply at him. "What do you mean?"

Lucan raised his brows and looked away enigmatically as he staggered to his feet again, wincing as his injured foot touched the ground.

"I only mean that you might possibly be pressed into expressing your opinion on that very matter…ah, quite soon." He gave her a grin and turned to limp away.

And Iris noticed Padraig standing nearby.

"Good morning, Iris," he said with a bow.

She smiled. "Good morning, Master Boyd."

"May I join you?"

"How could I refuse such a gentlemanly request?"

Padraig sat down with a groan and a sigh, tossing his crutch to the side. "Ah, well, I had the finest tutor." He was quiet for a moment. "*Would* it matter to you? If I doona gain Darlyrede? If I leave Northumberland with nothing?"

He had been listening.

"Do you know," she said, looking back to the smoking rubble of the keep, "this is the second time in my life that I have watched a manor burn. Where people I held dear to me have perished, leaving me with no home.

No possessions. No thoughts of a certain future. It's only stones, Padraig. Why would stones matter to me, of all people?"

She met his eyes then, and if she had been standing, she thought her legs would have been unable to support her, his gaze smoldered so.

"Because all I can offer you with any certainty is more stones—a stone cottage on a poor fishing island. A hard life for a woman, even one who is not used to fine things. I watched my mother live it."

Iris forced herself to swallow. "Do you admire your father?" she asked.

A slight frown creased his forehead. "Aye. Tommy Boyd—Thomas Annesley, whatever you wish to call him—he is the most honest, strongest man I have ever known. He loved my mother, he loved me. He taught me well. If none of this"—he waved his hand about the lawn—"had ever happened, I know that he would have lived out his days on Caedmaray as a good husband. A good father. A good man, if nae a noble one."

"I cannot think of any finer thing a woman could ask for than a noble man—noble in character, if not in title."

He stared into her eyes for a long moment. "Even if I win Darlyrede, it is a ruin now. It will be years before it will be rebuilt."

"If there is anything else we are in certain possession of, it's time," Iris suggested, a smile beginning to creep along her face.

"I love you, Iris," he said. She opened her mouth to respond, but Padraig placed a finger against her lips. "Shh. Before you say anything, I will love you here at Darlyrede House, or on Caedmaray, or at Thurso, or in London. It is my thought that I might petition the king to enlist in his army. And then, regardless of his judgment, I can make a life for us. Whatever I must do from this point on, and nae matter where I must go to see it done, I will do that for you. For us. So doona vow it if you're nae prepared to go with me."

"Anywhere," she whispered. "I'll love you anywhere, everywhere. Always."

Padraig kissed her gently then, and Iris felt the swell of happy tears behind her eyes.

But then he pulled away, causing Iris to rock forward and catch herself with one outstretched arm. He raised a hand toward the milling people and a sooty and weary-looking Father Kettering came forward, lugging a golden trunk on his thigh.

"A yes it is, then?" he called.

"Aye," Padraig replied, using his crutch heavily as he helped Iris to her feet. "Let's get the thing done before she changes her mind."

"Padraig?" Iris queried.

He turned to her, taking both her hands in his while Father Kettering opened the little trunk now nestled in the snow. "As I said, I doona know what will happen later today, let alone a year from now," he confessed with that smile that had melted her heart since the first night she'd seen it. "But I doona ever want to wonder if you will be by my side. Iris Montague, will you marry me?"

Iris looked over to where Lucan was standing on the edge of the crowd, his own subdued grin on his face.

"He's already asked my blessing," Lucan said. "Of course I granted it—I'll no longer have to worry about what country you're in."

"Well?" Padraig's prompt drew her attention back to him. "Will you?"

"Yes," Iris said, her heart pounding in her chest. "Yes, I will. But...now?"

Father Kettering cleared his throat, and when Iris looked at the priest, she saw that he had set up the pieces for the service, saved from the blaze in the gilded box.

But he moved forward to stand before Padraig and held out his hand. In the center of his palm lay the small wooden pin.

"I believe you," Father Kettering said.

Padraig's throat convulsed, and he reached out and wrapped his large fingers around the priest's outstretched hand, closing Kettering's over the pin.

"Your father gave his life for mine," he said in a low, choked voice. "Without him, I would not be here. I am proud to have returned this to you, and I know—*I know*—Tommy would want you to have it back."

Father Kettering's face was strained, his chin flinching as he nodded, and he laid his other hand atop Padraig's. "Thank you."

They parted with much clearing of throats, and after Father Kettering had swiped at his face with a kerchief, he turned back, making the sign of the cross before them.

"*In nomine Patris, et Fillii, et Spiritus Sancti...*"

Iris went to her knees in the snow at Padraig's side. "Amen."

"Wait," a woman's clear voice rang out, and Iris looked around toward the fringey finger of wood separating the lawn from the wide moor beyond.

"Och, what now?" Padraig muttered.

A woman dressed in the garb of the woodland rebels stepped from the trees, surrounded by her band. The men to either side of her had their bows readied, and yet the weapons were aimed at the ground.

Padraig struggled to his feet again, his fingers sliding free from Iris's. "Euphemia."

Iris's stomach tumbled as proof of the fantastic story Padraig had told her manifested before her very eyes; it was without a doubt the girl from the portrait.

The first girl to have escaped Caris Hargrave, but Euphemia was a woman now.

"Effie, if you please." She walked up to Padraig, her right hand clenched into a fist. "You didn't think I'd miss my brother's wedding, did you?" she asked.

Lucan snorted. "I don't think anyone shall require being shot."

Euphemia rolled her eyes. "Is he always such a baby?"

"A wee bit demanding," Padraig admitted.

Euphemia held out her fist. "I thought you might like this." She glanced at Iris and gave her a saucy wink.

Padraig looked down into his hand and then back up at the woman.

"Good God, Padraig," Lucan exclaimed. "Do you wish to be thrown into jail as soon as the king arrives? You surely understand it's stolen?"

Euphemia ignored him. "It's not stolen," she assured Padraig. "It was my mother's. I want you and…well, you're not Beryl any longer, are you, miss?"

Iris gave her a hesitant smile. She wasn't sure what to make of this wild woman wearing the fantastic leather trousers and long blond braid. Some woodland Boadicea.

"Thank you, Effie," Padraig said. "Will you stay on?"

"When the king comes, perhaps." Euphemia's gaze skittered away. "I'll be nearby until then."

"I should think you'd avoid the king at all costs," Lucan interrupted. "You killed a noble in the wood, after all. There are witnesses. I should have you arrested at once."

"He only wishes to arrest me as a balm to his pride." Euphemia lifted an eyebrow. "But I daresay he wouldn't be able to rest with no criminal to chase after, so I shall do him a favor and resist."

"Mama, Mama!" a child's voice called, and then a young boy ran from behind the armed men to catch himself around Euphemia's legs. "I want to see too!"

The clearing was completely silent as everyone's gaze fell on the lad, perhaps seven or eight years, his red hair soft and curling about his ears. Iris recognized him as the lad from the woods, on the day of her and Padraig's picnic.

"Your son?" Padraig asked quietly.

Euphemia nodded.

Padraig squatted down and held out his hand. "Padraig Boyd."

The child came away at once and placed his hand into Padraig's much larger one. "George Thomas Annesley. How do you do?"

"Come along now, George," Euphemia said. "Uncle Padraig is rather busy right now."

"He's my uncle? Oh, look, Mama—the kitten I told you about!"

Iris brought her hand to cover her mouth. Satin—more black than white now, dirty and skittish—crouched in the brush, his tail swishing low.

Padraig rose as the child ran along the edge of the wood toward Satin, and there was a strange look on his face. Iris glanced at Lucan and saw a similar expression there.

But Padraig came back to where Iris still knelt and held open his hand. A ring boasting a bright, square emerald lay in the center of his palm.

Father Kettering cleared his throat. "Shall we continue?"

The impromptu guests milling about like weary orphans witnessed the wedding with proper solemnity, but after the Scotsman had slipped the large emerald onto Iris's finger and kissed her gently to seal his oath, they cheered. Several came forth offering both their congratulations and various odd trinkets from what little was left of their possession. It was strange and touching.

"We must all, to a man, carry on to Steadport Hall," a dirtied and disheveled Lord Hood announced. "Lady Hood and I shall be honored to be your hosts as we celebrate these fine young people and our rescue brought about by Master Boyd. Huzzah!"

At the kind lord's invitation, Iris looked around to where Euphemia and her band had been standing, but it was as if the wood had swallowed them up without a sound, leaving only trampled snow and Satin sitting regally where the woodland group had stood only moments before, watching them with his cool disinterest. Her gaze found Lucan and saw that he wore a dark expression as he too stared toward the shadowed, empty wood as the tired cheers rang around them.

Iris thought it very likely that her brother wasn't at all finished with Euphemia Hargrave.

Nor she with him.

* * * *

Padraig waited in the luxurious depths of the bed in a chamber in Steadport Hall. Iris was just out of his sight behind the silk screen, and it seemed as though she'd been there for hours. There were no more sounds of water splashing, however, and the maid who had brought a length of creamy silken cloth had long departed.

He was nervous, now that they were married. Would he disappoint her as her husband? Would she regret her choice tomorrow?

Would she regret it tonight?

"Meow."

Satin leaped onto the bed at Padraig's side and stepped daintily onto his middle, breaking the cycle of worry that had begun to turn in his mind. Padraig stroked the cat's head.

"You're nae so bad for a cat, Satan," he admitted. "You still reek of hell, though."

"It's *Satin*," Iris called.

Padraig turned his head and saw her standing there, her dark hair damp and brushed long over her shoulder, her body touched by the soft, thin, silky material of her robe. Padraig shoved the cat aside—ignoring his offended yowl—and sat up further in the bed.

"That's what I said," Padraig argued.

She walked toward the bed, a small smile on her shapely lips. "That's not what you said. You said Satan. And don't tell me it's only your accent again."

Padraig grinned at her. "I'll need some more tutoring if I'm to survive in the king's army past my first day," he said wryly. "The other soldiers will nae likely be pleased with a Scot in their ranks."

"I doubt they'll have little untoward to say to you once they see how you handle a sword," Iris said with more than a touch of pride in her voice, and it made Padraig love her all the more. "Ulric has promised to take you under his wing. You won't be the low man long."

"I only hope it shows the king my sincerity," Padraig confessed.

"The king could have no more noble a man than Padraig Boyd serving him. He'll be pleased. And we'll be fine." She laid her forearms on his shoulders, her fingers stroking the hair at the nape of his neck. "Once you're settled, we can begin helping Lucan search for your father."

"I wish Tommy could have been here today, to see us wed. To know about Euphemia."

"We'll find him, Padraig," Iris promised quietly. "There is no reason for him to be afraid now. The truth will all come out, and Thomas Annesley can come home at last. But for tonight…"

Iris drew away from him and undid the belt of her robe as she stood. It fell apart slightly, revealing the cleft between her breasts, the navel in her flat stomach, the dark triangle of hair at the juncture of her legs.

* * * *

Padraig reached out for her again, taking her waist in his hands and pulling her into the bed once more, this time across his bare chest. Their lips met at once, and his hands—strong and wide and rough—smoothed the robe from her shoulders, turned her onto the mattress, held her while he rose over her.

He broke away. "You are the most beautiful thing I've ever seen in all my life," he said hoarsely. "I knew it the first moment I saw you. And I'm so proud that you are mine. I'll never be prouder of anything."

"You honor me," Iris whispered, smoothing back his hair from his forehead.

He kissed her again, and then his hands suddenly were all over her body as his wide frame shook with desire. It was obvious that Padraig was trying to go slowly with her, and she loved him all the more for it. Her nerves were raw even as he touched her breasts, suckled her, dragged his hands down her body to between her legs.

In moments she had forgotten her nerves as Padraig brought her passion to life. She had wanted him for so long—this man she loved. And now as he moved between her legs surely, his trembling gone, she was ready to receive him as a woman, as his wife.

His thrusts were slow at first, short; then growing deeper, surer, as her body relaxed around him. Iris did not think she would gain her pleasure this first time, but her discomfort faded, and her peak was swift. Padraig's strokes rocked her, and the feeling of her breasts jarring with each thrust brought her just to the edge again.

And then he was pulsing within her, burying his face in her neck, cradling her head in his hands.

"I love you," he whispered over and over. "I love you, Iris."

Iris could not think of words with meaning enough to convey the depth of her love for the man who was now her husband, and so she answered him the only way she could think of in the moment, with her passion still so high—she rolled over atop him, still joined together, and began another lesson.

This time, as his wife.

Epilogue

Effie stood in the fringe of the wood for a long time after the last of the refugees from the burned-out manor had trudged over the moors toward Steadport Hall. The stones would smolder for weeks, and even the birds were still silent in the fading light of afternoon. She could just make out the only remaining window ledge of the large opening of what had been her chamber. The chamber where she had suffered for so many years.

And somewhere in the rubble beyond, her tormentors' bodies lay.

A mad part of Effie longed to stalk to the ruined house and dig through the smoking carnage like a madwoman until she found their blackened bones—she wanted to see the evidence of their deaths with her own eyes, needed it. She forced herself to swallow down the tears that threatened. She was no longer that weak, unsure girl who needed the guarantee of a thing already done. They were both dead. It was over. That was good enough for her.

It must be good enough.

Padraig Boyd, her brother, had come. He was a good man, Effie thought; she'd certainly seen enough evil to be able to tell a keen difference. Perhaps one day she would see that goodness reflected in her own father.

And yet Effie had not waited all these years, suffered for so long just to turn over the house, the people, she had looked after for so long to Padraig Boyd. Caris and Vaughn Hargrave had killed her mother and then ripped Effie from her womb. They had stolen from her not only her parents but her home, her life. She should have grown up knowing the joy of Darlyrede House, not its darkness. Even Lucan Montague had cowed to Vaughn Hargrave's evil power, allowing his home to remain razed, conferring with the king on Hargrave's behalf.

She was glad she'd shot him.

And, of course, there was George to consider. Effie was determined that her son would enjoy the benefits of the life denied to his mother. She would stop at nothing, and no one—not her brothers and certainly not Lucan Montague—would prevent her from doing it. Even if George was so very excited at the idea of having an uncle.

And an aunt too now, Effie supposed with a slight smile.

She turned away to circle back through the wood to the caves, treading through the snow. She stopped in the fading gray light halfway through to the stream, noticing the second set of small footprints tracking her initial trail, and crouched down with a wry smile. She'd told him no.

She looked around her through the dark slashes of trees. "George Thomas?" Her chiding inquiry was met with silence.

"George, where are you?" She rose and followed the prints. "It's all right—I'm not cross that you followed me. Only come out now so we might go home before it's dark. George?"

Effie walked faster now through the twilight until the footprints halted in a jumble of trampled black mud, contrasted with—

Hoofprints.

Effie turned her head to follow the black, dragging scuffs through snow now tinged pink from the last bursts of the setting sun. Horse tracks. A single horse, coming from the direction of the smoldering rubble that was once Darlyrede House. Effie's heart stopped in her chest as her head snapped up.

The tracks headed north.

And George's footprints were gone.

George was gone.

Effie screamed up into the treetops as the sun slipped behind the far-off, rolling hills of Northumberland. She screamed and screamed, but the silence around the moors swallowed up her agony with an indifferent sigh of wind.

Printed in the United States
by Baker & Taylor Publisher Services